The sirens getting closer

Bolan leapt over the body as the car door swung open. He jumped in as Katz took off. But at the end of the alley, a police car suddenly came into view.

Katz threw the Mercedes into reverse and stomped on the pedal. They were halfway to the other exit when two more cop cars pulled in, blocking their path.

When the first round struck the windshield, shattering the glass, Bolan realized the cops weren't waiting for explanations.

MACK BOLAN ®
The Executioner

#177 Evil Code
#178 Black Hand
#179 War Hammer
#180 Force Down
#181 Shifting Target
#182 Lethal Agent
#183 Clean Sweep
#184 Death Warrant
#185 Sudden Fury
#186 Fire Burst
#187 Cleansing Flame
#188 War Paint
#189 Wellfire
#190 Killing Range
#191 Extreme Force
#192 Maximum Impact
#193 Hostile Action
#194 Deadly Contest
#195 Select Fire
#196 Triburst
#197 Armed Force
#198 Shoot Down
#199 Rogue Agent
#200 Crisis Point
#201 Prime Target
#202 Combat Zone
#203 Hard Contact
#204 Rescue Run
#205 Hell Road
#206 Hunting Cry
#207 Freedom Strike
#208 Death Whisper
#209 Asian Crucible
#210 Fire Lash
#211 Steel Claws
#212 Ride the Beast
#213 Blood Harvest
#214 Fission Fury

#215 Fire Hammer
##216 Death Force
#217 Fight or Die
#218 End Game
#219 Terror Intent
#220 Tiger Stalk
#221 Blood and Fire
#222 Patriot Gambit
#223 Hour of Conflict
#224 Call to Arms
#225 Body Armor
#226 Red Horse
#227 Blood Circle
#228 Terminal Option
#229 Zero Tolerance
#230 Deep Attack
#231 Slaughter Squad
#232 Jackal Hunt
#233 Tough Justice
#234 Target Command
#235 Plague Wind
#236 Vengeance Rising
#237 Hellfire Trigger
#238 Crimson Tide
#239 Hostile Proximity
#240 Devil's Guard
#241 Evil Reborn
#242 Doomsday Conspiracy
#243 Assault Reflex
#244 Judas Kill
#245 Virtual Destruction
#246 Blood of the Earth
#247 Black Dawn Rising
#248 Rolling Death
#249 Shadow Target
#250 Warning Shot
#251 Kill Radius
#252 Death Line

DON PENDLETON'S
EXECUTIONER®
DEATH LINE

BOOK III

THE
BORDER FIRE TRILOGY

A GOLD EAGLE BOOK FROM
WORLDWIDE®

TORONTO • NEW YORK • LONDON
AMSTERDAM • PARIS • SYDNEY • HAMBURG
STOCKHOLM • ATHENS • TOKYO • MILAN
MADRID • WARSAW • BUDAPEST • AUCKLAND

First edition December 1999
ISBN 0-373-64252-0

Special thanks and acknowledgment to
Jerry VanCook for his contribution to this work.

DEATH LINE

History teaches us that the great revolutions aren't started by people who are utterly down and out, without hope and vision. They take place when people begin to live a little better—and when they see how much yet remains to be achieved.

—Hubert H. Humphrey

A little rebellion now and then is a good thing.

—Thomas Jefferson

A leader is one who has the courage to look for a new solution and the support of his men to choose a different path.

—Mack Bolan

THE
MACK BOLAN®
LEGEND

Nothing less than a war could have fashioned the destiny of the man called Mack Bolan. Bolan earned the Executioner title in the jungle hell of Vietnam.

But this soldier also wore another name—Sergeant Mercy. He was so tagged because of the compassion he showed to wounded comrades-in-arms and Vietnamese civilians.

Mack Bolan's second tour of duty ended prematurely when he was given emergency leave to return home and bury his family, victims of the Mob. Then he declared a one-man war against the Mafia.

He confronted the Families head-on from coast to coast, and soon a hope of victory began to appear. But Bolan had broken society's every rule. That same society started gunning for this elusive warrior—to no avail.

So Bolan was offered amnesty to work within the system against terrorism. This time, as an employee of Uncle Sam, Bolan became Colonel John Phoenix. With a command center at Stony Man Farm in Virginia, he and his new allies—Able Team and Phoenix Force—waged relentless war on a new adversary: the KGB.

But when his one true love, April Rose, died at the hands of the Soviet terror machine, Bolan severed all ties with Establishment authority.

Now, after a lengthy lone-wolf struggle and much soul-searching, the Executioner has agreed to enter an "arm's-length" alliance with his government once more, reserving the right to pursue personal missions in his Everlasting War.

PROLOGUE

"Hello, Mr. President," Hal Brognola said into the receiver.

There was a moment's pause on the other end. Then the most familiar Southern accent in the world said, "Returning your call, Hal. What is it? I'm in a hurry."

Brognola cleared his throat. He had been dreading this call and had spent the last hour trying to decide how to inform the President on the current situation. Stony Man Farm, the base of operations for the most sensitive counterterrorist strikes, was the country's best-kept secret. Outside of the Farm's personnel, the President of the United States was the only person who knew of its existence. Brognola had served under half a dozen of the men who had occupied the White House, but the man currently in office had proven to be far more difficult to work with than his predecessors. This President had no understanding of clandestine operations; in fact, he had no military background whatsoever. As if that hadn't made things hard enough, at the moment he was under scrutiny for being caught publicly in multiple lies.

Add all that to the trouble spilling into the United States from Mexico, and Brognola suspected he was dealing with a man more concerned with saving his ass than solving the country's current problems. He didn't like to believe it, but he knew there was always the chance the man in the White House might stage something dramatic to shift the focus from his personal problems.

"It's my operative in Mexico," Brognola said. "He was kidnapped and—"

"What!"

The director of Sensitive Operations took a deep breath. "He's okay," Brognola continued. "He escaped, but he's going underground. The Mexican president thinks he's dead."

The voice on the other end of the line grew stern. "That's unacceptable. President Fierro Blanco asked for an American bodyguard he could trust. He asked it as a personal favor, and I agreed to send the best man we had. That's your operative, isn't it?"

"Yes," Brognola answered.

"I gave Fierro Blanco my word," the man in the White House said.

"But Mr. President—"

"And I gave you direct orders, Brognola."

The Stony Man director sighed inwardly. "Let me refresh my mind as to exactly what those orders were, Mr. President," Brognola said. "The orders were twofold. First, to protect the Mexican president during a period when Fierro Blanco didn't even know if he could trust his own federal bodyguards. The second part was to find out if Fierro Blanco is dirty—find out if he's tied in to the Mexican terrorist groups and drug cartels—and if he's really responsible for the assassinations of political foes and journalists as some are claiming. All of this was in order for you to be able to evaluate whether or not Mexico should be recertified as cooperating with America's antidrug efforts, was it not? Wasn't this, in turn, to determine if you would continue to grant funds to Mexico?"

"Of course it was," the president said testily.

"Well, sir, as good as my man is, he has been unable to complete both missions at the same time. He's convinced that he needs to be in the field. You're right—he's our best man. But we have a number of good men who are also capable of keeping President Fierro Blanco safe. But no one, and I repeat no one, can operate in the field the way my main operative does. If you are intent on finding out about Fierro Blanco, he's the man for the job."

"All right," the President said. "Do it. But if it goes wrong, I'll have your ass." He paused to cough, then continued. "I think you should know, I'm sending more troops to the border. And I've been discussing another possibility with the Joint Chiefs."

Brognola felt the hair on the back of his neck rise. He was afraid he knew what was coming. "And what's that possibility, sir?"

"An invasion," the Commander-in-Chief said. "With the intent of setting up a provisional government until the people of Mexico can hold new elections."

Brognola closed his eyes. An invasion of Mexico. There, the words had been said. Was the President considering such drastic measures because he believed it was sound strategy or, as the Stony Man director feared, was he willing to lose American lives just to get the news cameras pointed away from his current personal problems? Brognola didn't know. But it didn't really matter, either. An invasion of Mexico, for whatever reasons, might well open the door to disaster for America. "I must advise against that, Mr. President," he said.

"Your reasons?"

"First, we'll turn the Mexican people into our enemies for the next hundred years. And we—Stony Man Farm—are going to get things straightened out sooner or later without it. I have Able Team running down the cartel assassins along the border. Phoenix Force just located and put an end to a second drug tunnel. That should cut into the drug traffic considerably. The DEA-Military task force is enough to finish locating the rest of the tunnels and handle them similarly. And there are already eighty thousand troops assigned to the Border Patrol—they're doing a good job of slowing the illegal immigrations.

"There's another reason I must advise against sending more troops."

"And that is?"

"It's because we're spread too thin already, Mr. President. If something breaks out in another part of the world while this is going on, we can't—"

"I don't need political advice from you, Brognola," the man in the Oval Office said. "Nor do I need thinly veiled criticism of my military budget cuts."

"Sir, I'm not offering political advice," Brognola said, clenching his fists around the receiver. "It's military matters that concern me. There are any number of our enemies around the globe who are just waiting for us to get too busy to interfere with their agendas. North Korea and China are watching South Korea like wolves eyeing a lamb with a broken leg. Saddam Hussein is refusing the UN inspectors again. Even Russia and Japan are possible—''

''Thank you, Director Brognola,'' the president said. ''Let me rephrase my statement to make it clearer. I don't need, or want, your advice *at all.*'' He cleared his throat again, then said, ''All right, you tell your man to proceed in the field if you want.''

''Yes, sir,'' the Stony Man director said into the phone.

The other end of the line went dead.

Brognola dropped the phone in the cradle and sat back in his chair. He had told the President they would get things under control without an invasion. In truth, he wasn't so sure. Mexico was in chaos, with drug smugglers running rampant across the borders. Gang wars were breaking out in Houston, El Paso, San Diego and other cities; threatening to claim innocents in the cross fires. In Tijuana, American movie megastar Ronnie Quartel and several of his friends had been kidnapped and were being held for ransom by the *Ciudadano para Democracia Mexicana Legitima.* Around Mexico City and in the southern states the *Partido Revolucionario Marxista* had overrun the presidential mansion known as *Los Pinos,* destroyed President Don Juan de Fierro Blanco's summer house on the Yucatán coast, and mounted a half-dozen other assassination attempts aimed at the Mexican president. And now it looked as if someone—maybe the *Marxistas,* maybe the *Legitimas,* or maybe some other group—had zeroed in on Bolan. They had finally figured out that to have a reasonable chance of killing Fierro Blanco, they would have to get rid of his American bodyguard first.

Which was sound intelligence, Hal Brognola thought, as he shuffled a stack of papers into his briefcase and prepared to drive home for what was left of the short night. But he wasn't worried. Bolan was the best. Regardless of what name he went under. They were all one and the same. Striker. Mike Belasko. Mack Bolan.

The Executioner.

1

Mack Bolan squinted into the cracked mirror above the sink. The light from the naked bulb in the ceiling was so dim he could barely make out his reflection. But the Executioner watched a hard smile curl his lips in the fractured reflection. Because as far as anyone outside of the crew at Stony Farm knew, Mack Bolan was dead.

The soldier stepped into the dark, seedy bedroom and sat on the bed. He was just now fully recovered from the tranquilizer darts the two men who had kidnapped him had shot into his body. The events which had transpired after the abduction were finally focusing into a logical sequence instead of the dreamlike bits and pieces in which they had first been remembered.

The soldier reached for a bottle of drinking water. Twisting off the cap, he brought it to his lips. He remembered the two men—men who appeared to be brothers—firing the tranquilizer darts into him just outside the gates to *Los Pinos*. The next thing he knew, he had awakened on the floor in the cargo area of a delivery truck. The brothers, ahead in the driver's area, had made bizarre references to their mother and some kind of sacrifice they were going to perform on him. But Bolan had escaped when they stopped for gas.

Taking another drink of water, the soldier let it trickle down his throat. The tranquilizer darts had left him dehydrated; a common effect of such drugs. He squinted, coaxing his memory back to life.

After notifying Stony Man Farm that he planned to leave his assignment protecting the Mexican president to pursue the mission in the field, and informing Hal Brognola that he would need new weapons and equipment—his guns and other weapons had been taken by the kidnappers—he had purchased new clothing and other gear. The brothers hadn't taken his money, which proved that their motive had not been robbery. But the Executioner had never suspected that it was.

Rising from the bed, Bolan moved to the dresser where the lone weapon the brothers had overlooked now rested. He was grateful the men had missed the Gerber Applegate-Fairbairn Covert folding knife. Without it, he wouldn't have escaped. And until new weaponry arrived from the Farm or he could procure arms elsewhere the knife was, along with his hands, feet and, of course, his brain, his only line of defense.

The faded denim shirt and near-matching jeans he had purchased at the marketplace lay on the bed. Bolan pulled on the jeans, tucked his T-shirt inside and slid the wide Western belt through the loops. On the end of the belt was a large silver buckle. Chips of turquoise, red coral and gray abalone had been inlaid to form a picture of two cocks engaged in battle. The black belt matched the black Mexican-style cowboy boots he had picked up at the same place. Silver wing tips glistened on the sharp toes, with additional silver ornaments on the heels. He stepped into the boots and pulled his pant leg down over the tops.

Leaving the denim shirt unbuttoned and untucked as a jacket, the Executioner dropped his money into his left front pant pocket. The Gerber Covert clipped into the pocket on the right.

The mirror above the dresser wasn't cracked like the one in the bathroom—just dirty. The soldier looked into it and another smile curled the corners of his mouth. He looked exactly like he wanted to look. Like a down-on-his-luck-and-not-particularly-honest gringo expatriate in Mexico.

Dropping the clothes he had worn earlier into the cheap black canvas bag he had also purchased, Bolan exited the room and walked out to the street. His eyes scanned the lanes for a taxi in the fading daylight, but he didn't see one. He looked at his wristwatch and frowned. Grimaldi would wait for him at the airport for as long as it took him to get there. That wasn't a problem. The problem was that the Executioner wanted to get started.

A car without markings suddenly pulled over and stopped beside the curb. Bolan wasn't surprised when the driver motioned him inside. Unlicensed "gypsy" cabs were prevalent in all large cities and particularly those in Third World nations. Mexico was no exception. He opened the door and tossed his bag onto the back seat.

"Where to?" the driver said cheerfully as the soldier climbed in and closed the door behind him.

"Benito Juarez," Bolan said.

"Ah, the airport," the driver said, as he pulled away from the curb. "You're leaving us?"

Bolan shook his head. "Going to meet a friend," he said.

"A man or woman?" asked the driver.

"Man," Bolan said, then wished he could bite back the words. As soon as he'd spoken them he realized why the question had been asked.

"You and your friend will want entertainment?" the driver asked. The sun was almost down now and he switched on his headlights. "Some señoritas, no?"

"No," Bolan said. The cab had no air conditioner and he rolled the half-open window the rest of the way down.

"Boys? I can get you boys," said the driver without hesitation. The soldier shook his head.

Another cab rounded the corner and came within inches of sideswiping them. After the obligatory horn battle and angry, raised fingers and fists, the driver said, "Ah, just a quiet evening between two old friends then? Would you like some marijuana? Crack cocaine, perhaps? I can get you heroin, too."

Bolan shook his head again. The conversation was a little tiring but at least it proved his gringo look was working. "Nothing, thanks," he said.

The cabbie drove on, as dusk became night, navigating the streets of Mexico City with ease. Lifting a scarred plastic CB-radio microphone from where it was clipped to his dashboard, he thumbed the button and spoke in some Indian dialect the Executioner couldn't understand. In the rearview mirror, Bolan saw the man glance at him several times as if even in the strange language he was afraid he might be understood. They drove up an access ramp to the thoroughfare leading to Benito Juarez International as a male voice came back over the radio in the same tongue. Passing several exits, the conversation ended when the driver suddenly pulled into the right lane and drove down an exit ramp.

Bolan leaned forward. "This isn't the way to the airport," he said.

"Please sir," the driver said. "I must pick up my little sister from her work. It's right off the highway and won't take long. Don't worry—I won't charge you for it."

Bolan sat back, the warning light going on in his head. Something about the man's story didn't ring true. It might be something as simple as the "little sister" being a prostitute he thought Bolan wouldn't be able to resist. On the other hand, it could be far more sinister.

The cab stopped at the bottom of the ramp, then turned right toward a heavy commercial area of town. They passed a garage, a machine shop and then a crumbling factory that would have been closed by safety inspectors had it been in the United States. A neighborhood market stood on the corner just past the factory, the only business on the street that appeared to be open still.

"She works there, at the market," the driver said, pointing. "We'll pick her up at the back."

Bolan didn't answer.

The cab cut down the alley behind the store and stopped. The Executioner saw a young woman in her early twenties walk forward in the headlights. But she had taken no more than a half-dozen steps when a pistol came sliding into the window next to him.

Bolan turned slowly to face the weapon. He found himself looking into the .45 caliber barrel of an Argentinean-made copy of the Colt Government Model 1911. Barely visible in the shadows, Bolan could see the outline of a muscular man bending over to the window. Two eyes shone in the dim light like a jungle cat's.

"Your money!" the man whispered gruffly. "And your watch! Give them to me now or I'll kill you!"

Bolan glanced toward the front seat. A phony look of surprise covered the driver's face. He shrugged as if to say, "What can I do?"

The Executioner scanned the area. No one else was in the alley except the girl—the bait—and she had already started to back away.

"Do you want to die?" the man with the pistol said, his voice rising louder in anger. "Do as I say!"

Bolan looked back at him, then twisted to the side, his left hand shooting out to grab the slide of the cocked .45. Pressing it downward, he pinned the man's hand and weapon against the window ledge. One round fired, drilling into the seat behind him. As the big Colt boomed, the Executioner's other hand dropped to his pocket, and the Gerber Applegate-Fairbairn knife appeared. Thumbing the stud, he opened the blade, twisted it in his hand into an ice-pick grip and brought the point down into the back of the hand holding the gun.

A sickening crunch sounded as the sharp dagger struck a bone in the back of the would-be robber's hand. The blade slid through the fractured bone and exited through the palm, wedging itself into the upholstery just below the window.

The man began to scream.

The Colt had fallen from the wounded hand, and now dangled from his limp index finger through the trigger guard. The Executioner ripped the gun away. Slapping the butt of the gun, Bolan racked the slide and chambered a round.

The pistol came up pointing at the mugger's face. "Step back," the Executioner ordered.

Tears filled the robber's eyes as he whispered, "I...can't...."

Bolan looked down at the man's hand still skewered into the car door. Reaching, he jerked out the knife.

The robber screamed again, then stepped back as he'd been ordered.

Bolan turned to the driver. "Get out of the car and go stand next to your friend."

"Sir," the cabbie pleaded. "He isn't my friend. I didn't know—"

"Do it!"

The man reached for the keys in the ignition.

"Leave them! Get out."

The driver obeyed as complacently as the other man.

Bolan wiped the Covert's blade on the car upholstery, closed it, and reclipped the knife in his pocket. He kept the Argentinean automatic trained on the men as he got out.

When he had both men up against the side of the car, he frisked them. Finding no other weapons, he wheeled them both back to face him.

"Please, sir," the driver said. "We're normally honest men."

The burly man held his wounded hand in his other. "These are hard times in Mexico," he pleaded.

"They're hard times everywhere," Bolan said. "For everybody."

"Are you going to kill us? Please—"

"Maybe I should kill you," Bolan said, "to make sure you don't try this on somebody else." He paused a moment and looked at the fear on the other men's faces. It wasn't something he enjoyed. But it was necessary.

Flipping the manual safety of the Colt to block the firing pin, Bolan brought the weapon around in an arc that struck the driver in the jaw. The man's knees buckled and he crumpled to the ground.

A moment of relief passed over the face of the man who had wielded the pistol. Then he closed his eyes tightly in preparation for what he knew was coming.

The gun struck him in the same place.

Bolan dragged the men out of the way, got behind the wheel and drove slowly down the alley. When he came to the corner, he saw the girl who had been the lure for the trap and stopped. She was halfway down the street but started toward the car when she saw it.

The Executioner kept his face shielded by the shadows as she approached. A few feet before she reached the vehicle, she called out in Spanish, "You have the money, Ramon?"

Bolan aimed the Colt through the window. "I've still got my money but I'm not Ramon," he said.

The woman stopped in her tracks.

"Find another line of work," the Executioner said. Then, pulling the gun back into the car, he drove away in the hot Mexico City night.

TRAFFIC WAS STOPPED at the intersection. The van, rented by Stony Man Farm's Able Team leader Carl Lyons, pulled into the shopping mall parking lot. The lot was emptying as the stores closed for the night. Men and women, keys and packages in hand, were headed across the asphalt toward the few remaining vehicles.

Houston Police Department Detective Dirk Anderson rode shotgun next to Lyons. "There," he said, pointing toward a Ford Bronco. "That's Keener."

Lyons followed the cop's finger toward the black sport-utility vehicle that had just turned in and stopped beneath one of the overhead lights. He guided the van toward it as two men, both wearing white cowboy hats, exited the Bronco.

As the men walked toward the slowing van, his thought was that he and the other men of Able Team might have stumbled upon the set of *Walker: Texas Ranger*. In addition to his white Stetson, the older of the two men wore a denim jacket, blue jeans and Western boots. Long graying hair fell to his shoulders, matching the salt-and-pepper whiskers that covered his weather-beaten face.

As the men neared the van, Lyons took note of Keener's black gun belt with the gold-and-silver buckle that featured the Texas Rangers's emblem. His denim jacket was short enough to see the Bill Jordan-style drop holster on his right hip which carried a stainless steel .44 Magnum Smith & Wesson Model 29 with stag grips. The gun on Keener's left was a beautifully engraved and inlaid Colt Government Model .45, toted in cross-draw fashion.

Lyons grinned. Texas Rangers were known for many things, among them courage, toughness and intelligence. But they were almost equally well known for their love of fancy personalized weaponry.

As Keener and his partner reached the van, Lyons extended his hand to the older man and Dirk Anderson said, "Ironman, meet

Ranger Bud Keener." Lyons gripped the callused right hand in his and introduced his fellow Able Team members, Hermann "Gadgets" Schwarz and Rosario "Politician" Blancanales.

"Who's your new friend, Bud?" Anderson asked, nodding toward the younger man.

All eyes turned to the man who had ridden into the parking lot with Keener. His Ranger status and tender age combined to bespeak the fact that he had worked his way up the Texas Department of Public Safety ladder quickly, and Lyons knew that could mean either one or both of two things: He was sharp and talented or he had political connections.

"Ranger Mark Harsey," Keener said.

The clean-shaven Harsey looked like a rodeo cowboy in town for the Saturday night dance. He wore a black Western shirt adorned with red flames, what appeared to be yet-unwashed Wrangler jeans and lizard-skin Roper boots.

Keener answered Lyons's unasked question by saying, "Don't let his age fool you. The kid's all right."

Like Keener, Harsey wore one of the small Texas Ranger badges—badges that were still forged after first melting down Mexican pesos—on the left side of his chest. His belt rig was just as fancy as his partner's, but in brown. On his right side rode a .357 Magnum Colt Python not unlike the one Lyons himself carried. The Browning Hi-Power opposite it was engraved and inlaid in gold like Keener's colt pistol.

"Pleased to meet you," Harsey said to the other men. Lyons saw the stub of a well-chewed matchstick barely visible in the corner of his mouth. The circular print of a can of smokeless tobacco was visible in the breast pocket opposite the badge.

The preliminaries over, Ranger Bud Keener didn't waste any time. "You said on the phone you got an *in* to Gonzales," he said, looking Anderson in the eye. "That really true?" Lyons noted that the Ranger didn't use the infamous brothel owner-drug runner's nickname, "Lone Wolf." The real Lone Wolf Gonzales had been one of the most well-respected Texas Rangers in the history of the organization, and the fact that a scumbag like Gonzales had stolen the appellation was a sore spot with the Rangers.

Anderson looked at Lyons quickly, then turned back to Keener. "Bud," he said, "what we're going to do requires a little explaining. Then, if you both want out, all I ask is you keep it to yourselves." The Houston detective glanced at Harsey.

"He's a Ranger," Keener said, answering another question that hadn't been asked. "You can trust him to keep quiet."

Lyons had been watching Anderson out of the corner of his eye, and now he noted that the Houston officer looked nervous. The Able Team leader wasn't surprised. Anderson had already told them he was a few short months from retirement and pension. He could lose that pension if convicted of a crime or even a serious breach of Houston PD policy.

And what Able Team, Anderson and maybe Keener and Harsey were about to do was technically a crime and definitely against policy.

Lyons studied Anderson's face briefly. He could see the detective trusted Keener to keep his mouth shut even if the Rangers chose not to participate. But the look in Anderson's eyes said he wasn't so sure about Harsey. Lyons understood that, too. Keener was of the old school—he knew there were times when the law had to be bent if society didn't want the animals of the world to take over. But Harsey was young, and younger cops appeared to take a much more by-the-book approach. Which could mean Harsey might even feel it his duty to report technically illegal activity on the part of fellow officers.

The Able Team leader decided to take Anderson off the hook. If worse came to worse, it would look better if Lyons had been the one to actually speak the words. And while Anderson didn't know it, if worse came to even more worse, Stony Man Farm would find a place for him that would more than compensate for any lost pension.

Lyons stepped in. "We don't have a warrant and we don't have probable cause," he said. "At least enough probable to make it stand up in court." He paused a second, then added, "We just know where Gonzales is, and what he's doing. And we're about to hit his place, kick ass and take names. We'd like you with us if you want to be, but we'll understand if you don't."

Slowly, Keener began to grin. He turned to his young partner. "You up for a little bull riding, kid?" he asked.

The young Ranger's face didn't change expressions. His answer was to reach up slowly and deliberately and unpin the star from his shirt and drop it out of sight into his pocket.

Keener did the same, then both men drew their elaborate handguns, shoved them into their waistbands and unbuckled the identifying Texas Ranger belt buckles.

"Want to ride in the van with us?" Lyons asked.

Keener nodded. "The plate on the Bronco registers to 'not found.' But the dispatchers advise headquarters any time it's out. In other words, if somebody calls it in, it'll eventually be traced back to us."

Lyons and the other two Able Team men climbed into the van. Anderson and his fellow Texas law enforcement officers followed. As the vehicle pulled out of the parking lot toward Gonzales's whorehouse, Lyons heard Ranger Bud Keener speak behind him. "You're about to see how we used to do it in the old days, kid."

"Looking forward to it," Harsey answered. "The only question I have is why we took our badges and belts off." Before anyone could answer, he went on. "If we do it like I heard you old-timers did it in the old days, there won't be anybody left around who can ID us anyway."

An arm in a faded denim sleeve came through the opening between the bucket seats and rested briefly on Dirk Anderson's shoulder. "What'd I tell you, Dirk," Ranger Bud Keener said. "The kid's all right, huh?" He leaned back again. "Of course, the boy could have left out that 'old-timer' part."

THE BLADES OF THE Apache helicopter whirled over David McCarter's head as the dry Baja Peninsula flatland appeared below. The leader of Stony Man Farm's Phoenix Force squinted into his binoculars. Far below, he saw what looked like a white Cadillac parked just off the dirt road. Next to it, also white, was what appeared to be a man.

"Take us down," McCarter ordered the young army pilot behind the controls of the chopper. "This is the place."

As the Apache descended, McCarter thought back over the past few hours. He, Gary Manning and Thomas Jackson Hawkins had discovered and helped fellow teammates Calvin James and Rafael Encizo, along with the DEA-Military task force, locate and destroy an underground tunnel between the U.S. and Mexico, though which millions of dollars worth of drugs had been traveling daily. Trapped inside the tunnel, he and Manning had miraculously escaped unharmed.

Hawkins hadn't been so lucky. Shot through the shoulder during an initial attack, and through the thigh during subsequent fighting, the youngest member of Phoenix Force had been flown to a hospital in Tucson, Arizona. The last word was that T.J. was still in surgery.

While they worried about Hawkins, and before they could congratulate themselves on the destruction of the tunnel, the remainder of Phoenix Force had learned from a surviving cartel drug mule that it was only one of multiple underground passageways linking the two countries. An attack at a second tunnel closer to California had taken out the delivery trucks picking up the shipment.

How many more tunnels were there? McCarter didn't know. But it was no longer his immediate concern. Members of the *Ciudadano para Democracia Mexicana Legitima*—the Citizens for Legitimate Mexican Democracy—had kidnapped American movie star Ronnie Quartel, his friend, former U.S. Army Intelligence officer Scott Hix, the mayor of Tijuana and several other people who had been at a party at Hix's house outside Tijuana. The right-wing Mexican terrorist group had finally come out with their demands— ten million dollars for Quartel's release and an additional million for the mayor. Hix, who Stony Man intelligence had confirmed was a close-quarters combat-expert-turned-expatriate importer-exporter, rated only half a million. And the others—prostitutes from Tijuana and a number of women brought down from Hollywood by Quartel—would be thrown in for free.

What a deal, McCarter thought sarcastically as the helicopter set down on the ground. Today's special: Buy three, the rest are free. In any case, Mack Bolan, who was running the overall operation from Mexico City, had decided to pull Phoenix Force off the tunnel search and send them to Tijuana to help the Stony Man agents already undercover there. The DEA-Military task force was being left in the capable hands of its original leader, Winston "Pug" Nelson. Nelson was an old Navy SEAL buddy of Phoenix Force's Calvin James. James had faith in the man, and after meeting Nelson himself, McCarter did too.

The Phoenix Force leader opened the door and dropped out of the chopper. Manning, James, and Encizo followed. Hawkins's absence was more than noticeable, and left a hollow feeling in McCarter's belly. Would he pull through? The Briton didn't know.

The figure next to the white Cadillac turned out to be Leo Turrin wearing a light cotton suit. An old friend from Bolan's days fighting the Mafia, Turrin was now a successful Washington lobbyist, while still occasionally acting as an undercover specialist for Stony Man Farm.

"David, Gary, Rafe," Turrin said, extending his hand to each man in turn. When he got to Calvin James, he grasped the black warrior's hand in both of his and said, "I heard about T.J. from Stony Man. Any news?"

James shook his head. "Still in surgery, Leo. He lost a lot of blood."

Turrin nodded, his expression reflecting concern but also the knowledge that there was nothing any of them could do. He nodded toward the Cadillac. "You guys ready?"

"Give us a rundown on what you've been doing," McCarter said as Turrin slid behind the wheel and the others jammed their equipment into the truck.

Turrin sighed. "Stony Man probably told you," he said, starting the engine and pulling onto the road, "I've got two blacksuits with me. One's from Columbia's new counterterrorist outfit. Name's Bernhardt. Jaime Bernhardt. But he's going by the name Pompei down here."

Gary Manning's big shoulders leaned forward from the back seat. "Who's the other guy?" he asked.

"Martinez," Turrin said. "half-Mexican and half-black. He's a good man. Big and strong. And when I say big and strong I mean that." He paused, chuckled a moment, then added, "And he's smart, too. Comes from the Oklahoma Bureau of Narcotics and Dangerous Drugs. Call him Toro like everybody else in Tijuana is doing these days," Turrin said as the Cadillac reached the top of a small rise and the city appeared in the distance. "We've been laying some groundwork, and Toro and Pompei are getting quite a rep among the bad guys down there." The packed dirt road became gravel for a few hundred yards, then turned to a black-gray asphalt as cracked and dried as the ground on both sides of it. "Anyway, these guys are having the time of their lives—particularly Toro. No paperwork, no bureaucracy, no rules except getting the job done."

"So what exactly have they been doing, Leo?" McCarter asked.

"Basically, Toro's been beating the hell out of every bad guy he's come across in every cantina in town," Turrin said as they entered the outskirts of Tijuana. "This guy fights like he's a possessed demon. He boxed and played football in college, has black belts in about any martial art you can name and, most importantly, he knows the difference between the dojo and the street."

McCarter understood. Few of the techniques promoted by Oriental forms of fighting were effective in real hand-to-hand combat. But he couldn't help wondering at Turrin's strategy. He was sure this Toro was doing a lot of good by leaving some of Tijuana's criminal element bleeding on barroom floors, but he failed to see how any of it was furthering the mission. On the other hand, he had faith in Turrin. The man was a master of undercover work, and he knew how to create illusions that led to successful operations. "So where's this leading, Leo?" he asked.

Turrin grinned. "I was hoping you'd ask," he said. "You ever heard of Julio Conde?" he asked.

When McCarter shook his head, Turrin continued. "Neither had I until I started snooping around. Conde's supposed to be the biggest badass in Sonora. He fights the underground club circuit—when he can get somebody to fight him—and that's not easy anymore."

McCarter had heard of Tijuana's underground bare-knuckles club circuit. Operating in the dingiest, seediest of the border town's cantinas, the fights took place in the early hours of the morning.

There were no rules whatsoever, and the bouts were reported to make the *Ultimate Fighting Championships* look like afternoon tea with the Queen Mum. It was common for the loser to leave the ring without an ear or an eye, and deaths were frequent. Thousands of dollars traded hands between gamblers, and while the fights were technically illegal, it was rumored that a good half of those in attendance were Mexican police. "So," the Briton said. "You're going to set up a fight between Conde and Toro?"

Turrin nodded.

"Why?"

The Stony Man undercover ace grinned again as the Caddy rolled slowly into Tijuana, passing shacks of plywood and other scrap lumber painted yellow, pink and any other color the owners could get their hands on. "It's the beginning of an overall plan that will lead to the *Legitimas*," Turrin said.

McCarter was getting impatient. Like most undercover specialists, Leo Turrin had a flair for the dramatic and he was building the tension. The Phoenix Force leader wanted to get to the bottom line. "Give me a quick summary, Leo," he said.

Turrin caught the restless tone of his voice and said, "Okay, David. Like I said, Julio Conde is having trouble getting anybody to fight him. He killed the last guy and bit the nose off the one just before that. After Toro beats him, no one, and I mean no one, is going to willingly fight our man."

McCarter started to speak again but Turrin went on. "So what does that get us?" he said as he turned a corner into the tourist-business area of Tijuana. "A man who will be *forced* to fight him. There's only one man in Tijuana who has a chance of beating him. Scott Hix."

McCarter shook his head. "How do you plan to pull that off?" he asked.

"Simple," Turrin said. He pulled the Cadillac to the curb in front of a cantina, threw the transmission into park and killed the engine. "What do the *Legitimas* want?"

"Well," McCarter began, "according to Stony Man intel, they want to replace the current government and—"

"No, no," Turrin said. "What do they want right now? Why did they pull the kidnappings?"

"For the money."

"Right. They need money. They need it now. And the hostage negotiations are likely to take time. So we put up a five-million-dollar prize to anyone who can stay in the ring with Toro for three minutes. A quick five million is pretty good walking-around money while they work out the details of the hostage release. And what do they have to lose? Hix gets killed? What do they care?"

"Leo, this plan has holes big enough to drive a Hummer through," McCarter argued. "The *Legitimas* can't just bring Hix out in the open. It would be inviting arrest."

"Not under the name Scott Hix, they can't," Turrin said. "But how hard is it to call him John Doe or Jim Smith?"

"But the five-million-dollar prize doesn't make sense," McCarter said. "You've got nothing to win."

"We aren't planning on any takers to last three minutes, right? So we won't have to pay the prize money. And we can make a lot of money on side bets. Besides, if everything goes accordingly, there's not even going to be a fight between Toro and Hix."

On the sidewalk, McCarter saw heartbreakingly deformed beggars in front of several doors. They held their hands out as American men, women and children strolled by in shorts and T-shirts with cameras around their necks. Most of the tourists turned their heads from the pathetic sights.

"Do you want me to point out the other obvious problems with this plan, Leo?" McCarter asked.

"Please do," Turrin said, grinning. "It'll be fun telling you how I've already worked them out."

"First, what if Martinez—Toro—doesn't beat Julio Conde? And what if he leaves the ring minus his eyes or ears or nose, or doesn't leave the ring at all?"

Turrin shrugged. "Martinez is a grown man, David," he said. "He's aware of the danger and he's willing to chance it—I didn't pressure him. But if he loses to Conde, you're right, the game's over. That's one of the calculated risks that comes on any assignment. You know that."

McCarter nodded. "All right, let's assume Toro beats Conde. What if the *Legitimas* still don't bring Hix out? What if they think it's too dangerous, or they don't even hear about the prize money? I imagine they're a little too busy right now to be staunch fans of Tijuana's version of a Jean-Claude Van Damme movie."

Turrin shrugged again. "Once more, a calculated risk," he said. "But we're going to do everything we can to make sure they're aware of the prize. While Toro has been kicking ass, little Pompei has worked his way into TJ's criminal element. He's pretty sure some of his new friends have ties to a *bandido* who recently linked up with the *Legitimas*." He paused to clear his throat. "Pompei will talk the thing up and get the word out that way. But I'm even going to run ads in the newspapers, just in case."

"The papers?" McCarter said, frowning. "Won't the cops—"

"Like I said, a lot of them are fans, David," Turrin interrupted.

McCarter nodded slowly, more to himself than to Turrin. "Okay, but don't forget there's going to be other men wanting this prize, too," he said. "And it's not like Hix is going to contact you himself. It'll be somebody representing him— one of the *Legitimas*—and they'll be using an alias for Hix. How are you going to know which offer is the right one?"

"Oh ye of little faith," Turrin said, shaking his head in mock sadness. "We're going to interview people and we're going to ask questions. Then we're going to demand, not request, demand to see the actual fighter before the match."

"On what pretext?"

"That we don't want to look like buffoons in front of everyone," Turrin said. "We're promoters, we're putting on a show, and we can't have some wimpy-assed SOB who doesn't even last three seconds, let alone minutes. It's bad for business."

"You think the *Legitimas* give a damn about your business?"

"No, but I think they'll want the five million. At least I'm counting on it."

"So we snatch Hix at the interview, then force the revolutionaries guarding him to take us back to the other hostages?"

Turrin nodded. "Or just leave him with the *Legitimas* and follow them all back. Whichever looks better when the time comes."

He smiled at McCarter. "You know, you're catching on to this stuff, David," he said in the voice of a grade-school teacher praising a student. Both he and McCarter chuckled as Turrin opened the door and got out.

The Phoenix Force leader and his men followed. Turrin led the way through a narrow doorway and up a flight of splintered stairs.

"Where are we going?"

"To meet Toro and Pompei," Turrin answered. "I think you'll have more faith in my plan after you do." He reached the top of the stairs and rapped three times on the door, paused, then struck it four more times. A few seconds later, the door cracked open and an eye appeared.

"It's us, Pompei," Turrin said. "Let us in."

The door opened the rest of the way and a man barely five feet tall stepped back. McCarter guessed he didn't tip the scales at over a hundred and ten pounds, and he was grateful that Turrin had called him by name as soon as the door opened. Pompei looked more like a racehorse jockey than a fighter, and the Phoenix Force leader suspected his heart might have stopped if he'd thought that this was Toro.

Turrin led everyone into the living room of the dingy apartment. The room was completely devoid of furniture, and wrestling mats had been spread across the floor. From the rear of the dwelling came an erratic pounding sound; someone was working out on a heavy bag.

"One final question then," McCarter said.

"Shoot," said Turrin said. "Not literally, of course, although you may be tempted to if your next question is what I think it is."

"What do you want us to do while you're setting all this up?"

A smile that looked like it had been borrowed from Satan spread across Turrin's face. Rather than answer immediately, he turned toward the hallway and shouted, "Toro!"

The pounding sounds stopped. A moment later, heavy footsteps plodded along the hallway's wood floor. Then one of the largest, meanest looking men David McCarter had ever seen stepped into the living room.

Toro's head had been shaved to expose a shining coffee-colored scalp that glistened with the sweat of his workout. He wore only a skintight pair of bright red sweat shorts, and his chest dripped with perspiration.

"Martinez, Oklahoma Bureau of Narcotics and Dangerous Drugs, meet David McCarter and his men," Turrin said.

Toro nodded to each of the men.

"Well," McCarter said, staring at the huge man. "You look like you might be able to take care of yourself. What do you weigh in at?"

Toro shrugged.

"You've done some fighting in the ring before, I understand?"

The giant nodded but again kept mute.

The Phoenix Force leader turned to Turrin. "Can't he talk?" he asked bluntly.

"He can," Turrin said. "He just doesn't like to." He turned to Toro and said, "Go on, Toro. You're going to have to eventually. Might as well get it over with."

Toro looked down at the mats on the floor and suddenly all of the menace drained from his face. He looked very much like a frightened schoolboy being forced to speak against his will in class. McCarter guessed he must have some sort of speech impediment of which he was ashamed, and prepared himself accordingly.

Finally, with a deep breath, Toro said, "Pleased to meet you guys."

The room fell into silence, and McCarter realized however well he had prepared himself, he hadn't been ready for what he'd just heard. For a moment, he even wondered if the voice that had just spoken might have come from a ventriloquist rather than the hulking monster he saw before him.

Before any of the others could respond, Toro looked up. "Okay," he said. "Now you know. I've got the body of the Incredible Hulk and I can fight like Mike Tyson and Muhammad Ali combined. I was an all-American linebacker at the University of Nebraska, and I've got more black belts than I can mention." He took another deep breath. "But the good Lord has a sense of humor sometimes. He gave me the vocal cords of Shirley Temple.''

''You'll get used to it,'' Turrin said. ''Pompei and I did.''

McCarter turned to Turrin, thankful that he had broken the ice. ''You still haven't answered my question, Leo,'' he said. ''I assume you've got some part in all of this for us?''

The evil smile returned to Turrin's lips. ''Oh yes,'' he said. He turned back to the embarrassed giant before them. ''Toro's been doing great work on the punching bags.'' He paused and, although McCarter wouldn't have thought it possible, the leering smile became even more wicked. ''He fights Conde late tonight, and he'll need to rest between now and then. But right now, he needs some live training partners.''

2

The old witch brought down the end of the belt across her son's bare back and watched the area she had struck swell into a bright crimson welt. As she had already done ten times before, she took a short half step to the side, raised the belt again and slapped it across her other son's back.

Roberto remained silent. But a soft, kittenlike mew escaped Santiago's lips. Both men's eyes were filled with tears, their skin now covered with the ugly bumps the leather had brought on.

The old woman stepped back, her breath coming in short tight gasps. A strange excitement filled her bony chest. She looked down at her sons, on their hands and knees before her, and struck them both again. Finally, Roberto let out a short whimper. An angry series of strikes, one after the other, turned the whimper into cries and left the old witch-woman so breathless she was forced to stop. It was several moments before she even managed to say, "Get up."

Roberto and Santiago rose, blood dripping from the more severe wounds.

"You have failed!" the old woman shouted. "Failed!" she brought the belt around in an arc that caught Santiago just below the ribs and released another wail of pain from his lips.

"You had this man, this president's bodyguard, and you let him get away!" said the old woman, shaking her head.

"Please, mama," whispered Roberto. "It couldn't be helped."

The old woman brought her arm back and whipped the belt across his abdomen. Another bright red welt appeared, and with a scream her oldest son fell to his knees.

"Tell me again, Roberto," the old witch said. "Tell me again what happened."

He looked up from his knees afraid any word he spoke might bring on another stinging blow. But after a few seconds, he saw in his mother's eyes that his continued silence was certain to do so. "This man isn't human, mama," he risked. "He was shot with enough tranquilizers to bring down a rhinoceros. I was even worried that he'd die before we got him home."

The old woman waited.

After a few gasps for air and a grimace, Roberto continued. "He must have awakened in the truck. When we got back in after pumping the gas, he was gone."

The old woman frowned. She had loaded the tranquilizer gun herself and supplied the extra darts. Her sons had used all of them on the man, and indeed by all rights it should have killed him. But it hadn't.

Not only had he lived, he had escaped.

Did the American bodyguard known as Mike Belasko have his own magic? Was his magic stronger than hers? It was possible.

Looking down at her son again, the old witch motioned for him to rise. She had known this man Belasko was strong—only a strong man could have kept the president alive throughout all of the assassination attempts. And she had hoped to incorporate his strength with her own after killing him through the proper ritual. But now, she had to wonder if that was possible. If his strengths came from magic, and that magic surpassed her own, he might well kill her and her sons instead.

The old woman looked around the ritual room, seeing the threadbare furniture, daggers and other ornaments. She turned to the coffee table, reached down and picked up a newspaper. On the front page, she saw President Fierro Blanco looking back at her. His bearded face was a mask of sadness. Lifting the paper, she turned the headline toward her sons. "*El presidente* presumes Mike Belasko is dead," she said.

Roberto's eyes brightened slightly. "Perhaps it is so, mama," he said. "He had such an enormous amount of tranquilizer in his system, he could have escaped but then died."

The old woman stared at her son with the expression of some-one eyeing a centipede. Suddenly, she brought the belt around, striking him across his face. Roberto's arms flew up a second too late as he recoiled backward. The back of his knees struck the couch and sent him spilling over the top.

"You fool!" the old woman screamed as Roberto scrambled to his feet. "I said 'presumes'! Whoever it was that kidnapped Mike Belasko, *el presidente* reasons, has killed him. Well, idiots," she went on, looking back and forth between the two boys. "We know who the kidnappers were, don't we? And we know they didn't kill this man. Because you, my dim-witted sons, let him escape!"

Both men now stood side by side again, dripping blood, looking down at the floor.

The old witch threw the paper on the floor in front of them. "We're the only ones who know he isn't dead," she said, more to herself than her boys. "So we must ask ourselves why has he not returned to *Los Pinos?*"

"Perhaps he *did* die, mama. Perhaps they haven't yet discovered the body."

A sharp look and a short movement of the belt brought another cringe from Roberto. He clamped his lips tightly in silence.

"No," said the old witch. "Mike Belasko isn't dead. He didn't return to the presidential mansion because he is looking for *you.* He is the kind of man who wouldn't forget a thing like this. Look-ing for you means looking for *us.*" She paused, and the excitement she had felt earlier turned to a blood-freezing fear. "And he is the kind of man who will find us."

Santiago rarely spoke, letting his brother do his talking for him. But now it was he who broke the silence. "Mama, what do you want us to do?"

The old woman looked up at him. For a brief moment, she remembered him as a little baby suckling her breast. The image flew quickly away. "Clean yourselves up," she said. "Then come back. I need time to think." She waved them out of the room and sat on the couch.

Idly, the old witch picked up the stone dagger on the coffee table and twirled it in her hand. She had planned to use it on

Belasko as she performed the ancient ritual that would transfer his strength and power to her before leading to his death. She had been ordered to kill the president's bodyguard by the bearded man; the powerful man who was, in one way or another, behind all of the turmoil Mexico was currently experiencing. And the bearded man had been explicit about the fact that he wanted Belasko dead without delay. She had been lured, however, by the power that kidnapping him first and performing the ceremony might bring her. She had gambled and lost. And now, if the bearded man found out, she would pay. With her life and the lives of her sons.

Roberto and Santiago returned wearing clean clothes. The corners of gauze bandages could be seen beneath their open collars.

"Sit beside me," the old woman said.

The men complied as if ordered by God Himself.

The woman looked first at Santiago. He was hard to figure out. He seemed only interested in eating, drinking, smoking marijuana and, of course, sex. Santiago wasn't stupid. But he was limited.

Turning to Roberto, the witch examined him. Roberto was the more intelligent of the two. But he would be no match for the American.

The old woman's mind returned to the direct orders the bearded man had given her: She was to kill the president's bodyguard outright and not risk attempting to steal his magic first. She knew what the bearded man would do to her and her sons if he found out that the American had escaped because she had violated those orders, and suddenly, the acquisition of Belasko's strength didn't seem nearly as important as it had the day before. Not compared to what the bearded man would do if he found out the bodyguard still lived.

Standing, the old woman shuffled slowly across the room to where Roberto's and Santiago's machetes hung from nails in the wall. She lifted one in each hand. How many times had she seen her boys use these blades on a human sacrifice? How many times had they killed others for the money supplied by the bearded man? She didn't know.

Turning back to her sons, she handed them their weapons of choice. Roberto started to speak but she held her finger to her lips.

She then shuffled across the floor to the splintered sea chest against the wall.

It took both of the old woman's spindly arms to raise the lid. She began digging until she reached the bottom. Then, with a grunt of anguish, she lifted the suitcase out.

Roberto appeared by her side and took the heavy case from her trembling hands. "What is it, mama?" he asked. "I didn't know there was anything inside the box but junk."

The old woman didn't answer. She pointed at the floor next to the couch and Roberto set the suitcase down. Taking her seat again, the witch unfastened the clasps and opened the lid. Out of the corner of her eye, she saw Santiago smile.

Roberto reached in and lifted the Winchester 1200 12-gauge shotgun and unfolded the plastic pistol-grip Choate stock. He pressed the butt into his shoulder and grinned like an idiot.

"Be careful, you fool," the old woman said. "It's loaded." She turned to Santiago. "Take the other one," she said.

Santiago lifted the Rossi Model 92. With it's sixteen-inch barrel, the .357 Magnum lever-action carbine would be almost concealable under a long coat.

"You still have the pistols you took from the gate guards at *Los Pinos?*" the old woman asked.

"Yes," Roberto said. "A .45 automatic and a .357 Magnum revolver. And we have the American's weapons as well." He pointed to the .44 Magnum Desert Eagle and Beretta 93-R select-fire pistol on a table in the corner of the room. "But we'll need extra ammunition for all of the guns."

"That isn't in my line," the old woman said. "My weapons are from the spirit world. I wouldn't have had these guns had your father not left them. But I'm sure you know men who can supply the proper bullets."

"Yes, mama," Roberto said, still admiring the shotgun. "I'll have ammunition within the hour. But where do we find Belasko?"

The old witch couldn't suppress a sigh. What would happen to her two poor boys once she was gone? They were such idiots.

"He'll be looking for *you*, my babies," she said. "And he'll start his search at the last place he saw you."

"The gas station?" Roberto asked.

"Where else?" the old woman answered, considering a few more whacks with the belt out of sheer frustration at their witlessness.

"Then we'll go there," Roberto said, his head bobbing. "And we'll be well-armed this time when we take him prisoner."

Again the old witch sighed. "Don't try to kidnap him again, Roberto," she said. "You have already proven incapable of doing so. Just go to the gas station and wait. When he arrives, kill him."

SECURITY AT BENITO JUAREZ airport was similar to what the Executioner had dealt with at most installations in Mexico. It appeared to be in place simply for the personal benefit of those operating it.

Bolan rolled down the window as the uniformed guard approached. The man was a good hundred pounds overweight, and the stripes down the legs of his skintight trousers zigzagged back and forth under the strain of his massive thighs. He leaned to rest a flabby arm on the window as he said, "May I help you?" in Spanish.

"I'm meeting a friend who just flew into one of the private hangars," Bolan answered in the same language.

The guard's hairy eyebrows rose slightly. "Ah," he said. "I'm not sure I can permit this. We have had much trouble in that area recently. Drug smugglers, you know." His eyes beamed with greed.

Bolan sighed. Call it graft, bribery, or whatever you liked, payoffs were a way of life in Mexico. And while it went against his grain to be part of it, the Executioner had found playing the game was sometimes a necessary evil. Reaching into his pocket, he produced his money clip and peeled off a hundred-dollar bill. "This is for going in," he said, handing it through the window. "And this is for coming back out without being stopped." Another hundred passed from his hand to the guard's.

The uniformed man's eyes widened to the size of dinner plates as he stuffed the bills into his trousers. It was far more than he had anticipated.

Bolan pulled through the gate and onto an access road, bypassing the lighted area of the passenger terminal. The private hangars stood at the edge of the airport just inside the security fence illuminated by lights atop tall wooden poles. As he neared, the shadowy form of a man standing next to the nearest shed came into view.

The Executioner pulled to a halt in front of the hangar and got out. Jack Grimaldi extended his hand. "Having fun down here, Striker?" Stony Man Farm's ace pilot asked, grinning.

Bolan chuckled. He and Grimaldi went back a long way, all the way to the days when the former U.S. Army fighter pilot had made a "wrong turn" in life's skyways and begun flying for the Mafia. The Executioner had been right in the middle of his personal war with the Mob, and had helped the basically honest Grimaldi see the error of his ways. The pilot had gone to work for Stony Man Farm, and since then Bolan had never had a truer and more loyal friend and fellow warrior.

"You bring me a care package, Jack?"

"Several," Grimaldi said, stepping back and indicating the entrance to the hangar. "Step inside my parlor said the spider to the fly."

Bolan opened the hangar door and held it for his old friend. He saw the large trunks Grimaldi had already unloaded onto the floor next to the wall and headed that way.

Grimaldi cleared his throat. "There's a little essential explanation that comes with some of the gear Cowboy sent."

Bolan laughed. "There usually is, Jack," he said. He dropped to one knee and unsnapped the catches on the nearest trunk. John "Cowboy" Kissinger, Stony Man Farm's chief armorer, stayed on the cutting edge of technology. Which meant that along with the Executioner's usual weapons and other gear, there were almost always a few "surprises" Kissinger wanted field-tested. Bolan didn't mind. By the time Kissinger passed them on to him, they had already been though so many tests that the Executioner knew they would work.

Flipping the lid, Bolan found a medium-sized black leather briefcase. Opening it, he found a Heckler & Koch Personal Defense Weapon. The newest version of the world-renowned MP-5K, included a folding stock and was only fourteen and a half inches overall. The Executioner lifted the weapon, checked the action, then set it on the concrete floor next to the trunk.

"Cowboy has altered the select-fire mechanism," Grimaldi said as Bolan stacked the extra 30-round 9 mm magazines that had come with the submachine gun next to it. "You've got semiauto, fullauto, and a hammer feature rather than 3-round burst."

Bolan nodded. The hammer feature was a concept Kissinger had been playing with for several weeks now. Some of his tests had indicated that the third round in bursts of three often went astray. Even if the last of the trio stayed on target, for a marksman of the Executioner's degree, it was overkill and the waste of a perfectly good 9 mm round that might be needed later. A double tap to the chest or head was almost always more than enough if the shot placement was on target. On the rare occasions that more shots were needed, Bolan had only to pull the trigger again.

The foam rubber insert on which the briefcase had rested came out of the trunk next. Bolan looked down to see that the next layer contained an SIG-550. Arguably the finest assault rifle in the world, it too wore a folding stock. Also like the MP-5K, a dozen extra magazines accompanied it.

"Ever shoot one before?" Grimaldi said in an innocent voice behind Bolan. "An assault rifle, I mean?"

Bolan chuckled again. "Maybe you could give me a few pointers, Jack," he said. "And when we're through, I'll teach you how to fly an airplane." Replacing the weapons and magazines, he moved to the second trunk.

Smaller in size, it too was packed in layers. The top yielded a replacement for both the .44 Magnum Desert Eagle and Beretta 93-R. Just below them Bolan found another Boker Applegate-Fairbairn dagger and Gerber's version of the folder—the big brother to the Applegate-Fairbairn Covert that had enabled the Executioner to escape from his kidnappers and the would-be rob-bers in the taxi. He had ordered and expected these blades. But the third knife he saw gleaming up at him was unanticipated.

"It's called a Hell's Belle Bowie," Grimaldi said as Bolan lifted the blade and drew it from the leather sheath. The huge clip point weapon featured an eleven-and-one-third-inch blade and a double guard, both sides of which curved gracefully toward the tip to work in conjunction with the Spanish notch cut into the blade near the hilt. With these features, a skilled man could actually trap an opponent's blade, twist slightly and disarm his attacker. Inferior blades would even snap in two. The Spanish notch and guard were wasted on anyone short of the expert knife player. But in the hands of someone like the Executioner, they became another asset.

Opening the third trunk, Bolan found an assortment of holsters, a blacksuit, boots, folded civilian clothing and various other gear. He took off the denim shirt and slipped a black leather shoulder holster over his black T-shirt. The new sound-suppressed Beretta 93-R slid between the spring clip retainer. The Desert Eagle went into a Helweg speed rig on his right hip. The Kydex sheathed Boker found a home at the small of his back, and the Gerber folder—also housed in Kydex—slid horizontally into his belt on the left side for a fast left-hand presentation. The Covert he kept where it had been since the kidnapping—clipped to his right front pocket. Donning the faded denim shirt once more, Bolan covered the body arsenal.

Grimaldi reached into his pocket and pulled out a large passport case. Bolan opened it to find a passport and credit cards in the name "Michael Belasko" and the equivalent of fifty thousand dollars in pesos in the money compartment.

"We forget anything?" Grimaldi asked.

"Yeah," Bolan said, glancing over his shoulder at the equipment. "A warehouse to keep all this stuff in."

"Sorry, big guy," the Stony Man pilot grinned. "You're on your own there. I'd suggest the trunk of your car."

The Executioner shook his head. "Not big enough," he said. "Besides, I've got to ditch the rig I brought here before it's turned in as stolen. But I've got another idea." He turned, lifted the trunk containing the SIG and Heckler & Koch, and started toward the door.

Grimaldi grabbed another of the boxes and followed. "Care to share it?" he asked. "Or is it one of those deals where you could tell me but then you'd have to kill me?"

Bolan laughed. "I think you can be trusted." He told the pilot what he had in mind.

Now it was Grimaldi's turn to laugh. "That ought to fit your new image," he said. "You look like a broken-down old rodeo cowboy-turned-drug dealer."

"That's the idea." Bolan opened the trunk of the cab and deposited the container with the rifle and submachine gun. It filled the trunk and he opened the door to the back seat, holding it while Grimaldi deposited the second box. Together, they returned to the hangar for the last equipment container.

"Anything else, Striker?"

Bolan shook his head.

"Then I'm out of here," Grimaldi said. He extended his hand. "I've got to standby for Able Team in Houston. They're hitting a whorehouse and they may find leads to somewhere else."

Bolan took his old friend's hand. "Where's Mott?" he asked, inquiring about one of Stony Man Farm's other pilots.

"Charlie's cooling his heels in Tucson, trying to split the difference between you and Phoenix Force—depending on who needs him first." He paused, frowned in thought, then added, "We may be cutting it pretty thin on pilots. I'll radio Brognola and see if he can put Bill Humphrey on alert."

The Executioner nodded. Humphrey, now in his seventies, was a veteran World War II fighter and glider pilot, and an old friend of Brognola's. He still had the reflexes of a man in his twenties, and was called in to take up the slack when Stony Man ran short of flyers.

"Charlie's in Tucson?" Bolan said, more statement than question. "Any word on T.J.?"

"He's staying in touch by cellular phone. Last word was that Hawk was out of surgery and in the ICU. He's still listed as critical."

"The doctors giving any odds?"

Grimaldi's face covered in pain, then went deadpan again. "Yeah," he said. "But you don't want to hear them."

The Executioner felt the same pain of concern for the wounded Phoenix Force warrior flow through his body. He pushed it aside. There was nothing he could do, and worrying would only get in the way of his own mission. "Be careful, Jack," Bolan said.

"You too, Sarge," the pilot answered.

Bolan got behind the wheel and drove off. The same guard stood at the gate and he waved the Executioner through without stopping him.

Two hours later, the sun rose over southern Mexico. An hour after that, the Executioner saw the first salesman arrive and unlock the glass front doors to Ramone's Boat and RV Center on the edge of Mexico City. And forty-five minutes after that, he paid the salesman for a 1969 Chevy bus that had been converted into a camper. The salesman had been delighted that the gringo hadn't haggled over the price, and even happier when there was no argument about the cost of the second vehicle purchase. The Executioner's overpayment, and an additional five-hundred-dollar "tip," had insured that the paperwork on both acquisitions would be lost.

Thirty minutes after leaving the RV lot, Bolan had stopped at a lumberyard and procured a pair of two-by-twelve planks. Another stop at a hardware store got him the tools and nuts, bolts and screws he needed.

By noon he was on his way to find the brothers who had kidnapped him, discover why the *Marxistas* had attempted to kill President Fierro Blanco of Mexico so many times, and the truth about the president himself.

ABOVE THE RUMBLE of the crowd, the brassy sounds of a Mexican quartet playing the old Herb Alpert song "The Lonely Bull" could be heard. Barmaids worked the floor fetching whiskey, beer and tequila, and giggling whenever a drunken hand ran up their short tight skirts. Cigarette and cigar smoke clouded the room, giving it an almost unworldly ambience.

Seated at a table with McCarter, Encizo and Manning, Calvin James raised his arm to scratch his head and felt the pain shoot through his shoulder. It wasn't bad, really. In fact, it was somewhat reassuring. The pain was the result of the two rounds he'd sparred with Toro earlier in the day, and reminded him that the Oklahoma State Bureau of Narcotics agent could hit like the bull for which he'd been named. This, in turn, helped James believe that the young man at least stood a fighting chance of defeating the behemoth who had just stepped in through the front door of the Roho Cantina.

James watched through the smoke as two trainers led Julio Conde confidently through the bar, turning over tables that stood in their way rather than walking around them. Occupants of those tables who didn't see the procession in time to move went sprawling onto the dirty floor along with bottles, glasses and ashtrays.

James studied the underground bare-knuckles circuit fighter. Conde was huge for a man of any race and enormous by Mexican standards. Standing a good six foot six in the heavy work boots he wore, he had to weigh in at close to four hundred pounds. But he moved with a grace that seemed to contradict his size, and beneath the flab James knew there was still far more muscle than could be found on any other man in the room.

With the possible exception of Toro.

James watched Conde's face as the no-rules fighter climbed into the ring that had been set up in the center of the big cantina. He had deep sunken eyes and the broken veins of a drinker's nose. Heavy lines creased the man's forehead beneath a distinct widow's peak hairline. But no matter which feature the Phoenix Force warrior looked at, he was always drawn back to those eyes.

They were like the eyes of a shark. Dull. Deadly. The eyes of a killer.

The regulation boxing ring, the Phoenix Force warrior knew, was the only thing that would even remotely resemble a boxing match. In the underground bare-knuckles fighting circuit anything went; eye-gouging, biting, everything was permitted. The only restriction was that weapons weren't to be used, and James had even heard stories about that rule being violated.

Cheers rose from the drunken crowd as Julio Conde climbed through the ropes onto the canvas. One of the men with Conde, looking like an over-the-hill fighter himself, set a three-legged stool in the corner. James had no idea who he was.

But the other man, dressed in a well-cut beige linen suit, who now leaned through the ropes and whispered into the seated Conde's ear, was Pedro Hernandez. A midlevel Tijuana drug cartel boss, Hernandez managed Conde's fighting career as a hobby. In turn, Conde did odd jobs for his boss—like breaking arms, legs and necks.

Conde listened to whatever Hernandez was whispering, then laughed. He reached out and grabbed a handful of air at testicle level, twisted and then jerked his arm back.

All eyes in the room turned toward the door on the other side of the ring as it swung open. The brass quartet halted in the middle of "The Lonely Bull" and went into a Hispanic version of the theme from the *Rocky* movies. James saw Leo Turrin, wearing a freshly pressed off-white suit similar to the one he'd had on earlier in the day, enter the room and step to the side. Pompei came next, his little head barely visible over the tabletops. Toro followed, wearing the same skintight sweat shorts he had worked out in earlier in the day. On his feet were black Adidas martial-arts shoes. The half-black half-Mexican's chest glimmered with sweat; the muscles in his arms and legs rippled in shadowy light.

Turrin led the way to the ring, holding the ropes while Toro climbed through. Pompei set a stool similar to the one Conde's man had brought in the corner. Toro ignored it. He began dancing and punching, staying warm.

A middle-aged Hispanic man in a frayed black tuxedo now entered the ring as a microphone lowered from the ceiling, and then the man began to speak in Spanish. He welcomed the crowd, made a joke about buying more tequila, then said, "In this corner, the champion, Julio Conde." He went on to announce a record of 101 victories, no defeats and eighteen kills.

The crowd seemed to take the kills statistic as another joke.

Turning to Toro, the announcer said, "And the challenger, new to Tijuana, we know little about him. Toro is his name, but he is indeed a mystery to us all." He paused, then said, "Señor Toro, can you at least tell us from where you come?"

James held his breath. Toro's little-girl voice would bring hoots of hilarity from the crowd if heard, and the way Martinez had acted when he first spoke to the men of Phoenix Force, that laughter might kill his confidence right there and then. At the very least, it would set him back a few paces.

But Toro had evidently considered this possibility himself. Rather than answer, he leaned in and whispered to Turrin. A moment later, Turrin looked toward the center of the ring and yelled at the top of his lungs, "Toro would like me to tell you he comes from Hell. But it's your Julio Conde who will be there before the night is over."

The room exploded with applause, screams and the stamping of feet.

"Then let us begin," the announcer said, and hurried out of the ring. A bell just beyond one of the neutral corners chimed. It was the only time the bell would ring until the end of the fight. There was only one round—and it lasted until one of the men surrendered, could fight no longer or died.

Toro moved into the center of the ring first, dancing, bobbing and weaving. James knew that part of his attack plan was to make it appear as if he planned to box. The intelligence reports Pompei had picked up indicated that the last man Conde had fought had been a champion boxer. Conde had taken his best punches as if they have been delivered by a child, moved through them to take the stand-up fighter to the canvas before crushing his larynx with a forearm.

Conde shuffled his bulk forward slowly, looking like a grizzly bear still stiff from a winter of hibernation. But James had seen the big man's gracefulness earlier when he walked into the cantina. The awkward gait was as much a game on Conde's part as the boxer's ruse was on Toro's.

With Toro's feet moving like lightning and Conde's plodding along, the two men began to circle in a counterclockwise direction. Conde stepped in, faking as if to punch, then stepped back out. The movement had stayed well out of Toro's reach, and been designed solely to test the other man's reactions. The result had been that Toro threw a short jab toward Conde's head that fell short.

Now Toro moved in more aggressively, jabbing two lefts, then a right cross that drove the bigger man backward toward the ropes. The flab around Conde's middle danced a jig as he backpedaled, deftly raising his arms to slap away the punches. Shuffling along the ropes a foot inside the ring, he had soon maneuvered out of the corner and back to the center of the canvas.

Conde faked three punches in a row. James could see his face, and saw the evil, deadly eyes now flickering with light and excitement as they carefully watched Toro's reaction to each movement. The big Mexican bare-knuckle fighter was refining his game plan even as he fought. Waiting. Watching. Ready to move in with just the right technique as soon as he saw a weakness.

Toro suddenly slid forward, threw a short right that he never intended to land, then raised his right leg and brought it around in a roundhouse kick. Conde caught the agent's shoe on the forearm. Without hesitation, he stepped forward, faked his own right at Toro's nose, then dived under the man's blocking arm and dropped to his knees.

Conde's arms wrapped around Toro's knees and the hands clasped together at the rear. Conde stood, and suddenly Toro was rising through the air backward.

James drew in a breath. If Conde maintained his hold, Toro would be thrown to the canvas on his back. Conde's four hundred pounds would land on top of him.

The fight would be over.

But Toro had seen what was coming, too. While still in midair, his right fist moved over his head, the second knuckle of the index finger extended. Bringing the fist around behind him, he drove it into the back of one of Conde's hands.

A howl of pain shot from the Mexican giant's mouth. His hands unclasped behind Toro's knees in time for the agent to fall backward on his own, then roll to the side a split second before Conde plummeted to his hands and knees on the canvas.

Toro rolled to his feet, turned back to his opponent and shot out a front kick. The toe of his shoe caught Conde squarely in the ribs. But inches of padding—both fat and muscle—sheltered the fragile bones, and Conde took the force of the blow as if it had come from a child.

Taking another half step in, Toro brought his leg up in the standard Thai boxing knee kick. But Conde had rolled, flying out of the way to bound to his feet on the far side. The slow, lumbering ruse was gone now as he moved forward with the grace of a ballerina. James watched his eyes again. In them, he saw a combination of anger, hatred and humiliation. He guessed that Julio Conde wasn't accustomed to having this much trouble with an opponent.

When he had closed the gap to arm's length, Conde's foot suddenly shot out. The toe of his work boot struck Toro just below the knee and the crack of the strike echoed throughout the cantina. Toro grimaced and stepped back awkwardly. But Conde had gained the advantage he sought, and wasn't about to give it up. Looking like an NFL linebacker about to sack the quarterback, he ducked his head and threw his entire body into the agent from the Oklahoma Bureau of Narcotics and Dangerous Drugs.

This time, Conde's arms encircled Toro's waist. The Fed was driven backward, valiantly struggling to maintain his balance on his injured leg. But Toro's effort was futile. The tackle slammed his back into the canvas.

And now, Conde's four hundred pounds did follow on top of him.

Calvin James felt the pain as if he'd been struck himself as Toro's head hit, then rebounded off the canvas. The agent's eyes rolled up in his head and his body went limp. Conde leaned over his victim, the flab of his belly almost hiding Toro's chest from view. The Mexican giant leaned farther, and placed his left forearm across Toro's throat. His right hand went to the wrist crossing Toro's larynx for support, then he began to raise his buttocks to force all of his weight forward.

James felt his own hands tightening into fists. This was the stranglehold he had heard about—the one with which Conde had killed eighteen men. He could see how. There appeared to be no way anyone could displace a man of Julio Conde's size once he had gained the position he now maintained.

James turned to McCarter. He, Manning and Encizo watched the ring, their eyes glued to what was about to take place. "David!" James shouted above the roar of the excited spectators awaiting Toro's death. "We can't let this happen!" His hand moved under his shirt to where the Beretta 92 was hidden.

McCarter turned to face him and nodded. The former British SAS officer's own hand was reaching for the Browning Hi-Power beneath his lightweight safari jacket. Encizo and Manning made similar movements for their weapons as all four men of Phoenix Force stood around the table.

James turned his eyes back to the ring and saw Leo Turrin watching them. The Stony Man Farm undercover expert began shaking his head.

The Phoenix Force warriors paused.

And that brief moment of hesitation saved both Turrin's plan and Toro's life.

In the ring, Conde had leaned so far forward that he'd risen off his knees and onto his feet. Suddenly, Toro's leg shot upward, his shin catching Conde squarely between the legs. The bigger man's girlish scream echoed above the cheers of the crowd. But he didn't release Toro from his grasp.

Toro's leg shot upward again, then again and again. Each time it struck Conde in the testicles the man squealed. He tried to close his knees together, which threw him off balance. Toro reached up and rammed two fingers into his eyes while his other hand grabbed Conde's sweaty hair. Twisting both his own hips and Conde's head, Toro threw the bigger man to the side.

Toro moved over Julio Conde now, bringing his right arm high over his head. His hand came down in a hammer-fist blow, striking Conde squarely on the nose. Blood spurted from both of the giant's nostrils, but by then Toro's arm was above his head once more. The next hammer-fist caught Conde in the jaw. Again, again and again, like some steel forger's hammer striking an anvil, Toro's fist rained down upon the Mexican champion's face.

Streams of blood and several of Conde's teeth flew through the air around the two entangled bodies. It looked like only a matter of time until the reigning champion of Tijuana's underground fight circuit lost consciousness.

But Julio Conde hadn't become champion by being weak or giving up easily. And he had one last card to play.

James saw it coming and felt helpless to stop it. Even if Toro could have heard him over the roar of the crowd, the Phoenix Force warrior knew there was no way to warn the Fed in time.

While Toro continued to batter Conde's head, James watched the Mexican champion's hand slide to the pocket of his soiled khaki work pants. His fingers disappeared inside for a moment, then returned holding a cheap Mexican switchblade. Holding the knife to his side, beyond Toro's range of vision, Conde thumbed the button and the blade flew open. With a mighty grunt, he brought the stiletto point in an arc toward Toro's ribs.

Nothing but luck, and the fact that he was tiring, saved Toro's life.

A split second before the blade entered his ribs, Toro sat back on his heels to take a deep breath. As he did, his arm moved back to cover his ribs and the cheap Mexican blade struck his biceps. Blood spurted from the wound as Toro shrieked in surprise. His Shirley Temple voice went unnoticed under the circumstances.

What James saw next sent a shiver down his spine. The same killer look that had been in Conde's eyes fell over Toro's face. With a grunt, the Oklahoma Bureau of Narcotics agent reached across his body with his right hand, grasped the wrist still holding the switchblade and bent it downward at a forty-five-degree angle.

Conde screamed as the bone snapped.

Toro didn't pause. Jerking the knife from his hand, he grabbed Conde's hair with his other hand and forced his head back. Then, touching the switchblade's tip to the soft pallet under the giant's chin, he started to drive it up into Julio Conde's brain.

James heard voices behind him screaming, "Down in front!" and realized that he and the other Phoenix Force warriors had remained on their feet.

But no one sat. The room grew quiet as Toro froze on his knees, the tip of the switchblade just under the skin of Conde's throat. A thin trickle of blood began to run down the Mexican fighter's neck as he awaited death.

Then, suddenly, Toro drew back the knife, twirled it from a saber grip into an ice-pick grip, and raised his arm over his head yet again. This time, when the hammer-fist came down, the hilt of the switchblade struck Conde on the chin—right on the "knockout" button. The giant's eyes closed in sleep rather than death.

Toro crawled to the side of the unconscious body, raised his arm again and drove the switchblade into the canvas in front of him. Twisting the knife, he snapped the cheap handle from the blade, rose and threw the broken plastic into the crowd.

Toro smiled, held out his arms and roared like a victorious bull. The crowd went wild then, screaming and applauding. Dozens of peasants who must have won small fortunes in bets rushed the ring, lifting the panting Martinez to their shoulders and carrying him off as a hero. The brass band struck up a rousing rendition of Spanish bullfight music, as the room began to chant, "Toro! Toro! Toro!"

Calvin James and the other men of Phoenix Force looked at one another in both relief and disbelief as they moved toward the door where Toro and the mob were headed. Leo Turrin and Pompei climbed down from the ring and began trying to fight their way through the crowd. Anyone wanting to be heard had to shout, and Gary Manning leaned into James and almost took out his fellow warrior's eardrums when he yelled, "This guy, Martinez...Toro...Oklahoma Bureau of Narcotics, right?"

James nodded.

"Remind me of something later, will you?" Manning said, grinning.

James frowned. "What's that?"

"Never sell dope in Oklahoma."

Behind the splintering wooden desk where he had set up the command-post office for the *Cuidadano para Democracia Mexicana Legitima* hostage operation, Jesus Hidalgo stared at Pablo Huertes. Short of both money and manpower, Hidalgo's CDML had been forced to form an uneasy alliance with Huertes and his *bandidos*. Right now, the *Legitima* leader knew he needed them. But the sooner he could get rid of the motley crew, the happier he would be.

At the moment, Huertes sat across the desk in the room's only chair. The sight and smell of the man disgusted Hidalgo.

But what the bandit had just said did not.

"Repeat that, please," Hidalgo said.

Huertes shrugged. "I said," he began, "that word in Tijuana is that Julio Conde was defeated. By some new fighter they are calling Toro."

"Not that part," Hidalgo said. He leaned onto his desk and crossed his arms. "The rest."

Huertes frowned, trying to remember. Finally he said, "Do you mean the rumor that now no one will fight this Toro?"

"Go on," Hidalgo prompted.

Huertes shifted in the chair, and the movement sent an acrid wave of the *bandido's* body odor floating through the air, causing Hidalgo to recoil involuntarily. "Word has it that the syndicate backing Toro is offering a five-million-dollar prize to anyone who can last three minutes with their man."

The CDML leader shook his head in disbelief. "That makes no

sense. Syndicates are in business to make money. How can they make money when they offer such a reward?''

Huertes shrugged again. He pulled a bottle of tequila from inside his filthy shirt and took a swig, then replaced it. His eyes took on a watery look as he said, "I suppose they don't believe anyone can beat Toro—or even stay in the ring with him for that length of time. So they won't have to pay the reward. And their money will come from side bets.''

Huertes frowned through the fog of alcohol that encompassed his brain, "I only mentioned this in passing. Why does it interest you so?''

"Because we have a man who might possibly defeat this Toro," Hidalgo said. "Or at least last the three minutes it will take to collect the five million dollars.''

Huertes burst into laughter. "Who?" he said. "You? Me? Which of our men? I have never even seen this Toro but I have watched Julio Conde fight many times. If Toro has beaten him, believe me, we have no one who would stand a chance.''

Hidalgo's eyes narrowed. His hatred of the revolting bandit he saw before him grew with each second he was forced to share with the man. "I was speaking of Hix," Hidalgo said. "Scott Hix.''

Huertes had taken the bottle from his shirt again and removed the cap. He stopped it halfway to his lips. "Yes..." he said slowly. "Perhaps the American could win, or at least last the three minutes." He took the drink before finishing. "You researched him carefully? And he was a...?''

"A close-quarters combat specialist," Hidalgo said. He flipped open a manilla file folder on the desk in front of him, a gift from a Mexican-American *Legitima* sympathizer in the U.S. Army. "Hix was the best the Americans had. He was assigned to U.S. Military Intelligence and was behind the lines in Iraq during the Gulf War. His dossier states that he was there to help locate the Iraqi SCUDs and also to pinpoint locations for the 'smart bombs,' as they called them. During that time, he killed several men with his bare hands, others with a knife." He watched the dumb look on Huertes's face grow dumber, as if the bandit was hearing this for the first time, which he wasn't. "Why do you think we have taken such extra pains to guard him?" Hidalgo couldn't resist asking sarcastically.

Huertes's answer was a sour belch, which caused Hidalgo to try moving even farther back. He tried to ignore the stench as the bandit leader said, "But what if Toro kills Hix? If Hix is dead we lose the half-million dollars of his ransom."

Hidalgo couldn't keep his head from shaking in awe at the bandit's stupidity. "The ransom will take time to collect," he said. "Perhaps weeks more of negotiation. The Americans have a saying that describes our situation well: 'A bird in the hand is worth two in the bush.' And I'll risk a half-million dollars for the chance to make five." He had seen Huertes's drunken eyes grow confused when he spoke of the birds and bushes. But it didn't matter. The man seemed to get the point.

"Hix will have to be guarded closely," Huertes slurred. "He'll try to escape at the fight."

"I don't think so."

Huertes's eyebrows rose in confusion once more.

"The woman," the *Legitima* leader said. "The West woman, Normandi. We'll use her to control him."

Huertes rubbed the stubble on his chin. "Yes," he said. "He's in love with her."

"Go get him."

Huertes frowned again. "Hix?" he asked.

It was all Hidalgo could do to keep from reaching across the desk and slapping the filthy, stupid drunk. Instead, he sighed. "Yes, Huertes," he said patiently. "Hix. Scott Hix. You do remember him, don't you?"

Huertes drained the rest of his tequila and dropped the bottle on the floor next to the chair. He rose and left the room.

Jesus Hidalgo sighed again, got up from behind the desk and circled it. He wished with all his heart that he was free of the bandits. But until he recruited more men, he couldn't be. And until he had money, he couldn't recruit more men. In the meantime, as distasteful as the meetings with the bandit chief were, he preferred to let Huertes believe he was second-in-command. That way the *Legitima* leader could keep a close eye on him.

Lifting the tequila bottle off the floor with a thumb and forefinger, Hidalgo carried it across the room as if lice, the HIV virus or some other yet-to-be-discovered disease might jump off it at any moment. He dropped it into the battered wastebasket next to his desk, then returned to his seat. He would have to give Hix another name for the fight. If not, word would leak to the public that one of the kidnapped Americans had challenged Toro. And it might also be necessary to disguise Hix in some manner—pictures of all of the hostages but the Tijuana whores had been in the newspapers.

Hidalgo caught himself nodding. These were minor problems; they could be easily dealt with.

Five minutes later, Huertes and five rifle-toting guards dragged a bound, blindfolded and limping Scott Hix into the office. Huertes and two of his slovenly men held Hix by the arms. They half dropped, half threw him into the chair in front of the desk, then ripped the duct tape from his eyes as the other guards took up positions along the walls.

Hix squinted into the light.

"Buenos dias," said Jesus Hidalgo.

"Fuck you," answered Scott Hix.

Hidalgo nodded sadly. "Señor Hix, I can readily understand your anger," he said. "I have, however, already explained that I regret what you and your friends have been through, and what you must continue to endure. But it's unavoidable and necessary for the cause."

"And I've already told you I think that's a crock of shit," Hix said. "If you're so sorry, let us go."

Hidalgo leaned forward again. "I can't do that," he said. "Not exactly. But what I'm about to propose is at least an improvement over your current situation."

Scott Hix sat in the straight-backed wooden chair, expressionless, as the revolutionary leader explained about Julio Conde, the new fighter Toro and the reward. But before he could make his pitch, Hix burst into laughter. "Wait a minute," the American said. "I see where this is going, and you can save your breath. I saw Conde fight once. If Toro beat him, I don't want any part of him any more than the rest of those bare-knuckle idiots in TJ. I'm not in shape for a fight like that, and I especially don't intend to fight him for your benefit.''

"But it would be to your benefit, as well."

"Lay your cards on the table, Hidalgo."

"If you defeat Toro, the CDML will have the much-needed funds to continue our fight for freedom. I can't release the other hostages, especially your friend Quartel. That would be like trading ten million for five. But I will release you, if you are victorious.''

Hix hesitated, and Hidalgo could see the former intelligence agent was trying to formulate an on-the-spot plan to get the most out of his cooperation. He waited.

A few seconds later, Hix said, "Here's the deal. I fight Toro. Win or lose, you release everybody except Quartel and the TJ mayor. Besides me, they're the only ones worth any money to you.''

It was precisely the offer Jesus Hidalgo had anticipated. He shook his head. "No. First, you must win. And although we have demanded no money for the other hostages, their very number keeps us in the headlines of the American newspapers and calls attention to our cause. I'll only release you." He waited for the next counteroffer, again, reasonably sure what it would be.

Scott Hix took a long time answering, and again Hidalgo could almost see the wheels turning behind his eyes. He had something in mind, some plan to outwit the leader. But what?

"I've got another idea," Hix finally said. "One that might well be satisfactory to both of us. But I don't see why I should waste my breath.''

"And that is because...?" Hidalgo asked.

"Because there are reasons your simple idea won't work," Hix said. He shifted in his chair as much as his bonds would allow. "For one thing, as soon as word gets out that Scott Hix is going to fight Toro, there's going to be a combined army of FBI agents and any other agency who can squirm their way into the fight.''

"We won't use your real name," Hidalgo said, surprised that the American hadn't thought of that himself. Or had he?

"I haven't seen a newspaper since you good old boys invited me along on this little adventure," Hix said. "But I wouldn't be at all surprised if my picture has been in them every day. You going to give me plastic surgery, too?"

Hidalgo chuckled. "Please, my friend Scott," he said. "With all due respect, don't allow your ego to get in the way of reality. Yes, your picture has been in the newspapers. But only once. And it was a very old picture of you in an Army uniform. You look very different now. A few minor cosmetic changes will disguise you beyond all recognition."

The American tried to shift again, but the chains and tape kept him almost still. "Okay, that might work," he said. "But you haven't even thought of the biggest problem."

"What's that?"

"The fact that in my current physical condition I can't win. And I doubt if I could stay in the ring for three rounds with any decent fighter, let alone this Toro guy." Hix glanced down at his hands and feet. "You see, Jesus, amigo," he said sarcastically. "I've been tied up in the same position for several days now and I can barely walk, let alone fight."

Hidalgo studied the face of the man in front of him, trying to look beyond the skull, see inside the brain. Scott Hix, he reminded himself, was an intelligence expert as well as a distinguished hand-to-hand fighter and instructor. He was running his own subtle game, even now. Hidalgo could sense it, feel it in the air. But he could not define exactly what it was. "If you agree to fight, you'll be unchained," the revolutionary said. "You'll be kept under lock and key and guarded at all times. But you'll be free to move around. And to regain your strength through training, of course."

Hix chuckled. "You give me that kind of freedom and you might as well say adios right now," he said. "I'll get away. You know that or you wouldn't have kept me in this state." He held up his chained and taped wrists for emphasis.

Hidalgo shook his head. "No, I don't think so," he said. "I don't think you'll try to escape."

"And what would stop me?" Hix asked. "Are you going to kill Ronnie if I'm gone? I don't think so, he's worth too much money. The mayor of Tijuana? Same thing. And the women? They're all whores I never met before the other night at the party, some from TJ, the blondes from Hollywood. Hate to let my hard side show, Jesus, but none of them mean jack shit to me." He glared confidently at the *Legitima* leader.

"That's only partially true," Hidalgo said. "One of the blondes is not a whore. And we both know you care very much what happens to her." He smiled inwardly as he saw the confidence suddenly drain from Hix's face. "You see, Scott Hix," Hidalgo went on, "as much as it goes against my grain, I'll put your beloved Normandi West through a hell on earth if you escape. Oh, I'll kill her all right. But first, I'll give her to Huertes and his men for a few days."

Huertes and the other two bandits still stood next to Hix. "Yes," Huertes said with wet shining lips. "It's an assignment we all would relish."

The American started to speak, then closed his mouth again.

Hidalgo leaned forward over his desk. "Enough banter," he said, determined to follow up now that he had Hix at a disadvantage. "I'll be generous. You'll stay in one of the rooms upstairs. We'll bring in training equipment and provide men with whom you can spar. You'll be guarded at all times by six men with rifles, and they'll be under order to shoot at the slightest provocation."

"And if I refuse to fight?" Hix said in what appeared to be a last stab at poise.

"Then Huertes and his men can get started with your woman immediately," Hidalgo answered.

Scott Hix looked around the room. Hidalgo could see the fear in his eyes; almost smell it wafting off his body. He had found the American's weak spot. He had him where he wanted him.

Finally, Hix turned back. "I guess I don't have any choice," he said. "But there's one more thing I want."

"Yes?" Hidalgo said. "If it's possible—"

"It is," Hix said. "I want Normandi kept in the room with me." He looked to the bandits again. "I don't trust these bastards when I'm not around."

Hidalgo refrained from laughing. Had he given Huertes's men

free rein to do what they wanted, Normandi West and all of the other women would have been raped repeatedly by now. And regardless of how tough he might be, there was nothing a taped and chained Scott Hix could have done but watched. He knew this and he suspected Hix knew this as well. But Hidalgo had no desire to break the man's spirit completely. He had to leave him with some dignity or the American would be worthless when it came time to fight Toro.

Nodding slowly, Hidalgo said, "I understand. It shall be as you request." He paused, then added, "But I regret that I can't give you the privacy I am sure you would like. Men will be watching you at all times. As you said, you're capable of escape if they don't. And with your woman in such close proximity, you might even escape with her."

The confidence returned to Hix's demeanor. "They can watch all they want," he said. "I don't plan to turn it into a honeymoon. I just want to make sure she's safe."

Hidalgo nodded his agreement. Good, he thought. The American had been torn down. Now Hidalgo must begin building him back up—under his rules. He turned to Huertes. "Release his chains and cut the tape," he ordered.

Huertes and one of his men stepped in and did so.

Slowly, the pain evident on his face, Hix began to stretch his stiffened limbs.

"Before you go, Señor Hix," Hidalgo said. "There's one last matter to take care of."

Hix had been rubbing his wrists. He looked up.

"As we discussed, we can't present Toro and his backers with your correct name."

The American nodded. His eyes told Hidalgo he had already anticipated the next question. "No, but it's got to sound real," Hix said. "And it has to be something I'll answer to naturally already. We don't have time for me to get used to a whole new name. That doesn't happen overnight."

Hidalgo nodded in agreement. "Yes," he said. "I understand. But it occurs to me that you might want to use a name that will draw the attention of your fellow American intelligence personnel.

So it can't be one you have used before that's in your dossier."
He patted the opened folder in front of him. "Of which I have a
copy, you see. So don't try such a foolish trick. If you do, I'll
know."

"Give them the name Sykes," Hix said without hesitation.
"*S-Y-K-E-S*. It's an undercover identity I worked up for a mission
in Europe several years ago. The mission never came off, so don't
worry, it was never official—I never even turned it in." His eyes
fell to the file on the desk. "Go ahead and check."

Hidalgo stared at the man. "I will." But he already had, and
Jesus Hidalgo knew that the name "Sykes" wasn't among the
false identities Scott Hix had used. He lifted a pen from his desk
and jotted the name on a piece of scrap paper. "We'll need a first
and middle name as well," he said.

"Rex," Hix said.

Hidalgo wrote it down. "And the middle name?"

"I didn't have one," Hix said. "Just two initials. W and E."
He paused, then added, "The full name was Rex W. E. Sykes."

Hidalgo raised an eyebrow. "Two initials? It implies two middle
names."

Scott Hix snorted. "That's a funny question coming from an
Hispanic. You guys seem to end up with a string of about fifty
names."

"Yes," he said. "Rex W. E. Sykes it is. But it is unusual."

"I'm an unusual man."

Hidalgo watched Huertes and the others lead Hix out of the
room at gunpoint. The American was right—he was unusual—and
the *Legitima* leader would have given his right arm to get Scott
Hix on their side. In fact, Hidalgo would have gladly traded Pablo
Huertes and all of his drunken idiots for a lone warrior of Hix's
caliber. It deeply saddened him that he had been forced to take
the American hostage, and what he was about to make Hix do
disturbed him even further.

If Toro was as tough as they said, there was every possibility
that Scott Hix would leave the ring as an invalid. Or never leave
the ring alive at all.

LYONS GUIDED THE VAN slowly down the street of the upper-middle-class Houston residential area. The houses were all relatively new—built within the last ten years. Successful, but not wealthy. A few millionaires, perhaps, most likely doctors, lawyers and businessmen.

And one whoremongering pimp who also dealt dope.

The Able Team leader slowed the van as they approached a three-story house slightly larger than the others. It was set back farther from the street and sported an eight-foot chain-link fence around the acre of land it occupied. But the gate was open. And no guards appeared to be watching it.

"Got any ideas on our approach?" Dirk Anderson asked from the shotgun seat.

Lyons nodded but didn't answer. He turned the van left, circled the block and squinted through the darkness at the rear of Gonzales's house. He needed one man on the inside, two for the front and two at the rear. He could have used two more men to cover the outside in case someone tried to escape through the windows. But he didn't have them.

Leaving the residential area, the Able Team leader spotted an all-night convenience store on the corner of a busy thoroughfare. Pulling into the parking lot, he turned in his seat toward Hermann Schwarz. "Gadgets, go get us a six-pack," he said.

In the semidarkness that engulfed the rear of the van, Lyons saw Ranger Mark Harsey frown. But it wasn't a frown of disapproval, more of curiosity.

"I'm going to send somebody inside first," Lyons said as Schwarz slid open the side door and got out. "Then we'll drive the van through the fence. We'll go in just like any other six guys who got horny after a night of beer drinking." He cleared his throat. "A beer can here and there adds to the illusion."

Schwarz returned with a brown sack. As Lyons backed out of the parking lot again, the Able Team electronics expert pulled a six-pack of Lone Star from the paper, jerked the cans from the plastic rings and began handing them around.

Ranger Bud Keener popped the top on his and a loud hiss echoed throughout the van. "What a shame," he said as he rolled down the window and poured the liquid onto the pavement. The others followed his example.

Lyons drove back into the neighborhood. "Gadgets," he said over his shoulder, "we'll drop you off. I want you to go on in as a customer and get an idea of the layout."

Rosario "Politician" Blancanales grinned. "Get an idea of the layout is a pun too easy to even mention," he said.

Lyons ignored the remark. "Take one of the walkie-talkies," he said. "As soon as you've got a make on the floor plan, find a hole someplace by yourself and radio us. Try to locate Gonzales. At least find out where his office is."

The van slowed two houses down from the brothel and then came to a stop. Schwarz slid a walkie-talkie down the back of his pants, covered it with the tail of his shirt and reached for the door handle.

"Gadgets?" Blancanales said, an innocent look on his face.

Schwarz looked back into the van.

"Don't get caught with your pants down."

The door slid shut.

Lyons turned in his seat. "As soon as we hear from him, I'll drive in. Pol, take Harsey and head to the back. Keener, you and I will go to the front." He turned to face Anderson. He wanted to keep the almost-retired Houston detective's hands as clean as possible. "Dirk, stay outside and watch the perimeter. I'd suggest heading around back with Pol and Mark, then moving back and forth to check both sides of the house." He scratched at the stubble of beard beginning on his chin, then added, "If things go well, nobody'll have time to get out the windows. But you never know."

Anderson shook his head. "Ironman, I know what you're doing and I appreciate it. But just because I'm about to retire doesn't mean—"

"No argument," Lyons said, then turned back in his seat to end the conversation.

Four minutes later, Lyons's walkie-talkie squealed. A second later, Schwarz's whispering voice followed. "Able Three to One," it said. In the background, Lyons could hear the sound of a toilet flushing.

Lyons held the radio to his lips. "One here. Go Three."

"The house has been remodeled inside," Schwarz said softly. "Downstairs rooms have been gutted and it's just one huge reception area with what I'm guessing is a kitchen at the rear." He paused. "Rear entry will have to come through that kitchen." The toilet quit flushing and a feminine voice in the background called out, "C'mon out, honey. You only paid for an hour and the clock's running."

"Just a second," Schwarz called out. "You don't want a man with dirty hands now, do you? Even one as cute as me?" Without waiting for the woman's answer, Lyons heard the metallic sound of twisting knobs and then water running in a sink.

"I'm on the second floor now," Schwarz said into the radio, whispering again. "It's been redone, too. Small cubicles. Maybe twenty. Just big enough to get the job done. One big hall down the middle."

"What about Gonzales and his men?" Lyons asked.

"Several hard types working the floor below, mingling and acting like hosts. Bulges under their tux jackets, though. No sign of Gonzales that I could see, unless he's one of them, and there was nothing to indicate that he was."

Lyons turned to Keener.

Keener knew the question ahead of time. "Fat guy," he said. "Short, five foot seven, probably 230 pounds."

Schwarz had heard the Ranger over the radio. "Haven't seen him, then," he said.

"How about the third floor?" Lyons asked Schwarz.

"That, I don't know," the electronics wizard whispered. "The little number I picked brought me to her room on two. I couldn't have gone up without really drawing suspicion. It's either another floor of these mini-screw-rooms or maybe Gonzales's offices." He paused. "Or something else. I don't know."

"Okay," Lyons said, unconsciously nodding his head. "Stall the new love of your life for another five minutes and we'll be inside."

"Sure you can't give me a little longer?" Schwarz chuckled. "She's not half-bad."

Lyons switched off the radio and dropped it into his pocket. He turned to the back of the van again, and said, "Pol, weapons."

Out of an equipment bag, Blancanales pulled a Calico 950 sub-machine pistol with a 50-round drum magazine mounted on top. He handed it to Lyons, who started to take it, then stopped. They weren't dressed to hide subgenus and they'd be noticed—probably by electronic surveillance cameras—as soon as they got out of the van. He planned to have a couple of the men throw out empty beer cans on the lawn to strengthen the illusion he was creating and get them to a parking spot. He might even be able to carry it even farther and get them all inside before Gonzales "made them."

But not if they were carrying submachine guns.

"Anybody uncomfortable going in with nothing more than side arms?" the Able Team leader asked.

"Oh, I've done such things a time or two before," Keener said "And I think the kid can handle it."

"You both have extra loads?"

Keener and Harsey nodded.

Anderson shook his head. "I didn't exactly realize I was going rat killing when you stopped by the video store," he said.

Lyons smiled in the semidarkness. They had begun the evening by picking Dirk Anderson up at the video-rental store he had inherited from his recently deceased father. The Houston detective would have had no reason to dress for war. Handing him the Calico, Lyons said, "Take this and trade places with somebody back there." He hooked a thumb over his shoulder. "Stay hidden until we're inside and you hear the first shot. Then carry on as planned and cover the sides."

Anderson and Keener exchanged seats.

"Any other questions?" Lyons asked.

No one answered.

Lyons threw the van into drive. "Then let's do it," he said.

BOLAN INSERTED THE KEY the warehouse's owner had given him, snapped open the padlock and slid back the sliding door. A hundred dollars a month was more than the place was worth. But like the salesman who had sold him the bus, the proprietor had considered it—and an extra fifty dollars up front—enough to keep his mouth shut concerning his new tenant.

The soldier climbed back up behind the wheel of the bus and drove it into the warehouse, leaving the headlights on until he'd spotted the light switches on the far wall. Then, killing the engine, he made his way through the semidarkness and illuminated the room. Swinging the door shut, he locked it again—this time on the inside.

The Executioner wasted no time unloading the planks, hardware and tools he had just purchased. A few screws, hinges and nails later, he had a serviceable ramp that would hook over the tailgate of the bus. He opened the double doors above the bumper, lodged the ramp firmly in place and climbed into the rear of the vehicle.

Kicking the Harley-Davidson into neutral with his boot, Bolan grasped the handlebar and rolled the big motorcycle down the ramp to the warehouse's packed dirt floor. He engaged the kickstand, then climbed back into the bus. The burned-out-rodeo-cowboy look that Grimaldi had immediately recognized was going to be his primary image during the remainder of his mission in Mexico. But he needed another look—another character—to do his dirty work.

Opening the trunk that contained the clothing from Stony Man Farm, Bolan pulled out a pair of scuffed black motorcycle boots and a black leather vest, which looked to be made more of zippers than leather. He dropped his denim shirt onto a chair in the converted camper and slid the vest over his black T-shirt. There was no mirror in the camper-bus but he could tell with his fingertips that the tail just covered the bottom of the Helweg holster housing his Desert Eagle.

The Executioner frowned. When he straddled the motorcycle, the cutoff jacket would ride up to expose the weapon. Pulling the Hewleg off his belt, Bolan jammed the big .44 Magnum into his pants at the small of his back.

The motorcycle boots replaced the cowboy boots next, and the soldier dug through the trunk for something that would cover his head. He found it near the bottom, carefully folded into a neat square. The large black bandanna was covered with skulls and crossbones. Gaudy and tasteless, but people would focus their attention on it, which was just what he wanted. Anyone seeing him in this outfit would forget the details of his face.

The Executioner was unfolding the bandanna when several rectangular pieces of paper fell out and fluttered to the floor. He bent to retrieve them, smiling as he stood. He hadn't requested that Kissinger include the press-on tattoos—he hadn't even thought of them. But Kissinger had, and one of them bore a note that read,

Hey, didn't think they could hurt! JK.

The Executioner's final stop before renting the warehouse had been at a supermarket to outfit the bus with food and other necessities. Grabbing a bottle of drinking water from the case he had purchased there, he dampened his arms and applied tattoos to both forearms and biceps. Like the skulls and crossbones, they would draw the eye of anyone watching him and take attention away from his face. The two on his forearms were elaborate dragons eating their own tails. The one on his right upper arm was a variation of the skull-and-crossbones theme—a grinning skull with twin daggers stuck into it.

But it was the tattoo the Executioner applied last to his right biceps that said it all. It had no picture. Just Old English letters that spelled out Born to Kill.

Rolling the Harley into the sunshine, Bolan slid the door shut again and replaced the padlock. A moment later, he had kick-started the big bike and was pulling away from the warehouse.

The Executioner had been drugged more than a little when he'd escaped the two brothers at the service station. But years of training and experience had overcome the dope. Although he had never been a cop, he had developed the mind of a good patrolman and well remembered the twists and turns that had taken him to the gas station. It took only ten minutes of shifting gears and cutting through the heavy Mexico City traffic to get him back there.

The station was busy when Bolan pulled up to the tanks. He hadn't seen an attendant when he'd been there before but now a teenager, built like a power-lifter, was busily pumping gas into the tanks. Bolan waited while he finished one, then another, then another. Each time it looked as if his work would slow, more vehicles drove up. Finally, Bolan walked up to the kid and said, "I need to talk to you. Private."

The young man looked at him as if he were from Mars. "Can't you see I'm busy?" he snarled in Spanish.

The Executioner pulled out a twenty-dollar bill and worked it into the man's skintight T-shirt pocket. "Tell them the place just became self-service."

The attendant had seen the rest of the money in the Executioner's roll and didn't even bother to do that. Setting the pump on automatic, he said, "Let's go," and started for the door of the building.

Bolan followed him inside and shut the door behind him. There was always a chance that the two brothers had used a credit card to purchase their gas the day before, and if they had, there would be a paper trail. It wasn't much but it was all he had to start with. And before he started asking questions from a guy who would be reluctant to answer, it was worth a try. "I need to see all of your credit card invoices for yesterday," he said.

The young man looked him up and down, bandanna to boot. "Who are you, gringo?" he asked. "FBI? CIA? Maybe DEA?" His eyes fell to the pocket where the Executioner had replaced his money. "I don't have to let you see shit."

Bolan smiled and reached into his pocket again. Handing the man another twenty, he said, "No, you don't. I'm just asking for a favor. And I'm asking nicely."

"Not nice enough," the muscle man said.

Bolan handed the kid another twenty.

The teenager indicated a battered green filing cabinet with his head. "Top drawer. Front file would be yesterday. I've got to get back." Without waiting for an answer, he headed out the door.

Bolan opened the filing cabinet and pulled out a well-worn manilla file. The title tab at the top had been written on and scratched out so many times it was almost illegible. Laying the file flat on the counter next to the cash register, he began to search through the receipts, taking careful note of the times each purchase had been made, which were printed in the yellow forms.

Three credit cards had been used within five minutes of the time the two brothers had brought the Executioner to the station. The first bore the name John Sawyer, and the inscription below was the Chrysler Corporation. Bolan discarded it. The brothers might well have been using a stolen card but if they had it would do him no good.

The second card was registered to a Manuel Chevez of Saltillo, the third to Maria Rodriguez of Mexico City. Even though he suspected they would be of little help, he memorized the information on the cards, then turned toward the door just as the young attendant strutted back through.

"You find what you needed?" the kid asked as he walked to the cash register.

The lot had cleared after the rush for gas, and the Executioner decided he would find no better time for the second part of his intel-gathering mission. It, too, was a long shot. But people—both honest citizens and criminals like the brothers—were creatures of habit. They bought the same brands of toothpaste over and over, shopped at the same grocery stores, and bought their gas at the same places. There was a chance the attendant might know the men who had kidnapped him.

"No," the Executioner said. "I wouldn't say I found what I was looking for. So—you want to make some more money?"

The young man snorted as if it were the stupidest question he had ever been asked.

"Were you working here yesterday?"

The kid nodded.

Bolan reached into his pocket and pulled out his money. "Two guys got gas in a parcel delivery truck. Looked like they could be brothers. Who were they?"

The young man's eyes had fallen to the money the Executioner held but they suddenly shot back up to Bolan. The blood drained from his dark-skinned face leaving it a sick-looking gray. The man shook his head. "I don't know," he said, his voice almost cracking.

Bolan pulled two hundred-dollar bills from the roll and extended them. "I think you do," he said.

For a moment, pure greed entered the attendant's eyes. But as suddenly as it had come, it was replaced with a combination of fear and self-preservation. "I told you, I don't know who you're talking about!" he almost shouted.

"You're getting a little too upset for me to believe you," the Executioner said. "Look, let's cut the bargaining. It wastes time. I'm prepared to go five hundred. No more."

The powerfully built young man's head shook back and forth violently on his heavy shoulders. "I...don't...know," he said, emphasizing each word.

Bolan sighed as he replaced the money in his pocket. It was more than evident that the young man did know more than he was saying but that he was too terrified to speak about it—even for more money than he probably made in six months at the gas station. Taking another quick glance through the glass walls to the pump lot, he saw it was still empty. Turning to the young man, he reached out with his left hand while his right darted under the leather vest behind his back.

The fingers of the Executioner's left hand grabbed a handful of the attendant's greasy black hair and jerked his head back to expose his throat as the Applegate-Fairbairn's six-inch dagger came out in his right. Pressing the razor-edge against the man's throat, he whispered, "I tried things the nice way. Now you're forcing me to lose my sweet disposition."

The powerful kid started to struggle. A little more pressure against his throat and he stopped. Bolan glanced down at the huge pectorals quivering in fear beneath the tight T-shirt. "I suggest you tell me what you know about the brothers."

"They...come in sometimes," he croaked. "I don't know them...don't know who they are."

"Then how come you're so afraid to tell me about them?" Bolan asked, moving the knife slightly to remind the kid it was there. "That doesn't make much sense now, does it?"

The attendant started to shake his head in agreement, then realized that to do so might cut his own throat. "I know who they are…" he sputtered "…by…reputation."

"Well, tell me their reputation," Bolan said. "What are their names?"

"Roberto and Santiago," the attendant whispered. "Roberto is the older one. Santiago, is the one who rarely speaks." He gave Bolan a complete description of each man.

"Roberto and Santiago what?"

"I don't know. Please, you must believe me."

"What is it that scares you about them?"

The young man hesitated, then decided that the devil who had him now was more dangerous than the devils who might get him later for talking. "They are killers," he spit out. "And they are demons. They worship Satan. Their magic is powerful, and it comes from the Prince of Darkness himself!"

Bolan relaxed the pressure slightly on the young man's throat. His gut instinct told him the kid was telling the truth—at least the truth the way he saw it. He had no further questions.

A split second later, an explosion sounded in the lot and the glass in the front of the service station building burst into pieces.

Bolan released the attendant and dropped to one knee, transferring the Applegate-Fairbairn to his left hand and jerking the Desert Eagle from his belt in one swift motion. Between the broken shards of glass still clinging to the corners of the window frame, he saw the two brothers—Roberto and Santiago, he now knew—in a white Chevy Corvette convertible. Based on the attendant's description, Roberto was the one behind the wheel and Santiago was the one aiming a Winchester 12-gauge pump with a folding stock directly at the Executioner.

Bolan dived forward as a second explosion came from the shotgun. He heard a grunt behind him and rolled to his side to see the powerfully built young attendant fly backward. A hole the size of a golf ball appeared in the center of the young man's chest as blood and bone fragments blew out his back to splatter the wall.

Rolling back to his belly, Bolan rose high enough to fire a double-tap from the big .44 Magnum pistol at the Corvette. But as he pulled the trigger Roberto jerked the car forward slightly and the rounds sailed between the two brothers. Return fire forced the Executioner back to the floor of the service station.

The Corvette's engine roared. Bolan rose again, Desert Eagle aimed through the window. All he saw was the rear of the vehicle as the convertible turned out of the pump lot and raced down the street.

The Executioner leapt to his feet, turned, and took a final look at the attendant. There was nothing that could be done. Half sitting, half lying against the wall, the 12-gauge deer slug had separated his spine. His eyes stared straight ahead in death.

Hurdling over the steel frame where the glass had once been, Bolan raced to the Harley, swung a leg over the saddle and kicked the starter. By the time he reached the street, he could barely see the Corvette two blocks ahead. At least twenty other cars stood between the two vehicles.

But that was one reason Bolan had wanted a motorcycle. Ignoring the honking horns, screams of displeasure and upraised middle fingers, the Executioner began to cut his way through the traffic.

4

David McCarter couldn't keep the grin off his face. So he turned to the wall, pretending to read one of the framed certificates that had been hung there less than five minutes before the office had opened that morning. Behind him, he heard Leo Turrin say, "All right, Señor Gorre. We've got your number. Don't call us, we'll call you." In the reflection of the glass covering the certificate, McCarter watched a hulking Mexican man who looked like he'd just stepped in off the bandit trail open the door and walk out to the hallway.

McCarter turned as the door slowly closed. The man had been a bandit, he'd bet his life on that. But he wasn't one of the right bandits. The man himself had wanted to fight, and there had been no mention of an American fighter under the name Scott Hix or any other. He hadn't come from Pablo Huertes's gang of cutthroats who had joined with the *Legitimas* as McCarter had hoped he might have.

The former British SAS operative took a seat in one of the chairs against the wall. Turrin gave him a wink as a brawny young peasant lad holding a straw sombrero in both hands opened the door and entered the room. Pompei, who stood to the side of the desk, handed the man a printed form and a pen.

The man's eyes fell in shame. "I'm sorry," he muttered under his breath in Spanish. "I...can't read or write." His eyes rose. "But I can fight, and fight very well."

Turrin smiled like an understanding father, pulled his feet down off the desk and reached for the paper. "Name?" he asked.

The young man gave it to him. Turrin finished filling out the form for the would-be fighter which included his height, weight, fight record and phone number. "I have no phone," the man said, again embarrassed. "But you can contact me through my brother's job." Turrin wrote down the number.

"Okay, that's it," the Stony Man undercover expert said. "We'll call you if you're chosen."

The young man nodded enthusiastically. "Thank you," he said. "Are you really offering five million American dollars to anyone who can defeat your fighter?"

Turrin gave him the fatherly smile again. "Not just that..." he glanced down to the page in his hand "...Joaquin. All you have to do is last three minutes."

A rapturous smile broke across the peasant's face and his eyes glassed over. McCarter could almost see the specifics of the better life he was imagining for himself, his wife, children and perhaps a mother and father. Then reality overcame the man again and he stared at Turrin. "Please, sir," he said. "Call me. I can fight well. I'll put on a good show for the fans. You have my promise."

"Thanks for coming in, Joaquin," Turrin said, and pointed toward the door.

As soon as it had closed, Turrin said, "I need a short break." He glanced at the coffeemaker he'd set up in the corner of the room, then to McCarter. The Phoenix Force leader shook his head. Turrin walked over and poured himself a cup, then turned to Pompei. "How many do we have so far?" he asked.

Pompei walked to the battered green filing cabinet against the wall opposite McCarter and opened a drawer. "Forty-five, fifty," he said.

"And not one of them was Scott Hix or anybody from the *Legitimas*," McCarter said.

Turrin looked over to the Phoenix Force leader as he took a sip of coffee. "Patience, my fine British friend," he said. "We've only been open for a couple of hours."

McCarter nodded. Turrin glanced to Pompei and nodded. Pompei opened the door and another street fighter walked in. This one could write, and he sat on the other side of the desk and began filling out the form.

The Briton's mind drifted. The five-million-dollar award had generated more interest than even Turrin had expected. The waiting line was massive. When they'd finally opened the two-room office complex on the third floor of the Sonora Insurance Building, the line had stretched down the hall all the way to the elevators.

And it was getting no shorter. Every time McCarter stepped out into the hall, new faces had arrived. It seemed that there wasn't a legitimate boxer, martial artist or barroom brawler in Mexico or Southern California who wasn't after the five million dollars.

Noon came and went, with Encizo, Manning, James and Toro taking a break from Toro's training schedule and dropping in with lunch. Even though the fight between the blacksuit and Scott Hix would never actually take place, word of where Toro was working out had hit the streets and people were dropping by to watch. Appearances had to be kept up.

When they'd finished eating, McCarter walked them down the hall to the elevator, noting that the line of wanna-be millionaires was still growing. "You guys having fun?" he asked his fellow Phoenix Force warriors as they stepped through the open door.

James looked at him beneath the swelling over his left eye. "Oh yeah," He grinned. "Nothing I like better than getting my head beat by this human tornado. How about you, Gary?"

Manning had a shiner on his left eye that wasn't yet in full bloom. "Isn't it about your turn, David?" he said.

McCarter laughed. "Rank has its privileges," he said as the door closed. "Besides, it's excellent training for you, guys."

The Phoenix Force leader returned to the interview office and sat patiently while the men wanting to fight Toro continued to file in and out. They had advertised that they'd be open between 0800 and 1700 hours, but when closing time came the line was still long.

And none of the applicants had appeared to be representing Scott Hix.

Another applicant had just left the room and McCarter was about to step into the hallway and announce that the interviews would continue for two more hours. But before he could even rise from his chair, a man wearing a serape walked into the office holding his sombrero in both hands. He looked for all the world like one of the *bandidos* out of the old Humphrey Bogart movie *The Treasure of the Sierra Madre.*

"*Hombres,*" the man said grinning. "I'm not here to fight myself. But I represent a man who I believe to be the one for whom you're searching. A man who I know can last three minutes with your Toro and whom I believe may even be able to defeat him."

Turrin waved him into the chair in front of the desk. McCarter was tempted to hold his nose. The odor emanating from the repulsive bandit was one of the most offensive he had ever encountered. A peculiar blend of stale sweat, cheap tobacco, tequila and either aftershave or cologne the man seemed to have doused himself in to cover it.

"This is a little unusual," Turrin said. "What's this man's name?"

"His name is Sykes," the bandit said. "Rex W. E. Sykes."

McCarter saw a split-second flicker in Turrin's eyes but it left the undercover expert's face as quickly as it had come. The Phoenix Force leader was a soldier rather than an actor, however, and he had to turn to the wall to hide the broad smile that broke out on his face.

The man was from the *Legitimas,* all right. And the man he wanted to fight Toro was Scott Hix.

Rex W. E. Sykes.

Hix had just sent them a message.

LYONS DROVE the van through the gate and down the white gravel drive past carefully manicured cactus plants and bushes. There were a half-dozen vehicles parked outside Gonzales's house in the circular drive. The Able Team leader parked as close as possible behind a Chevy pickup, pulled the keys from the ignition and stared through the windshield at the house. Four colonial-style columns rose from the front porch to the third floor of the building. Mounted into them just above the first floor, the Able Team leader could see the surveillance cameras. They were installed at angles to watch the entire front of the house, and he suspected other cameras would be mounted on the sides and at the rear.

Turning in his seat, he looked into the back of the van. Dirk Anderson had switched seats with Keener, who now rode shotgun. "Remember to wait until you hear the first shot," Lyons reminded the Houston detective. "That could be about the time we slide the van door open. Or it could be several minutes after Keener and I get inside." He shifted his gaze to Blancanales and Harsey. "You both saw the cameras?"

The two men nodded. "We'll stick with you as if we're going in the front until we get under them on the porch," Blancanales said. "Then we'll head around to the back."

"Just what I was about to suggest," Lyons said. "Unless there are more cameras mounted on the porch we haven't seen, we'll at least get the door opened before anybody realizes two of the four of us disappeared. With any luck, whoever is watching the camera won't have immediate contact with the guy who opens the door and he won't even know there were four of us."

Blancanales chuckled. "When was the last time Able Team had a streak of luck, Ironman?" he asked.

Lyons didn't bother to answer. He opened the door of the van and got out while the rest of the men, except Anderson, exited on the other side.

Keener held his beer can to his lips as the four of them stumbled toward the porch, drained what remained of the can, then threw it at the front of the house. "Warm it up for me, Mama!" he whooped like the drunk he was impersonating. "Daddy's home!"

The four men staggered up the steps and onto the porch beneath the cameras. As soon as they had, Blancanales and Harsey dropped their beer cans and their drunken stumbles and sprinted to the side of the house, disappearing around the corner. Lyons knocked loudly, using the brass knocker.

A few seconds later, the ornately carved door swung back. An American whose shoulders threatened to split the seams of his tuxedo stood in the opening, and Lyons saw the bulge under his arm that Schwarz had noticed earlier. "Evening, gents," he said in a slow Texas drawl. "Ready for a little fun?"

"Ready for more than a little," Keener slurred.

Lyons and Keener stepped past the man, and the Able Team

leader got a brief overview of the huge room. Beautifully gowned prostitutes, men, and a few women who looked more like lesbian patrons than whores, sat on expensive divans or stood sipping drinks and laughing. At the rear of the gutted first floor, a black man, who looked like Louis Armstrong, played the piano, and just to his side was a swinging door Lyons suspected, as Schwarz had said earlier, led to the house's kitchen.

But the American had continued to hold the door, waiting. And during the micro-second he did so, it told Lyons everything about the cameras.

Gonzales did *not* have more hidden cameras watching the porch, which meant no one had seen Blancanales and Harsey split off for the back. But the surveillance center inside the house was somewhere nearby. The man in the tight tuxedo had seen them get out of the van and approach the house. And he knew there had been four of them.

Frowning, the broad-shouldered man stuck his head through the door, looked both ways, then said, "Hey, where'd your—" Reality hit him midsentence and, as he whirled back around, his hand slid under his jacket toward the bulge beneath his left arm.

Lyons had already drawn the Colt Python. Double-actioning the smooth trigger, he placed a 125-grain semijacketed hollowpoint round directly between the man's eyes and into his brain stem. The explosion roared throughout the first floor of the whorehouse. All conversation ceased, and the men and women in the room froze in place.

Keener had already drawn his stag-handled .44 Magnum by the time Lyons turned back toward the room. The Ranger raised the big revolver and sent a trio of rounds into the chest of another tuxedo-clad man. The first-floor guard released his grasp on the automatic pistol he had gotten halfway out of his coat. The gun stayed half in, half out of his lapel as he plummeted to the thick carpet.

A crashing sound came from behind the swinging door to the side of the piano. It was followed by a series of gunshots in the kitchen, and the Able Team leader knew Blancanales and Harsey had entered the house. Lyons drew his Government Model 1911 with his left hand as he pivoted to face two men in black tuxes rushing toward him. Both men had already drawn their weapons, and one fired as he ran forward.

Nervous men tend to shoot high, and the round sailed a good two feet over the Able Team leader's head and out through the open door. Lyons heard a muffled "Ugh!" come from the front yard.

Had the stray round caught Dirk Anderson as the Houston PD detective got out of the van? Lyons didn't know. But this was no time to try to find out.

Raising the Python to shoulder level, Lyons stared at the second button of the guard's tuxedo and squeezed the trigger. Another .357 Magnum round roared from the Colt six-gun and drilled through the man's chest. Before he could hit the ground, the Able Team leader dropped his weapon slightly and swung it to the side, coming up in an arc with the gun pointed at the other guard's chest. A third round bore through the twists in the barrel and on through the second man's tux. He fell faster and both men hit the ground at the same time.

By now the initial shock had worn off and the men and women scattered throughout the room began to dive for cover. Screams in the voices of both sexes could be heard amid the gunfire.

The kitchen door swung open and Blancanales burst into the rear of the large room. Lyons watched the piano player reach inside the instrument and produce a small .380 automatic. He also watched Blancanales pause long enough to place a 9 mm slug in his head.

Schwarz had said the room was big. But Lyons hadn't realized how big until he saw Keener raise his pistol a little higher and shift his eyes to the sights. A good twenty-five yards away, against a side wall, another of the tuxedo-garbed hardmen was wildly firing a SIG-Sauer at them. Taking his time, Keener placed two rounds in the man's chest.

"Pol!" Lyons yelled at the top of his lungs.

Blancanales looked up at him.

"You see a back staircase?"

"Just this side of the kitchen!" he yelled back. "Harsey's covering it now!"

"Go back and go upstairs with him!" the Able Team leader shouted as he dropped another of the hardmen with the last two rounds in his Python. "I'm taking the front!" He slammed the empty revolver back into his holster as his eyes scanned the room. Seeing no immediate threat, he shifted the Government Model to his right hand.

Keener had drawn his elaborately engraved .45 automatic and performed a similar hand-switching maneuver. But for the moment, the gunfire on the first floor seemed to have died out.

"Bud!" Lyons yelled at the top of his lungs. "Stay here and make sure nobody gets out the front! I'm going up!"

The Texas Ranger nodded. As he did, a hand holding a pistol shot up from behind a couch. A head followed it.

Keener shot off most of it.

Lyons sprinted to the staircase and took the stairs three at a time, his own .45 leading the way. Halfway up the steps, a man wearing a business suit and toting a Heckler & Koch MP-5 appeared at the top. Lyons pumped two .45-caliber rounds into his chest, sprinted up the rest of the stairs and grabbed the subgun. A quick look down the hall confirmed what Schwarz had told him. The second floor had been divided into small cubicles. The hall was empty, and the doors up and down it all closed.

A quick look overhead showed no sign of activity on the third floor.

The Able Team leader heard more gunfire below. At the rear of the house, other rounds exploded. He thought of Schwarz as he dumped the MP-5's 30-round magazine and looked at it. By the weight, it appeared still to be fully loaded. His guess was that the man had come from the third floor and not yet fired a round. Pulling back the bolt slightly, the glimmer of brass told him that a round had already been chambered. Shoving the magazine back into the receiver, he flipped the selector switch to burst-mode and moved forward. He returned the Government Model to the shoulder rig under his arm.

Lyons moved to the first door on his right, lifted a foot and kicked. The door burst open and he found a man and woman huddled in the corner. The man was completely nude but the woman wore a black garter belt that held up matching fishnet hose. Her black boots extended to thigh height and a leather bra covered her breasts.

A short leather whip lay on the bed.

Both man and woman stared at the Able Team leader in horror.

"Stay there," Lyons said as he slammed the door and turned.

The doors along the hallway were offset, forming a zigzag pattern—none directly across from each other. That was good since he was by himself. Lyons could enter each door without having to worry that the one across the hall would open while he was preoccupied, and someone would shoot him in the back. Kicking the first door on the other side of the hall, he found the tiny room empty. Moving across the corridor again, he kicked and found two women with a man. One of the women was dressed like Little Bo Peep. The other had on Minnie Mouse ears. Shaking his head in dismay, the Able Team leader admonished them similarly to the couple he'd found in the first room, then slammed the door again.

In the next room, an attractive woman in panties and bra hid under the bed. Lyons reached under the frame, grabbed an arm and dragged her out. "Did you have a customer before all this started?" he demanded.

The woman trembled. "Are you going to kill me?" she asked.

"If you don't answer my question I just might," Lyons snarled. "Describe him."

The prostitute described Hermann "Gadgets" Schwarz. "He ran out as soon as the shooting started," she said. "He told me you'd come. He said he was going upstairs."

Lyons nodded, dropped her arm and shot back into the hall.

Blancanales and Harsey appeared at the top of the back stairs. Motioning them forward, the Able Team leader said, "I've checked the first five at this end. Finish up. I'm heading upstairs."

Blancanales nodded. "You seen anything of Gadgets?"

Lyons tilted his head toward the room he'd just checked. "Gal inside said he went up to three." He glanced overhead at the ceiling. So far, they had heard no shots or activity of any kind from the top floor of the whorehouse.

Without further ado, Lyons pivoted and rushed back to the stairs. He slowed, taking them carefully as he had with the steps from the first floor. This time, he met no resistance. It was easy.

Too easy.

Whatever its original purpose, Carl Lyons guessed that now the third floor had been converted into the business offices of Lone Wolf Gonzales. Sporadic gunfire on the floors below could be heard, but the third story was silent. The Able Team leader knew he wasn't alone, however. Though he could hear nothing, he sensed a presence.

Directly in front of him, Lyons saw a door. With the MP-5 gripped in his right hand, he moved toward it. The door was unlocked, and he swung it open, bringing up the submachine gun and sweeping it across the doorway. The room was empty. Inside, he saw pinball machines, video games, couches, chairs and a wet bar. The closet door was open. Shelves of video games and what looked from a distance to be porno magazines filled the space.

Slowly and quietly, the Able Team leader backed out of the room. Turning right, he passed the open door to a small second kitchen. At the corner of the hallway he saw another closed door and, taking a deep breath, swung it open. What appeared to have been a small bedroom had been converted into a storage area. Extra furniture, bathroom and kitchen supplies were piled from floor to ceiling.

The hallway turned to his left and Lyons followed it. He saw two doors ahead and guessed they both led into different areas of the master bedroom. Checking the first, he found it locked.

Why, he wondered, when all of the other rooms had been open? He knew the answer. The "presence" he had sensed knew he was coming. And wanted him to enter through the other door. Again, why? The answers could be many. But it could be as simple as just wanting to be sure all guns could focus on one spot.

Lyons moved to the second door. Slowly, quietly, he turned the knob until he confirmed his suspicion that this entrance was unlocked. Then, moving silently back to the first door, he kicked it open and burst inside.

"How predictable," a voice called out. "A stupid man would have chosen the unlocked door. Knowing you not to be stupid, we planned on you entering the hard way."

Lyons's eyes came into focus. He saw seven men occupying the room. The one who had spoken, a short overweight man with a pencil-thin mustache and greasy skin sat behind a large oak desk. Lone Wolf Gonzales gripped a Glock 21 in both hands. The four-teen-shot .45-caliber weapon was pointed at Carl Lyons's abdomen.

Five more men—men who might well have had "cartel" printed on their foreheads—were scattered about the room. In their hands, each had an MP-5 identical to the one Lyons had expro-priated earlier.

With the exception of one of the subguns, these weapons, too, were aimed at the Able Team leader. The gun that wasn't, pointed toward the seventh man.

The seventh man sat in a straight-backed wooden chair to the side of the desk. Handcuffs encircled his wrists, and the left side of his face was swollen and discolored.

Hermann "Gadgets" Schwarz.

"Hello, Ironman."

"Gadgets," Lyons nodded. He trained his own subgun on Gonzales.

"How nice of you to drop in," the greasy man behind the desk said. "But it appears you aren't here in search of a good time as most of our visitors are."

"Oh, I'd call this a damn good time so far," Lyons said. The MP-5 stayed unwavering on Gonzales. "Any time I can rid the world of a few maggots like you guys, I sleep real well all night."

Gonzales chuckled. "You'll sleep well from now on without awakening," he said, "if you don't lay down your weapon immediately."

Lyons paused. He needed to stall for time. There was no way he was going to take down Gonzales and the other five men before he or Schwarz took rounds. And Schwarz was the epitome of a sitting duck; unarmed, handcuffed and helpless. But sooner or later Blancanales, Keener, Harsey and maybe even Dirk Anderson—if he hadn't been shot in the front yard by that stray round—would arrive. That would even the odds. Lyons had left the door open behind him. The other men weren't as likely to stumble into the trap like he, and Schwarz before him, had.

Glancing at Schwarz, the Able Team leader said, "What happened?"

There was a short silence, then Schwarz said, "Oh, about the same thing that happened to you. Stumbled in here to find myself surrounded by cartel goons and a whoremaster who can't even come up with an original name." The electronics ace had spoken slower than usual, and now he paused again. Lyons knew he was on the same track, waiting for the rest of the men to arrive. "Of course, they weren't as nice to me as they've been to you." He paused again and then raised his handcuffed hands to point across the room. "That little guy there likes to hit people, Ironman. He's got the typical short-man syndrome. Thinks if he's tough he'll get taller or something. I swear, I don't understand why—"

"Enough!" Gonzales screamed. "Drop your weapon immediately or we'll kill your friend where he sits!"

Lyons took his time, bending to lay the MP-5 carefully on the carpet.

"Now your other weapons," Gonzales ordered. "And don't hold out. We'll check you."

Again Lyons moved at a snail's pace. The Colt Python came out of his holster in a thumb-and-index finger grips. The Able Team leader stopped with it still in his hand. "It's empty anyway," he said.

"Toss it on the ground just the same."

Lyons continued to move slowly, stooping to set it on the carpet. "It's a good gun," he said as he moved. "Hate to mess up the timing by dropping it too hard."

Gonzales laughed again. "You won't be needing it. What other guns do you have?"

"That's it," Lyons said, his mind on the Government Model in his shoulder rig. Gonzales had said someone would frisk him but there was no way he was giving up his last means of defense willingly. Particularly not with Schwarz in the state he was in.

"Go pat him down," the man behind the desk ordered, looking to the cartel man nearest him.

The little man Schwarz had spoken about—no taller than Gonzales's own reported five foot seven—moved across the room toward Lyons. The Able Team leader tried to remember how many rounds he had fired from the .45 before switching to the MP-5. In truth, he couldn't be sure. But there were six of the enemy in the room. And he strongly suspected he had shot more than two of the weapon's 8-round capacity.

The little cartel gunner let his MP-5 fall to the end of the shoulder sling as he neared Lyons. Then, squatting in front of him, he started at the Able Team leader's ankles and began tapping up his legs.

The ex-cop waited until the man had risen and was a tap away from hitting the holstered .45, then brought his knee up into the little man's groin with every ounce of strength in his thigh.

The short man screamed as Lyons ducked behind him, using the small body as cover. He wrapped his weak arm around the man as he drew the .45 pistol with his right hand and sent a snap shot into the nearest cartel gunner. Out of the corner of his eye, he saw Schwarz roll off the chair to the floor. Good, there was nothing he could do. The best thing was for him to get out of the line of fire.

Lyons turned the gun on a second cartel man and pulled the trigger. Another slug blew from the barrel, into the gunman's face. But by now the men had recovered from the initial shock and a 3-round burst of fire sailed his way.

Lyons had seen the man's hand tighten around the pistol grip of the MP-5 and moved just in time. The trio of 9 mm slugs struck the little man in the back and penetrated through his chest. Without cover now, Lyons dropped to one knee as another round burst over his head. He sent his third projectile into the nose of another gunner, his fourth into a burly cartel man next to the desk.

The Government Model locked on empty with two of the cartel men still standing.

Gonzales wasn't a gunman by trade, and it had taken him longer to recover from the surprise than the others. But now he saw what had happened and threw back his head in laughter.

To the side of the desk, Lyons saw Schwarz lying on his side. The Able Team electronics specialist was wildly trying to jam his handcuffed hands down the front of his pants.

Getting control of himself, Lone Wolf Gonzales said, "I regret we must kill you now, my friend. You have provided us with great amusement." He nodded toward the other two men who each raised an MP-5 to shoulder level and sighted down their bores at Carl Lyons.

Which was the moment Schwarz chose to rise over the edge of the desk with the .22 Magnum minirevolver he'd had hidden in his underwear.

The little gun barked as a .22 Magnum round drilled through the brain of the nearest of the two remaining cartel gunners. Lyons dived to the side as another burst of fire flew through the space where he'd been kneeling. As he rolled away from the attack, he saw Schwarz thumb the hammer of the tiny single-action weapon and fire again. The second man fell.

Gonzales had fired twice at the rolling Lyons, missing both times. In frustration, he now turned the gun toward Schwarz and jammed it into the electronic wiz's throat. "Say good night," he screamed like a madman, and Lyons heard the sickening roar of a .45-caliber bullet.

The sound made the Able Team leader want to puke. He stopped rolling and bounded to his feet. He knew what he would do. He would run forward through whatever rounds Gonzales fired at him. His righteous anger would be his shield, and no matter how many bullets struck his body he wouldn't die until he had killed the whoremonger with his bare hands.

He would avenge Schwarz's death, be it the last thing he ever did.

Lyons was halfway to the desk when he saw Gonzales lying across it facedown. Blood seeped from under the fat body, and Hermann "Gadgets" Schwarz stood to the side still holding the minirevolver. Schwarz grinned at something behind the Able Team leader.

Lyons turned to see Bud Keener gripping the fancy engraved 1911 Government Model. Only then did the Able Team leader realize that the .45 he had heard had come from the Texas Ranger's gun rather than Gonzales's.

As Carl Lyons shoved a fresh magazine into the pistol, Keener walked forward into the room. Blancanales and Harsey appeared in the doorway behind him. Blancanales shrugged. "Better late than never?" he asked.

Lyons chuckled. "You were almost too late," he said.

"Then it's good we aren't playing horseshoes."

A low moan came from the corner of the room and Lyons turned that way. The first man he had shot was still alive. A quick inspection showed he had suffered nothing more serious than a flesh wound, which they could treat themselves. Dropping to one knee, Lyons worked the slide on the Government Model and pressed the muzzle into the man's nose.

The cartel gunner closed his eyes and made the sign of the cross.

"I'm not going to kill you," Lyons said. "That is, as long as you do me two favors."

The man's eyelids shot up.

"First, tell me where your next little cartel war game is going to be played."

"San Antonio," the man said without hesitation. He gave Lyons an address and waited for the next order.

"Okay," the Able Team leader said. "Second favor. You're going with us."

The cartel man started to protest. Lyons raised the pistol and brought it down against the side of the man's head, administering an instant anesthetic.

Keener had moved to the desk, and Lyons watched him grab a handful of Lone Wolf Gonzales's greasy hair. Lifting the man's head back, he looked into eyes that could no longer see. "Well, you fat name-stealing son of a bitch," the Ranger said. "Guess you're about as dead as all your men now, aren't you?"

"Anybody seen Anderson?" Lyons asked. He still didn't know if the Houston detective was alive or dead.

Just then footsteps sounded in the hallway. All guns in the room turned that way.

Dirk Anderson made it to the doorway, then collapsed.

Lyons rushed forward and knelt next to the man. Anderson had a single bullet wound through the upper thigh. Miraculously, it had missed the femoral artery by less than an inch, and the bone by an even thinner margin.

"Somebody shot me, through the front door," Anderson said, gritting his teeth. "Right at the start."

Lyons nodded. It was that stray round that had been meant for him, and it explained the "Ugh!" he had heard from the front yard. But it hadn't stopped Anderson from doing his duty, and the Able Team leader felt a rush of pride. "We'll get you sewed up and good as new, Dirk," he said.

"That's not what worries me," Anderson said. "The hospital will report it, and the cops will come to investigate. I can kiss my pension goodbye."

Lyons shook his head. "You aren't bleeding bad, and we can stop that. Can you stand the pain a few more hours?"

Anderson nodded.

"Then we'll get you in the air. We've got doctors who don't report to anybody."

"I'll need to call in sick," Anderson said.

"We'll take care of that," Lyons said. He thought of Hal Brognola. The Stony Man Director could take care of that with a phone call.

Keener had walked toward Anderson, holding a bottle of tequila. "Have a bite of this Jose Gold," he said. "It'll take the edge off the pain."

Lyons rose to his feet. "We've got to get Dirk and our new cartel buddy out of here before the cops arrive," he said.

Schwarz and Blancanales came out through the door carrying the still-unconscious cartel gunner. Schwarz, still handcuffed in front, was nevertheless able to cradle the man's legs over his outstretched arms. Keener and Harsey squatted and lifted Anderson.

All of the men who had destroyed Gonzales and his operation began making their way as swiftly as possible back down the stairs. As they walked, Schwarz said, "Hey, anybody got a handcuff key?"

"We've got them," Keener said. "Let us get these guys to the van and we'll get you out of those bracelets."

As they proceeded, Blancanales's voice came from behind Lyons. "Tell me the truth, Gadgets," Blancanales said.

"About what?"

"It wasn't *really* Gonzales and his men who handcuffed you was it? I figure you let that little gal on the second floor do it."

5

The Executioner downshifted the Harley, picking up speed as he sailed around a rattling flatbed truck hauling caged and wildly clucking chickens. By the time he had started the motorcycle and turned out of the service station, the Corvette had been three blocks ahead of him. He had now gained a block on the brothers, and so far it didn't look like they'd noticed him. Roberto and Santiago had sped away from the service station with screeching tires. But now that they were away from the immediate area, they had slowed to avoid attracting attention.

Bolan cut around a Mercedes and the car's horn trumpeted. He glanced to his side and saw a uniformed chauffeur growling at him through the windshield. He couldn't help but smile when a well-dressed woman's immaculately manicured hand came over the front seat with the middle finger upraised. So much for ladylike behavior.

Weaving through traffic, the soldier drew within a block of the brothers. Two vehicles—a small economy car followed by a larger Ford pickup—still separated him from the Corvette. He continued to ride low in the Harley's saddle, staying out of sight by centering the motorcycle behind the Ford.

The procession continued down the busy street. Normally, Bolan would have hoped the biker's disguise would conceal his identity. But the mere fact that Roberto and Santiago had fired at him at the gas station proved that it hadn't worked—at least with them. It made sense that they would be looking for him, just as he was looking for them. And if the gas station had been the obvious place for him to begin his search, it was equally understandable that the two brothers would resume their hunt for him there, too.

So far, Roberto and Santiago hadn't noticed him yet. They were boxed in by traffic; the Harley had the advantage, and Bolan knew he could cut between the cars and overtake the Corvette at will. But he wanted to question the brothers. He needed to find out who had hired them. And the middle of the busy street was hardly an ideal place for an interrogation.

The Executioner downshifted again. On the other hand, this heavy traffic wouldn't last forever; they were fast nearing the fringes of the city. And once they hit open road his advantage would be lost. If Roberto and Santiago saw him then, the lightning-fast Corvette would leave the Harley in its dust.

Bolan stood on the foot pegs, risking a look over the pickup cab. In the distance, the traffic was already thinning. If his calculations were accurate, they were only a few miles from where the city began to gradually give way to the countryside. He sat back in the saddle. He had hoped to follow the two brothers all the way to their base of operations but that possibility was looking thinner with every block.

After considering all the facts of the situation, Bolan made his decision in a heartbeat. He would follow until he saw the first sign that they had spotted him, then cut around the vehicles in front and take them there and then.

Another mile went by, then two. The utility vehicle just behind the two brothers turned off. Bolan was more careful to stay low in the saddle and keep the pickup squarely in front. Through the cab of the Chevy, he could just see the tops of the two men's heads in the Corvette. He knew their ignorance of his pursuit couldn't go on forever and waited for the inevitable.

It came a mile and a half later, at the intersection of another busy street. The Corvette stayed in the middle lane but the pickup pulled over to the right to turn. Suddenly, the Harley was directly behind the Corvette.

The two brothers stopped at the red light and waited. Both men faced forward. Then Bolan saw Roberto look up into the rearview mirror. A split second later, he twisted violently in his seat to stare at the soldier. And a second after that, he floored the accelerator and sped through the red light.

Bolan popped the Harley's clutch and twisted the gas, narrowly dodging a honking semitractor trailer in the middle of the intersection. The truck's deep bass horn boomed in his ear as he flew forward.

A block from the intersection, Santiago turned in his seat and raised a 12-gauge shotgun. Bolan cut the handlebar to the right a second before the twin barrels boomed, sending deer slugs into the pavement where he'd been a moment before. Sparks lit up the concrete as the heavy rounds ricocheted and sailed off down the street. Santiago turned back to the front, and Bolan straightened the Harley again.

The Executioner raised his left hand from the handlebar, drawing the Desert Eagle. His thumb moved over the big gun's slide to take off the safety, then back around the grip. By the time that was accomplished, Santiago—and the sawed-off shotgun—were facing him.

Dodging the rounds this time was harder for several reasons. First, Santiago fired one barrel at a time, and each time he did, buckshot rather than a slug came out. When the lead shot reached the Harley, it had spread from the shortened barrels. Bolan cut the handlebar both ways, doing his best to keep control of the big machine and hang on to the Desert Eagle at the same time. Both times he almost crashed—first into an oncoming car in the opposite lane, the next into a fire hydrant mounted on a corner. A stray pellet ripped though the top of his leather vest. He felt a sting but could tell no major damage had been done.

Forced to reload, Santiago faced the front once more. The Executioner knew his chances of dodging the heavy shotgun shells grew thinner with each round fired. It was now or never.

Taking as careful aim on the bouncing motorcycle as he could, Bolan tried to align the sights on the right rear tire. The front sight jerked up and down, back and forth, as the two vehicles sped on. Timing it to the split second, the Executioner jerked the trigger quickly. The Desert Eagle boomed. But the round struck the pavement to the side.

Santiago turned again and fired before Bolan could dodge. Luckily, his speed had affected his accuracy, and the load went wide. Behind him, the Executioner heard a horn, and then he was cutting the handlebar hard to the right again as the second barrel exploded.

The quiet brother had more ammo and turned again to reload. Their speed had declined due to a vehicle in front of the Corvette, and Bolan heard the Harley sputter. He was forced to spend precious seconds jamming the hand cannon into his vest, hoping it wouldn't fall out while he downshifted and regeared. Retrieving the Desert Eagle as it started to slip, he pointed it toward the tire once more.

This time, the Executioner's aim was true, and when the big .44 Magnum exploded, so did the tire. The right rear end of the Corvette dropped a good six inches and the flattened rubber burned off in seconds. The Chevy went into a skid as the rim met the concrete, sending sparks flying as if from a welder's torch.

Bolan slowed the Harley, watching Roberto fight the wheel as he tried to regain control. The brother overcompensated and the Corvette slid across the road into oncoming traffic, barely missing an El Camino that ran its wheels over the curb. Roberto managed to get the vehicle back into the proper lane but then the rear end began to fishtail, and the Corvette moved onto the shoulder.

The Executioner accelerated slightly, ready to slide off the Harley and sprint to the vehicle as soon as it stopped. He wanted the brothers alive, needed them alive. His mission wasn't revenge for the kidnapping, it was a probe to find out who was behind the two. Who had hired them to get him? The *Marxistas? Legitimas?* President Fierro Blanco himself? If Bolan was ever to learn, once and for all, exactly who it was pulling the strings that caused all the current problems in Mexico, he had to take at least one of the brothers alive.

The Corvette suddenly began to spin. Each time the front of the vehicle whirled to face him, Bolan saw the astonished faces of Roberto and Santiago. He tightened his grip on the Desert Eagle, preparing to fire. But raising the shotgun looked like the last thing on Santiago's mind as his bewildered face watched the Chevy continue to pirouette.

Finally, the car spun off the shoulder, and the front bumper slammed into a telephone pole. Bolan watched Santiago catapult out of the convertible, over the hood and through the air. He crashed to the ground twenty feet away. The steering wheel had stopped Roberto, and as the Corvette shimmied to a halt in a sickening screech of dented metal, the man rebounded back and forth like a speed bag hanging in a boxing gym.

The Executioner laid the Harley down on its side and slid off running. Traffic had come to a halt around the accident, and the gaping mouths of onlookers could be seen through the windows and windshields. Racing to the mangled vehicle, Bolan pointed the Desert Eagle at the man in the driver's seat.

But Roberto wouldn't be talking. His head lay on one shoulder, his eyes staring ahead more in surprise than horror. Bright white vertebrae stuck sickeningly through his dark skin.

The Executioner turned to the spot where he'd seen Santiago hit the ground.

It was empty. He raised his line of sight and saw the other brother running, limping slightly, toward a crowd of astonished onlookers. Bolan raised the Desert Eagle and dropped the front sight on the man, then lined up the rear sight on a spot halfway between the shoulder blades.

His finger tightened on the trigger. Then relaxed.

Santiago was no good to him dead. But there was another reason the Executioner didn't fire. The big 240-grain semijacketed .44 Magnum pistol would have drilled right through the running man's body and into the crowd of spectators.

In the distance, the Executioner heard police sirens. He leaned across Roberto's limp body, opened the Corvette's glove compartment and pulled out all of the paperwork he found inside. The loose papers went into one of the zippered pockets of his leather vest. A quick pat down of Roberto's body came up with a slender tri-fold wallet in the back pocket. Bolan also found the Desert Eagle the brothers had taken from him during the kidnapping.

Dropping the wallet into his own pocket and jamming both

Desert Eagles into his jeans, the Executioner ran back to his over-turned Harley-Davidson as the police sirens neared. They were coming from both directions but the stalled traffic had slowed their approach. Lifting the motorcycle from its side, Bolan whispered a silent prayer of thanks when it roared to life on the third kick of the starter. He tapped it into gear with the toe of his boot, twisted the gas and let out the clutch.

The soldier was a block from the scene of the accident when he met the oncoming police car. The officers inside didn't give him so much as a glance in their hurry to get to the scene. Bolan returned their disregard. But he didn't stop the Harley until he had pulled it into the warehouse, parked it next to the camper bus and killed the engine.

Sliding the warehouse door back into place and locking it, the Executioner climbed into the bus and took a seat on the small couch in the back. He reached and turned on the overhead light.

All of the paperwork he had found in the glove compartment had been issued to a Dr. Francisco Guttierez and his wife, confirming the Executioner's suspicion that the Corvette had been stolen. He dropped it on the floor and pulled the wallet out of his pocket.

The tri-fold was packed with the usual odds and ends—scribbled notes, photographs and a driver's license under the name of Roberto Rodriguez. But the Executioner didn't jump to any conclusions. The name Roberto was as common in Spanish-speaking countries as José or Pancho. The billfold might have been stolen, too.

It wasn't until he came across the photograph of the two brothers standing on each side of an old woman wearing a scarf over her hair that Bolan knew he'd hit pay dirt. The picture looked to be at least five years old. But there was no mistaking the faces of the two brothers.

So their last name was Rodriguez. Roberto and Santiago Rodriguez. And the old woman was presumably the mother of whom they had spoken. The mother they seemed to fear.

The Executioner replaced the picture in the wallet and dropped it back into the pocket of his vest, closing the zipper over it. A thought played at his unconscious for a moment, then suddenly surfaced. And when it did, it brought a smile to his face. His mind had backtracked to the service station where the brothers had taken him, and where he'd returned to check the credit card receipts for gas.

Of the three credit cards that had been used during the time Bolan had been tied in the back of the brother's stolen delivery vehicle, one had been that of a John Sawyer who represented the Chrysler Corporation. The second had belonged to Manuel Chevez from Saltillo. But the third card had been issued in the name of a Mexico City resident. A woman named Maria.

Maria Rodriguez.

SCOTT HIX let the tiny speed bag rebound to a halt beneath the wooden frame. The rhythm had been soothing, lulling him into an almost meditative state in which there were no kidnappers, hostages, *Legitimas,* or *bandidos.* In the relaxing dream world he had entered for a few minutes while working the speed bag, there had been only two people. Scott Hix and Normandi West.

Hix glanced across the room to where the beautiful woman sat in an aluminum lawn chair that one of the revolutionaries had brought in. He smiled. She smiled back. But both held a trace of sadness.

The close-quarters combat specialist moved to the double-end striking ball suspended from the ceiling. Rather than fasten the elastic which extended from the bottom of the round leather sphere to the floor, Hix had instructed them to run it though the barbell hole of a ten pound disk and then tie it around the side. This provided two training advantages over the standard method of mounting such a device. It shortened and tightened the elastic cords, causing the ball to move faster. And the ten-pound weight shifted slightly each time the ball was struck, keeping him from getting into a recognizable rhythm or pattern. The striking ball became unpredictable. Like an opponent.

Hix began tapping the ball lightly, working on timing and speed rather than power. The fight in which he was about to engage wouldn't be a boxing match. But he knew of no better way to get into shape. The stiffness in his legs, back and arms—the result of all the time the *Legitimas* had kept him chained to the floor with the other hostages—had disappeared faster than he'd have guessed. Of course he'd worked at it. The first day he had done nothing but stretching exercises. They'd paid off. He was beginning to feel like his old self again.

The former U.S. Army intelligence officer began to bob and weave, sometimes punching the ball as it returned, other times letting it fly back at his head, ducking at the last second. Out of the corner of one eye, he saw West watching him. Out of the other, he could see the six guards. Their weapons never wavered away from him, following him around the makeshift gym as he moved from bag to bag.

Hix continued to move, increasing his footwork as he punched. Sweat broke out on his forehead and he felt it trickling down his chest. He intended to be in top shape; but not to fight Toro, as the guards thought. He wanted his wind, strength, timing and overall fighting ability at a peak for one simple reason.

Escape.

The striking ball shot back at his head and Scott Hix lifted an elbow. The leather orb struck it and rebounded like a basketball hitting the backboard. As it returned again, he caught it with an uppercut and the ball danced up and down on the cords.

The American stepped back and began to kick the head-level bag back and forth with roundhouse kicks. He had never found the move to be particularly useful in true combat, preferring to rely on lower front kicks. But the higher foot techniques were great stretching and conditioning movements. As he continued to kick, his mind drifted again.

Escape. An opportunity would come. Either while he trained, on the way to the fight or at the fight itself. When it did, he had to be ready. He had to see the opening and take it.

And he had to take West with him. He wouldn't go without her.

Hix suddenly felt the Applegate-Fairbairn combat dagger shift in his pants. He quickly dropped his leg. Turning toward West and away from the guards, he bent over as if winded, the bag gloves on his hands dropping to his groin and resecuring the knife in place.

He had been only a second or two from taking off the Applegate-Fairbairn for bed when the *Legitimas* had burst through his door the other night. They had overlooked it and the knife had been hidden in his underwear ever since. There was nowhere else, and he was afraid that even if he found a place, it wouldn't be accessible when the time came that it might be put to use.

West watched him readjust the knife through his pants. She knew the weapon was there—he had told her. If something happened to him, he still wanted her to have every possible chance of survival and there was never any telling when the fighting blade might prove useful.

The men behind Hix—especially the three filthy bandits who made up half his guard—guffawed like prison punks. "Hey, *hombre*," one of them said. "Your woman makes you want to play with yourself, eh?"

Hix ignored him. With the knife in place once more, he moved to the heavy bag mounted in the corner of the room and began practicing combinations. Over and over he struck the heavy canvas, pretending with each blow that the bag was one of the kidnappers.

The close-quarters combat expert struck the bag for a steady three minutes, then took a break. As his breathing returned to normal, he glanced at the closed door, then around the windowless room. He and West had both been brought up from the room below—the room where he assumed Ronnie Quartel and the other hostages still were—in blindfolds. They had been led up two sets of steps. Other than the fact that they were in a building that had at least three floors, he knew no more about where they were than he had before.

Hix's eyes moved back to the door as it opened suddenly. Jesus Hidalgo, the leader of the *Legitimas,* and Pablo Huertes, the fat *bandido* whose men seemed to have formed an alliance with Hidalgo, entered the training room. Hidalgo walked forward and extended his hand.

Scott Hix narrowed his eyes as he looked at the hand like he would a snake he was about to kill.

Hidalgo dropped the gesture of friendship, and the expression that came over his face looked almost like hurt. Hix shook his head in disbelief. The leader was one walking contradiction after another. He kidnapped people, then he expected them to be friendly and like him?

Hidalgo cleared his throat. "You are well?" he asked.

"For a guy who's being held hostage and was tied up like an animal for several days, you mean?" Hix asked. "Yeah, couldn't be better. Just hanging out, punching the bags, entertaining myself and wondering when you're going to kill us all."

"You know that I pray that won't be necessary."

"Oh sure," Hix said.

Hidalgo let the words slide off his back. "Huertes has just returned from making the arrangements," he said. "You will fight Toro in two days."

"Then I'd better get busy," Hix said, turning his back to the *Legitima.*

Hidalgo reached out, placing a hand on the American's shoulder. Hix shrugged it off as he turned.

"I have brought you a sparring partner," Hidalgo said.

Only then did Hix really notice that a third man had entered the room behind Hidalgo and Huertes. His eyes narrowed again as he took in the bandit still standing by the door. The man's leering eyes were glued to West, and his lips were curled in a vulgar grin.

Hix felt the anger and hatred come over him in a rush. He recognized the man. One of the men who had guarded them below, he was the one who had run his hands all over West's legs before a *Legitima* guard had put a halt to it.

He was the one who had promised Hix he would have West sooner or later, and that when he was finished he would turn her over to the others.

Hix looked back to Hidalgo. "You couldn't have picked a nicer guy," he said.

Hidalgo shrugged. "Cervantes volunteered," he said. "It seems he doesn't like you or think you are as good as we do."

Hix felt himself smiling. "Why don't we find out?" he asked. "What are the rules?"

The man Hix now knew to be called Cervantes tore his eyes away from West and stepped forward. "No rules," he said. "I'm here to help you train." He threw back his head and laughed as if he'd made some hilarious joke. When he got control of himself, he looked back to West. "You are about to see a real man at work," he said. "Then, later, you will see what other work I'm good at, eh?"

West stared him in the eyes. Her expression was that of a woman viewing a worm.

"That's enough!" Hidalgo said. "Go put on a pair of gloves."

Hix followed Cervantes to the corner where several sets of well-used boxing gloves had been dumped. He took off the bag gloves he had worn and worked the more padded coverings over his hands. One of the guards dropped his rifle to the end of its sling and began lacing them for him.

The man hadn't quite finished the task when Cervantes tackled him from behind.

Hix flew forward, the stiffness in his lower back returning as he jacknifed through the air before being slammed face-first into the floor. Cervantes came down on him and blows from the bandit's gloves began to rain on the back of Hix's head and neck. Hix managed to roll onto a hip, took a punch in the side of the face that drove the other side into the floor, then whirled onto his back.

With his hand above him now, Scott Hix warded off Cervantes's next few blows, then drove a fist into the man's groin. Cervantes howled like a wounded wolf, and Hix threw him to the side and stood.

Hix forced the anger, hatred and frustration in his heart to simmer into a controllable rage. He knew from experience that the age-old tale of the "emotionless warrior" was a myth. Nobody—except maybe psychopaths and imbeciles—were able to rid themselves of all feeling during combat. Fear, fury, hope, despair—they were all there in the warrior's soul, and they volleyed back and forth, with each taking its turn in first place. But Hix knew the professional learned to control these emotions and make them work for him rather than against him.

Scott Hix knew one other thing, too. For days now, he had watched helplessly as these subhuman maggots mistreated and humiliated innocent people, not the least of whom was the woman he loved. He was furious. He was frustrated. If he didn't find an outlet for these emotions soon, he felt as if he'd explode.

Well, he had just been handed that outlet on a silver platter. And he intended to kill Cervantes. But not too fast.

Hix moved to the center of the room and waited for Cervantes to recover. He wanted the man back to one hundred percent of his abilities when they started fighting again. The man who wanted to rape Normandi West was going to provide his emotional release and the American wanted it to last.

Cervantes finally stood, took a deep breath and raised his gloves.

Hix stepped in and threw a jab. The guard blocked it and shot out a right. Hix raised a glove to parry, and the two men stepped away from each other again.

Slowly, carefully, Hix and Cervantes began to circle, taking stock of each other. The Mexican had some training, Hix could see. And he was mean—Hix could see that in his eyes. He was the kind of man who would rather force his will on others than reach an agreement. The kind who would enjoy rape far more than consensual lovemaking.

Hix stepped in, feinted a left and threw a right that connected with Cervantes's jaw. The bandit dropped his guard and the close-quarters combat expert started to throw a left out of instinct. No, the blow would have finished the fight. And that wasn't what he wanted. Not yet. There was still too much fire raging within Scott Hix's soul.

Dancing back to the middle of the room, Hix waited. He didn't just want to beat Cervantes, he wanted to treat him the way the hostages had all been treated. Humiliate him. Torture him, both physically and mentally. Cervantes wanted to rape West but that wasn't the only reason the American wouldn't let him leave this room alive. How many women had Cervantes raped in the past? How many innocent women's lives had been ruined to pleasure the bastard? How many more times would he commit the vile act in the future if he lived?

Cervantes moved in and threw a series of rights and lefts. Hix didn't even bother to block. Dropping his gloves to his sides the way Muhammad Ali used to do, he simply bobbed and weaved out of the way as if he were on a planet with less gravity than the Mexican. "What's wrong, Cervantes?" he taunted. "Didn't get enough sleep last night? Out fucking a goat or something? Or won't the goats have anything to do with you either?"

The guard cursed but saw through the attempt to make him lose control. He stepped away, caught his breath, then suddenly shot a foot at Hix's knee. The American got his leg off the ground just in time to take the kick on the side of the calf rather than the weak knee joint. It hurt, but no damage was done.

Hidalgo had said there were no rules. And Cervantes was taking the leader at his word. So Hix would, too.

The close-quarters combat expert moved in, faked a right, then a left, then swept his right leg across the floor and into Cervantes's ankles. The Mexican's feet flew out from under him and he suddenly found himself on his back. Hix took a half step in and came down with a stomp-kick to the nose. Not hard enough to kill the bandit or knock him out. But enough so that bone and cartilage snapped loudly.

Blood ran from Cervantes's nostrils as Hix threw back his head and laughed. "Got a cold, you filthy bastard?" he asked the man on the ground. "Your sinuses are running. Come on. Get back up, faggot!"

Few places in the world take a slur to a man's masculinity as a compliment. But nowhere is it considered more of an insult than in Mexico.

Scott Hix, of course, knew this well.

Cervantes bounded to his feet, his eyes radiating the insanity behind them. He was beyond control now. Maddened with humiliation and hostility. Ravenous for revenge. He howled like a wolf, then rushed Hix, both arms outstretched.

Hix waited until the man was a foot away, then stepped to the side and let him run into the wall.

Cervantes caught himself with his gloves and twirled back around. Hix slid forward and tapped him on the nose with a glove. Both of the man's gloves came up to protect the bleeding nostrils and Hix shot a straight left under them into the Mexican's gut. Cervantes wheezed for a second and then cursed. His gloves dropped. Hix punched him in the left shoulder, then the right. The gloves fell farther. Cervantes's entire head was now open, but that was too easy—too fast. Hix hit him three times in the ribs and heard a cracking sound.

The guard moaned like a sick kitten. "Enough!" he cried. "I am beaten."

"You pussy!" Hix cried. "Hit me! Go on, hit me! I'll give you a free one!" He stuck out his chin and closed his eyes.

As soon as his eyelids lowered Hix knew it had been a mistake. He was grandstanding now for West's behalf. She wasn't going to be impressed—she wasn't the kind of woman who would be. And tactically, such actions were inexcusable.

Hix opened his eyes in time to see that Cervantes had jerked off his gloves and drawn a huge folding knife from his back pocket. The eight-inch blade came clicking out with a sound like a ratchet. Hix jumped back as Cervantes threw a wild slash that would have disemboweled him had he remained motionless. The American threw off the right glove which hadn't been properly laced when Cervantes's initial tackle started the fracas. His hand started to move to the Applegate-Fairbairn in his pants, then stopped. No. He needed it for later.

"Stop it!" Hidalgo cried. "If you kill him, Cervantes, I will kill you!"

But the bandit was beyond listening or caring.

One glove on, the other off, Hix backpedaled as Cervantes moved forward. More slashes arched through the air like a windmill. In his peripheral vision he caught a glimpse of West. The stoic expression she had maintained since the kidnapping was gone. It had been replaced by a look of sheer terror as she waited for her lover to die.

Hix didn't intend to let that happen. Ducking under a slash meant for his throat, he drove his bare fist up into Cervantes's sternum. The bandit coughed. But he brought the big blade down in a thrust aimed at the top of Hix's head.

The American got his glove hand up just in time to slap the side of the curved blade. He felt the pressure of the razor-sharp edge as it cut into the leather and padding. Enough was enough. The balance of power had changed as soon as Cervantes drew the weapon. He could no longer play games with the man.

Scott Hix's bare hand reached up and into Cervantes's throat, his thumb digging into the right side while his fingers did the same on the left. Grabbing as if he was holding a softball, he squeezed until he felt the fingers touch his thumb behind the larynx, windpipe, tendons and ligaments.

Cervantes's eyes bulged in pain and shock.

Hix held his grip and jerked with all his strength. Sounds not unlike violin or guitar strings popping filled the room. A brief choking sound issued forth from Cervantes's lips, then stopped.

The bandit was dead before he hit the floor.

Hix stepped back and turned to Hidalgo. "Why don't you bring me somebody who's at least a little competition?" he asked.

Hidalgo's face showed no emotion. But Pablo Huertes was grinning ear to ear. "Yes," he shouted. "I'm a believer now! I truly believe he can last the three minutes."

Scott Hix turned to Normandi West. He saw the relief in her eyes. But he saw something else as well, something he hadn't seen during the entire hostage situation. Fear. And it wasn't the *Legitimas* or *bandidos* who frightened her.

It was Scott Hix himself.

THE EXECUTIONER had taken on many chances over the years. He knew that certain calculated hazards were part of the game but the cardinal rule of danger was that every aspect of a mission could be controlled. A wise operative prepared for every possible twist and turn that a mission might take ahead of time.

And sometimes that meant recruiting backup.

Bolan turned the bus onto the street of the presidential palace and cruised past the presidential mansion. The usual guard outside had been tripled since his kidnapping, and it was made up of both uniformed police and men who were obviously plainclothes feds. They watched the bus go by but didn't appear to give it any closer scrutiny than the other vehicles.

The Executioner stared straight ahead as he passed but scanned the men out of the corner of his eye. It was unlikely, but there was always the chance that Captain Juanito Oliverez, the one fed that he trusted, might be on the grounds. He wasn't.

Bolan's mind moved back a few days in time to the assault on the palace and the many attempts to assassinate President Fierro Blanco of Mexico. Oliverez had proved over and over that he could be trusted. Most of the other bodyguards had proved that they were incompetent or could be bought. The Executioner knew good men existed among their rank and file. But he didn't have time to weed them out.

Parking the bus too near the *Los Pinos* would be asking for trouble, Bolan knew. While it was a perfect hide-in-plain-sight vehicle in general, it would draw attention among the cars and pickups that surrounded it. And he couldn't risk driving by the president's residence another time, either. The bus would be remembered.

Bolan turned the corner, drove six blocks down the street and pulled the vehicle into three parallel parking spaces along the curb. A police officer standing on the other side of the street immediately yelled in Spanish, checked both ways for traffic and began to cross. By the time he reached the bus, the Executioner had rolled down the window. He reached into his pocket, pulled out a ten-dollar bill and handed it down to the man.

The Mexican officer took the money, spun on his heels and disappeared down the block without a word.

The cellular phone the Executioner had used at *Los Pinos* was still at the mansion, but Jack Grimaldi had brought along a replacement with the other equipment. Rising from the driver's seat, the soldier moved to the rear of the bus and dropped onto the threadbare couch as he tapped numbers into the instrument.

A moment later, an accent that betrayed a history in both France and Israel answered the call in Spanish. *"Buenos tardes."*

"You alone?" Bolan asked.

"Hardly," Yakov Katzenelenbogen said. The former leader of Phoenix Force and current tactical advisor to Stony Man Farm, Katz had replaced the Executioner as Fierro Blanco's American bodyguard.

"When will you be?"

"About fifteen minutes," Katz whispered. "My shift ends and I return to your old room."

"Can you get out without being seen?"

A soft chuckle came over the airwaves. "I retired from full-time duty because I was getting old, Striker. Not stupid."

Now it was Bolan's turn to chuckle.

The Executioner glanced across the street to a furniture store. Inside the front window he could see tables, chairs and a dining room suite. "I'm a block south, six blocks east," he said into the phone. "Look for the bus across the street from the furniture store." He hung up.

Twenty minutes later, Yakov Katzenelenbogen opened the passenger's side door of the bus and climbed in. His eyes surveyed the layout before he looked into the back where Bolan still sat on the couch. "Well, it's not exactly the old War Wagon now, is it?" the Stony Man advisor said, referring to the specially equipped and armored vehicle the Executioner had used years before in his war against the mafia. "What are you doing? Moonlighting as a Mexico City tour guide?"

Bolan laughed. "Take a seat, Katz," he said. As quickly as possible, he ran down the situation with the Rodriguez brothers and their mother. "I don't know exactly how they tie in to the overall situation. But they're in it somewhere," he finished.

"So we're going to pay Mama Rodriguez and her sole surviving bad little boy a visit?" Katz asked.

Bolan nodded. "Mother, son and whoever else is there. I need you to cover the outside while I go in." He paused, frowning. "The Harley's still too hot to take out—cops'll be watching for it. And the bus is perfect for the road but it'll attract too much attention in their neighborhood. I think we're going to have to go boost a car."

"Nonsense," Katz said. "I already did. Got one from the *Los Pinos* parking lot when I left."

Bolan's eyebrows rose. "Good thinking."

"It's a Mercedes, and it won't look like something the neighbors just bought. But it won't draw the notice this thing will, either." He tapped the bus window behind him.

The Executioner laughed as he rose. Snatching a Mexico City map off the table next to the couch, he climbed out of the bus.

The Israeli led Bolan to a Mercedes parked a half block behind the bus and the Executioner slid behind the wheel. Bolan started the vehicle as he handed the map to Katz and gave the man the address of the Rodriguez house. He pulled the Mercedes out into traffic. They left the *Los Pinos* area as Katz located where Maria Rodriguez lived. He directed the Executioner up an access ramp onto a major thoroughfare.

"What's Fierro Blanco been up to?" Bolan asked as he drove.

Katz shrugged his shoulders. "Same old, same old," the Stony Man advisor said. "He faded from sight again about an hour before I left. So I'm guessing he's off with his singer again."

Bolan kept the Mercedes below the speed limit. The president's mysterious absences had been commonplace while Bolan had been guarding the man, hoping to find out if he was honest or actually behind the Mexican unrest. Finally, he and the men from Able Team had followed the Mexican president to a clandestine meeting with Margarita Felice, a famous Mexican singer and actress. Which hadn't solved the puzzle about Fierro Blanco's involvement in Mexico's unrest in the least. Just because he was meeting the woman some of the time during his absences didn't mean it was her he was meeting all of the time.

Thirty minutes later, they left the highway and drove into a lower-income residential area. Bolan turned a corner. Two blocks down, he saw a light-brown Mercedes pull away from a house and drive off. It was almost identical to the one in which he and Katz now rode.

The Executioner squinted. *Los Pinos* had an entire fleet of Mercedes. Was the one he saw ahead another of them? Katz had said

Fierro Blanco had disappeared again. Might it be the president behind the wheel?

Bolan watched the address numbers as they neared the house. He was hardly shocked when the number they were looking for turned out to be the house where the Mercedes had been. There were no other vehicles parked in the drive or yard. Driving to the corner, the soldier jerked the Mercedes to a halt. "Change of plans," he said.

"I follow the other Mercedes and see if it was Fierro Blanco," Katz said, anticipating his orders.

"You got it," Bolan said as he exited the driver's side. "If I'm not waiting when you get back it means it already hit the fan."

"Who watches your back now?"

"Me."

Katz nodded and slid over behind the wheel. A moment later the wheels burned rubber as the Israeli took off to try to find the other Mercedes.

Even dressed in his ragged jeans and denim shirt, the Executioner expected that a strange gringo would draw attention in the neighborhood. So he was somewhat surprised when the men, women and children lounging on the broken-down front porches of the other houses in the area didn't seem to give him a second glance. As he walked toward the Rodriguez house, it appeared to Bolan that the neighbors were accustomed to outside visitors.

Two houses away, the Executioner cut between a pair of crumbling adobe shacks and sprinted to the alley. He kept low, using the trash cans as cover, as he neared. Just because the driveway was empty didn't mean Santiago hadn't found his way back home. And home to Mama was exactly where the Executioner expected the man would flee. Both to report his brother's death and lick his own wounds.

Just because the neighbors had appeared listless on the surface was no guarantee that they hadn't noticed him and hurried to warn the Rodriguez family. Bolan increased his pace now, vaulting a low fence into the backyard and sprinting past a row of chicken houses. The frightened birds announced his arrival with frantic clucks as effective as any trained watchdog. Drawing the sound-suppressed 9 mm Beretta from beneath his shirt, the Executioner jumped the two steps to the back porch and landed on splintering, unpainted wood—promptly falling through the rotted lumber to his knees.

Not only had the wood cracked as loudly as a gunshot, the Executioner lost precious seconds climbing out of the hole. He kicked the back door open and found himself in a strange room that looked as if it was used for some sort of ritual. Daggers, pentagrams and other pseudoreligious items were scattered around the worn out-furniture. Crucifixes hung upside down on the walls. What appeared to be pools of blood had dried across the floor and coffee table. But the main thing that took his notice was the room itself.

It seemed to have its own personality. And its aura was evil incarnate.

Santiago appeared suddenly in the doorway. The second brother held the Beretta he had taken from Bolan during the kidnapping, and he now tried to line up the sights on the Executioner. He fired too soon, sputtering off a burst of 9 mm slugs that missed Bolan by a good three feet.

Again, the Executioner knew he needed Santiago alive for questioning. Raising his replacement Beretta and aiming toward the man's legs, he squeezed the trigger and sent his own three-shot volley toward a hipbone. But just as his finger triggered the burst, the soldier saw Santiago drop to one knee. Under normal circumstances, it would have been sound gunfight strategy. But the three rounds meant for the brother's hip caught him squarely in the face.

Santiago Rodriguez fell to the dirt floor inside the ritual room, adding his own blood to whoever else's had been spilled there in the past.

The Executioner cursed silently as he scooped the Beretta from the dead fingers. He stepped over the man and into a hallway. Movement sounded through another door ten feet away and he made his way toward it. Turning into a small kitchen, he saw an old woman leaning back against the cabinet. She held a Rossi lever-action carbine in her hands, the short barrel pressed beneath her chin. Her feet were bare, and one of her dirty toes was inside the trigger guard.

"Don't!" Bolan said. He dropped the twin Berettas to his sides. With her sons dead, the old woman was his only link to whoever had been behind the Executioner's kidnapping and possibly the assassination attempts on Fierro Blanco. Or maybe his link to the president himself, and his involvement with the drug cartels and political upheaval.

The truth was, Bolan didn't know what the old woman was. But he knew she was all he had.

"Don't do it," he said in a softer voice. "I'm not going to hurt you."

A strange mixture of humor and fear covered the old woman's face. "Your magic is strong," she said.

"I don't have any magic."

"You aren't aware of it, perhaps," came the crackling voice. "But you have it. I feel it. I feel it strongly now that you are near."

"I mean you no harm," Bolan said. "I just want to talk to you. Set the rifle down. Carefully."

The old woman's eyes fell to the Beretta 93-Rs in both of the Executioner's hands. "Put your guns down first," she croaked from above the carbine's barrel.

Bolan hesitated. There was every chance in the world that it was a trick on the old woman's part to disarm him. But he saw no way around doing what she'd asked if he didn't want to kill her, or have her kill herself. And her eyes told him she was more than ready to pull the Rossi's trigger and end her own life. In any case, he would still have both Desert Eagles hidden beneath his shirt. Using them on the old woman, of course, was the last thing he wanted to do. He needed to find out who had hired her and her sons.

Slowly, Bolan let both the Berettas fall to the wooden floor of the kitchen.

As soon as they left his hands the old woman twirled the carbine with a dexterity that defied her age. The Executioner was suddenly looking down the .357 caliber barrel of the lever-action carbine.

"You possess strong magic," the old witch said. "The strongest I have ever seen. I want it, and by killing you, I'll have it."

The old woman's knurled and wrinkled finger tightened on the trigger and the weapon exploded.

6

There had been a change of plans.

Carl Lyons looked across the cabin of the plane and saw Pancho Montoya strapped in his seat. The cartel gunner they had captured alive at Gonzales's house was naked from the waist up except for the bandages on his shoulders. His eyes were closed, and a slight grimace of pain covered his face. The Able Team leader wasn't sure whether he was faking or if the superficial wounds he had sustained might have hit a painful nerve. But he didn't care. The man wasn't in danger of death, and Lyons would be damned if he wasn't going to get every bit of help he could out of him.

The change of plans had come only a few minutes after Able Team, Texas Rangers Bud Keener and Mark Harsey, and Dirk Anderson had left Gonzales's demolished whore and drug house. As they got the injured Anderson into the air with Charlie Mott, who would fly him where doctors could mend his gunshot wound, Lyons had made a quick scrambled cellular call to Hal Brognola. The director of Sensitive Operations had informed him that the U.S. president was preparing to amass nearly seventy-five percent of America's available military personnel along the Mexican border. Military cutbacks by the man in the White House had dropped the fighting force to such sparse levels that if any other hostilities broke out around the world Washington would be as impotent as a eunuch in a porno flick.

The roar from the plane's engines quieted slightly as Jack Grimaldi, at the controls, prepared to land in San Diego, California. According to Brognola's reading of the President, a lot of the pressure to invade Mexico was coming from the Man's powerful

Hollywood friends. They wanted movie megastar Ronnie Quartel safe and sound and ready as soon as the next director said, "Action." And Brognola theorized that if they could solve that problem quickly there was a good chance of at least delaying the President's insane police action south of the border.

Therefore, Able Team was on its way to give the men of Phoenix Force a hand finding Quartel, former U.S. Military Intelligence Officer Scott Hix, and the other hostages kidnapped by the *Ciudadano para Democracia Mexicana Legitima.*

The wheels hit the runway, and the men around the cabin began unbuckling their seat belts. Lyons glanced at Bud Keener. The Ranger's eyes were still closed, and it looked to the Able Team leader as if the gray in his black beard might have doubled over the past few hours. Keener was no longer a young man. But he had proved himself to be everything the Texas Rangers had gained their reputation of being: Tough, smart and competent to get the job done. His young partner, Harsey, obviously idolized him the way most young officers did a good training officer. They made a good team, and they weren't afraid to bend the rules a little to get the job done.

That's why Lyons had invited them to go to Tijuana with him, Schwarz and Blancanales. Keener and Harsey hadn't hesitated to call Ranger headquarters and take some of the many overtime "comp" hours they'd amassed and say, "Why not?"

The plane taxied to a halt but Lyons and the other men didn't rise from their seats. While Grimaldi dropped out of the front to do the necessary paperwork and rent them a car, Lyons said, "Gentlemen, we've got a few problems to iron out." He glanced at Montoya, whose eyes were still closed. "Open your baby-browns, Pancho," he said. "Nobody believes you're really asleep."

Montoya's eyes opened, but the grimace of pain stayed on his face.

"We've got to cross the border with weapons," Lyons went on. "And under the current conditions both sides—Mexico and the U.S.—are practically strip-searching every vehicle." He turned to Montoya again. "There's another of the drug tunnels somewhere close by. Where?'' Although it didn't show on the Able Team leader's face, inwardly he held his breath. The statement and question had been total bluff. He had no such intelligence information about any tunnel.

But the bluff worked.

"It's outside the city to the east,'' Montoya said. "But you can't go through it. There will be drug shipments coming the other way and if you encounter one you will be vastly outnumbered.''

"Pancho,'' Lyons said, leaning forward in his seat. "Two things. First, no editorial comments from you. I ask the questions, you give the answers. End of story. Second, get that phoney-ass-oh-I-hurt-so-much expression off your face or I'll give you a real reason to wear it.''

The grimace left Montoya's face immediately.

"Okay,'' Lyons said, straightening in his seat. "We've got our side arms, and three Calico subguns. We're going to need more firepower. How's everyone stand on ammo?''

Ranger Bud Keener glanced down at the hand-tooled rig on his belt. "Down to two .45 mags and a couple of speed-loaders for my Smith,'' he said.

Lyons looked to Harsey. "No better,'' the young clean-shaven Ranger said.

The Able Team leader nodded. He had checked the ammo lockers onboard the plane and they were running low as well. With both Jack Grimaldi and Charlie Mott in the air almost since the Mexican problem had begun, the Stony Man planes hadn't had time to return to the Farm and replenish their stores. And Able Team didn't have time to wait now. "Then we better find guns and ammo here,'' he said. Before he could speak again, he heard a car engine pull up outside the plane and stop. A second later Grimaldi opened the door to the cabin. Reaching up, he handed a key ring, a San Diego phone book and a city map to the Able Team leader. "Here's your stuff, bwana,'' the ace pilot grinned. "Any more orders?''

"Yeah,'' Lyons said as he stepped down from the plane. "Have the beer waiting when we get back.''

"I'll get some and make sure it's cold," Grimaldi said, chuckling.

Lyons looked up to see a bright red Chevy Suburban idling a few feet away. "Talk about drawing attention," he muttered. "Couldn't you find one in neon yellow?"

Grimaldi shrugged. "Last large rental they had left," he said. "Maybe I should have taken the GEO Tracker for all of you? It was black."

Lyons slid behind the wheel of the Suburban as Schwarz and Blancanales escorted Montoya into the back seat. Keener and Harsey were transferring the canvas bags containing the arms and what little ammo remained to the rear of the vehicle.

A few moments later, they were leaving the airport. Lyons watched Schwarz, riding next to him, thumb through the phone book's yellow pages until he came to the *G*s. "Ah, 'Guns,'" he said. "And where one finds guns, one will usually find bullets."

Blancanales had leaned forward directly behind Schwarz and held open the city map. "Your investigative instincts are truly amazing, Gadgets," he said. He stared between the seats at the yellow pages.

Schwarz glanced at the map. His index finger tapped the phone book. "The closest place looks like the Krazy Kolonel's Kombat Korner. And with a name that corny, they deserve to be robbed." He quoted Lyons the address, and Blancanales extended the map into the Able Team leader's vision.

A few minutes later, they were pulling into a shopping center where a hundred-foot red-white-and-blue sign announced Guns! Guns! Guns!

Lyons threw the transmission into park in front of the store and turned in his seat. "Keener," he said. "Take the wheel. Harsey, look after our cartel buddy there." He took a deep breath, then glanced at Schwarz and Blancanales. "Let's go guys."

The men of Able Team got out of the Suburban.

"I always wanted to pull off an armed robbery," Schwarz said.

"Me too," Blancanales said. "But I feel cheated that we don't even get to wear ski masks."

DAVID MCCARTER set the phone down in the cradle and leaned back in the chair Leo Turrin had occupied the day before during the interviews. He looked around the now-deserted office, saw the phoney certificates, business awards and photographs on the wall. All of the little things that had gone into making Toro Enterprises had been an illusion. Quickly put together, they had been part of one of Leo Turrin's elaborate schemes to make things appear to be what they were not.

For a brief moment, McCarter thought about Turrin. What kind of man did it take to pull off such hoaxes? A man much different than himself, he had to admit. McCarter preferred the straightforward approach. He would work undercover when necessary, and had proved so many times over the years. But as Turrin himself had teasingly pointed out earlier, deceit wasn't part of his natural makeup. To Turrin, however, it seemed to be second nature. Did that make him a bad man? No, McCarter thought as he listened to the silence in the now-vacant office.

The Phoenix Force leader caught himself grinning. He supposed the same moral question might be asked of him. Did his ability to kill outright make him evil? No. Not until he began using that talent for the wrong purposes.

The grin left McCarter's face as he glanced back at the phone. Toro Enterprises might be an illusion but the phone call he had just made was all too real. Thomas Jackson Hawkins, the youngest and newest member of Phoenix Force, had been critically wounded in one of the Mexican drug tunnels. The call McCarter had just made had been to the hospital in Tucson. Hawkins was still in ICU. The doctors were doing everything they could. But they gave him less than a fifty-fifty chance of pulling through.

McCarter stood behind the desk. Should he tell the other men? How would it affect their performances in the mission ahead? They were all top professionals but T. J. Hawkins was closer to all of them than a brother, and as good as they were, the men of Phoenix Force were only human. Bad news sometimes drive human beings to even greater achievement; other times it paralyzed them. For a moment, McCarter wished that Katz was still leading

Play TIC-TAC-TOE and get FREE GIFTS!

HOW TO PLAY:

1. Play the tic-tac-toe scratch-off game at the right for your FREE BOOKS and FREE GIFT!

2. Send back this card and you'll receive TWO brand-new, first-time-in-paperback Gold Eagle novels. These books have a cover price of $4.99 each, but they are yours to keep absolutely free.

3. There's no catch. You're under no obligation to buy anything. We charge nothing — ZERO — for your first shipment. And you don't have to make any minimum number of purchases — not even one!

4. The fact is, thousands of readers enjoy receiving books by mail from the Gold Eagle Reader Service™ months before they're available in stores. They like the convenience of home delivery, they like getting the best new novels before they're available in stores, and they love our discount prices!

5. We hope that after receiving your free books you'll want to remain a subscriber. But the choice is yours — to continue or cancel, any time at all! So why not take us up on our invitation, with no risk of any kind. You'll be glad you did!

YOURS **FREE**

A FABULOUS **MYSTERY GIFT!**

We can't tell you what it is… but we're sure you'll like it!

A FREE GIFT – just for playing **TIC-TAC-TOE!**

DETACH AND MAIL CARD TODAY!

With a coin, scratch the gold boxes on the tic-tac-toe board. Then remove the "X" sticker from the front and affix it so that you get three X's in a row. This means you can get TWO FREE Gold Eagle novels and a **FREE MYSTERY GIFT!**

PLAY TIC-TAC-TOE

YES! Please send me the 2 Free books and gift for which I qualify. I understand that I am under no obligation to purchase any books, as explained on the back of this card.

366 ADL CX9G

166 ADL CX9F
(MB-12/99)

Name:
(PLEASE PRINT CLEARLY)

Address: _____ Apt.#: _____

City: _____ State/Prov.: _____ Zip/Postal Code: _____

The Gold Eagle Reader Service™ — Here's how it works:

Accepting free books places you under no obligation to buy anything. You may keep the books and gift and return the shipping statement marked "cancel." If you do not cancel, about a month later we'll send you 6 additional novels and bill you just $25.20* — that's a saving of 15% off the cover price of all 6 books! And there's no extra charge for shipping! You may cancel at any time, but if you choose to continue, every other month we'll send you 6 more books, which you may either purchase at the discount price or return to us and cancel your subscription.

*Terms and prices subject to change without notice. Sales tax applicable in N.Y. Canadian residents will be charged applicable provincial taxes and GST.

Phoenix Force. Then the decision would have been his. It was lonely at the top.

The Phoenix Force leader was still kicking the question around in his mind when the phone rang. He stared at it, almost afraid to answer. He had given the number to the hospital along with that of his cellular phone. Were they calling back now to tell him the worst-case scenario had been played out? Was Hawkins dead?

With the strange thinking that men sometimes have at times like this—thoughts such as this is the last time I will answer a phone without knowing T.J. is dead—filling his mind, McCarter reached for the receiver. "Toro Enterprises," he said.

"Buenos días," an unfamiliar voice said back, and McCarter was relieved not to recognize the voice.

"Who is this?" the Briton asked.

"My name isn't important," the voice said. "My words are."

McCarter waited.

"I represent Rex W. E. Sykes."

McCarter almost laughed into the phone, both in relief and genuine humor. Like the men of Phoenix Force themselves, Scott Hix was a professional warrior. An intelligence expert, well-trained at sending messages people didn't want sent. And this message he hadn't only sent right under the noses of his captors, he had even tricked the *Legitimas* into delivering it for him.

Scott Hix had been a close-quarters combat expert and, according to his army personnel file, a student and close friend of World War II Office of Strategic Services CQC instructor Colonel Rex Applegate. Applegate, still going strong in his eighties, had received some of his training from two of McCarter's fellow Britons.

W. E. Fairbairn and Anthony Sykes.

Rex W. E. Sykes. Scott Hix couldn't have made it more clear who he was if he'd sent a photograph.

"We're in the process of setting up the fight now," McCarter said. Continuing the illusion, Leo Turrin was negotiating with several Tijuana cantina owners even as they spoke.

"That won't be necessary," the voice on the other end of the phone said. "The fight can't take place in Tijuana."

McCarter's hand tightened around the phone. "And why not?" he asked.

"We have our reasons," the voice said. "I'm sorry but it's necessary."

McCarter tapped the phone with a finger, creating a click. "Excuse me a moment," he said. "I've got another call. May I put you on hold?"

"*Si,*" the voice said.

McCarter pressed a button and lay the receiver on the desk. He closed his eyes, wishing for a moment that Turrin had taken the call. This was his forte, after all. But Turrin wasn't there, and McCarter knew he had better step into the undercover man's shoes and fill them well.

The Briton began to massage his temples with both hands. Okay, he thought, here's what you know that they don't. They don't want to fight at a prearranged place because they know it could always be a trap. So they're going to set up the site and not let you in on it until the last minute. But you're the one putting up the five million dollars, which gives you the advantage. You can simply refuse and tell them you'll find another fighter if they won't fight in TJ.

McCarter was about to take the call again when he stopped. Unless the *Legitimas* were idiots, and they certainly hadn't proved to be so far, they would know a new fighter to face Toro was an option. They would have thought that through already and decided that losing the five million was better than getting caught. So they had decided that calling the whole thing off was preferable to taking the chance of getting caught and losing their hostages.

Which put the ball back in their court.

McCarter looked at the blinking red light on the phone. There was one other possibility. The call could be a test. Assuming the fight was on the up-and-up, and not a trap, then Toro Enterprises would use the five million to make Rex W. E. Sykes fight on their terms. If he agreed to a change in locations, it might prove to the *Legitimas* that they were setting a trap.

The Phoenix Force leader suddenly felt damned if he did, damned if he didn't. And if he kept the man on the other end of the line waiting much longer, that in itself would prove that something was amiss.

McCarter lifted the receiver and tapped the button. "Hello?" he said.

"I'm still here."

"Look," McCarter said. "That other call was from my associate. He's already made arrangements for the fight here in Tijuana. It's all settled."

"I have told you that's impossible."

"I'm afraid you've got it wrong," McCarter said, allowing his voice to become more stern. "It is possible and it will happen whether it's with your boy or some other fighter." There. He had thrown his weight. Now he waited to see where it had landed.

"We're very sorry to cause you any inconvenience," the voice said. "But Señor Sykes can't fight in Tijuana. There are warrants out for his arrest, and he simply can't show his face in that locality."

"So we get another fighter," McCarter said. "It's that simple." He paused for a moment. He had to make this look good. If the revolutionaries had set their own countertrap, he couldn't spring it. "Thank you for calling," he finally said, and hung up.

The Phoenix Force leader sat back in his chair, wondering if he'd done the right thing. He prayed with all his soul that the phone would ring again, but he also prayed that before it did he would come up with some logical reason to go along with the demand to change locations.

A few minutes later the phone rang.

The former-SAS operative took a deep breath as he forced himself to let the bell ring three times before answering. "Toro Enterprises," he said again after finally picking up the receiver.

"Sir," the voice said. "Please, hear me out. I wasn't at your office yesterday but my associate has advised me that there were few, if any, other suitable candidates in the long line outside your door. And if you didn't find decent competition for your fighter then, how can you now? Will it take you another day? A week? Perhaps a month or two?" The voice paused and McCarter heard the man take a nervous breath. The voice on their end of the line wanted the fight to take place—wanted it badly. Which meant he might accept a less-than-perfect reason for McCarter to agree to the change.

The Phoenix Force leader smiled. The balance of power in the negotiations was shifting again, this time back to the good guys.

"Sir," the voice finally went on. "Time is money. But our fighter doesn't want to go to jail, and the local law enforcement officers can't be paid off. We have tried. They'll arrest him if he shows up."

McCarter took in a deep breath and let it out slowly and with exaggerated exasperation. "So what do you have in mind?" he asked boredly.

"We have a place," the voice said. "But we don't know you, and don't feel comfortable disclosing it at this time. You could be part of a police trap for Señor Sykes."

McCarter laughed into the phone. "I can assure you we're not part of any plot on the part of the Tijuana police," he said honestly. "But okay, I understand your concern." His gut instinct told him that to be convincing, however, he needed to make one more attempt at keeping the thing in TJ before giving in. "But you said the Tijuana cops couldn't be bought? That's a new one on me. You just didn't offer them enough money."

The man on the other end of the phone had been waiting for that answer. "It won't work," he said immediately. "It's not a matter of money but of honor. It seems that Señor Sykes was somewhat indiscreet with the wife of a high-ranking officer."

Brother, McCarter thought. It just got deeper and deeper. An imaginary man having an imaginary affair with an imaginary police officer's imaginary wife. But in the context of the whole imaginary story, it was the perfect answer. It couldn't be checked out. And it went right along with the Mexican cops' *machismo* image. A cop who had been dishonored by his wife wouldn't take a payoff. He would demand revenge.

"I see," McCarter said. "All right. It's a tangled web that you've woven but I do think this Sykes fellow is better competition than most." He paused. "What would you have us do?"

An only partially covered sigh of relief came from the other end of the line. "Will you be at this number?" the voice asked.

"Only off and on." McCarter gave the man his cellular number.

"We'll contact you again. Please be prepared to fly."

"This Sykes had better be one hell of a fighter," McCarter said. "We're going to a lot of trouble for you."

"He's a remarkable fighter," the voice said. "And I promise, the trouble will pay off."

The line went dead.

McCarter had just hung up when Leo Turrin walked through the door. The Phoenix Force leader ran down the new developments and arrangements.

When he had finished, Turrin smiled. "Not bad, David," he said. "You handled it pretty well." Then the smile faded and he shrugged. "You're just lucky it didn't get complicated."

David McCarter stared at the man. He wasn't sure if Turrin was kidding or not. With a man who's life was spent creating illusions and mirages, seeking out each individual's personal weaknesses and playing to them in order to achieve a goal, it was sometimes hard to differentiate what was real and what wasn't.

McCarter stood and the two men left the office, locking the door behind them. As they walked toward the elevator, the Phoenix Force leader wondered again if Turrin's last comment had been meant in jest or if, by the undercover expert's standards, the mind game between him and the voice on the phone really had been simple.

He still didn't know. But he was damn glad that Stony Man Farm and, in turn, the world had Leo Turrin fighting for them rather than against them.

THE EXPLOSION in the small kitchen threatened to bring down the crumbling walls. Bolan dived forward as the .357 Magnum slug left the Rossi's barrel. Behind him, he heard the sounds of breaking glass and then shards of the razor-edged substance flew through the room.

Hitting the floor on a shoulder, Bolan rolled back to his feet and came up just to the side of the old woman. The witch's bony hands were struggling with the lever of the unfamiliar weapon, and he reached out, snatching it away from her. The talonlike fingers brushed his, trying to claw the carbine back as he pulled it away.

The Executioner dropped the carbine to his side and grabbed the woman by her frail shoulders. Her hands flew toward his face, her long cracked nails searching for his eyes. He dropped her shoulders and circled his fingers around her wrists.

The woman's skin felt like a reptile's. An acrid, almost unworldly stench emanated from her body, as if some evil fungus grew within her soul and couldn't be restrained by her aged wrinkled skin. Resisting the urge to gag, he looked down into the old woman's crazed eyes.

"Who put you up to all this?" Bolan demanded.

The witch struggled to free herself but Bolan tightened his grip on her bony wrists. She stared up him like a bridled demon, and the voice that came from her mouth was low, sounding more like a man's. "Your magic—" she began.

Bolan shook her. "I have no magic!" he shouted into her ear. "Who hired you to kill me?"

The old witch started to speak again, then suddenly went stiff in the Executioner's grasp. Her eyes rolled up in her head as if trying to escape her face. She shuddered once, then both of her gaunt hands clutched her breast.

Bolan lifted the woman and lay her gently on the kitchen floor. "Talk to me," he said in a gentler voice now. "You're dying. Talk to me."

The old woman's chest began to jerk. Bolan reached down, placing both hands above her heart and pushing. He recognized the symptoms. Heart attack. He pushed down several times on her chest, then placed his mouth over hers.

The old woman promptly bit his lip.

The Executioner grabbed her hair, tearing his face away a split second before her teeth sank all the way in. "Talk to me!" he demanded. "Tell me who hired you!"

The witch grinned like some fiendish beast. "It will do you no good," she said. "Lord Lucifer will triumph!"

"Who hired you and your sons?" he asked again.

The old woman's eyes were vacant—distant white was all Bolan could see. She tried to speak again but the words choked in her throat. Then, rather than the demonlike voice that had spoken before, the words that finally issued forth sounded more like they came from a little girl. "The...bearded man..." she breathed.

Bolan's mind raced. Half the men he had come into contact with since coming to Mexico wore beards—including President Fierro Blanco. "Which bearded man?" he demanded. "Fierro Blanco?"

"The accent," the little girl voice said. "The strange accent..."

"Is it Fierro Blanco?" Bolan shouted in her ear.

The witch started to speak, her dry lips opening. But instead of more words, a shrill, high-pitched scream suddenly shot from her mouth. Her head shook back and forth crazily and she began to gag. Her eyes rolled back into the sockets. "No!" she screamed. She clutched Bolan's wrists with her bony fingers. "Don't let them take me!" the little-girl voice screamed.

And then, suddenly, she went limp.

The Executioner pressed a forefinger into her carotid artery. There was no pulse. He stood, looking down at the body. His last question had been about Fierro Blanco. The Mexican president had both a beard and an unusual accent from all the years he had spent in European finishing schools. Had the old woman's final "no" been meant to clear Fierro Blanco from suspicion? Or was it a protest against whatever horror she had seen coming for her in the afterlife? He didn't know.

All of which still meant that the man behind the murders and mayhem in Mexico and the U.S. still might or might not be the Mexican president. Whoever it was, he had a beard and an accent.

A memory that hadn't surfaced in his brain since he'd been drugged by Roberto and Santiago now struck him like a lightning bolt. Razon. The Executioner remembered the red hair he had found next to the bottle of poisoned wine left in his room at *Los Pinos*. General Razon sported a reddish-brown beard on his portly face. Was the bearded man behind it all Fierro Blanco's chief military advisor? Maybe. But what about the accent? Razon had been born and raised in Mexico City, and sounded no different to the Executioner than any other native of the area.

Outside the house, the Executioner heard the neighbors shouting. The gunfire had been heard, and he suspected it would be only a matter of minutes before police arrived. Would Katz be back by then or would he have to make his escape on foot? First, he had one last task.

The house was small, and Bolan searched it quickly. He found a multitude of evidence that satanic rituals and even human sacrifice had taken place within the crumbling walls. Books, desecrated religious symbols, even a necklace that appeared to be made of human finger bones were everywhere. But he found nothing that would indicate who the bearded man might be.

Over the shouts and cries of the neighbors, sirens now sounded in the distance now. The Executioner tore open the drawers of a scarred wooden dresser, dumping the contents onto the floor of the bedroom. Clothing fell to the floor. Knickknacks bounced across the threadbare rug. Nothing appeared to be of value to his search until he opened the last drawer at the bottom.

A black address book.

The sirens were nearing as the soldier stuffed the tiny book into his pocket. He sprinted to the living room and looked out the window, seeing the first Mexican police car roar to a halt. Turning, he raced back through the kitchen and hallway, vaulted Santiago's body into the ritual room, then leapt over the broken porch into the backyard.

The chickens clucked madly again as he dashed through the yard toward the alley. He had drawn even with them when he heard the screech of tires and saw the Mercedes roll into the alley. Katz floored the accelerator and shot toward him as Bolan hurried past the trash cans. The former Phoenix Force leader leaned over to unlatch the door as he hit the brakes, skidding the Mercedes to a halt and sending dirt and garbage flying through the air.

The passenger's door swung open and Bolan jumped in, closing the door as Katz took off once more. At the end of the alley, another police car suddenly came into view, skidding to its own halt broadside and blocking their path. Two more cars pulled in behind.

Katz stood on the brake, threw the Mercedes into reverse and stomped on the pedal. The car shot down the alley backward, knocking trash cans and other debris to the side as it fishtailed. They were halfway to the other end when two more cars pulled in to block the other exit.

Bolan and Katz were looking at each other when the first round struck the Mercedes's windshield, shattered the glass and then drilled through the seat between them.

GENERAL AVIA PORTILLA of the *Partido Revolucionario Marxista* bowed respectfully and took a seat behind his desk. The man who had just come through the door of the small office building of the *Marxista's* training compound, hidden in the Sierra Madres, had never done so before. Portilla knew what risk he had taken—he might easily be recognized by one of the men even in the white peasant garb he wore. The black sunglasses and floppy sombrero helped somewhat. But he had arrived in a chauffeur-driven Mercedes and he had carried a leather briefcase. The sharp contrast between his personal appearance and accessories would draw more scrutiny, Portilla knew, than if he had ridden up on a white horse wearing a suit of armor.

Coming there at all, under any guise, had been a tremendous gamble. Which meant he believed the man with the beard and the strange accent believed his mission was important enough that he had to speak with Portilla face to face. Which made the general more than a little nervous.

The bearded man on the other side of the desk took his time removing the hat and sunglasses. Portilla waited. Finally, in his strange voice, he said, "We have suffered some setbacks."

It was a statement, but Portilla knew he should treat it as a question. "Yes, sir," he said. "As you can see by the wounded, over half of my men are no longer able to fight. We are finished. At least for now." He paused. "The American. I understand he is dead now. But he did the cause great damage before he died."

The bearded man laughed sardonically. "He isn't dead," he

said, crossing his legs. "Belasco has gone into hiding. He's searching for the truth. And if we don't act quickly now, he'll find it."

Portilla leaned forward across the desk. "I'm willing, of course. No one is more willing than me." He glanced through the window and threw up his hands. "But what can I do."

"You must recruit more men."

Although he knew it unwise in front of such a powerful man, a laugh escaped Portilla's lips before he could suppress it. "Please," he said quickly. "Excuse my rudeness. But all of the men who believe in the PRM have already joined us. It's unlikely that there are a hundred more men who are still sympathetic to our cause. Even if there are, they won't rally to our side, considering our recent defeats."

"They don't have to be loyal to your cause," the bearded man said. "Only willing to fight."

"Sir..." Portilla said in bewilderment.

The bearded man uncrossed his legs and placed his hands on the knees of his white peasant pants. "Communist, Nazi, Democrat," the man said. "Christian, Muslim, Jew. What is it that they all seek, General Portilla? What is it that unites them and makes them, in the end, no different from one another?"

"I suppose," Portilla began, "that in their own way, however mistaken they may be in their road to achieve it, they are all seeking what they believe is right."

"Bullshit."

The bearded man was a man of culture. He had been educated in some of the finest schools in Europe, and Portilla had learned over the past several months that he rarely resorted to vulgarities. When he did, they were carefully calculated to induce the desired shock effect.

Portilla watched as he pulled the briefcase next to the chair to his lap, opened it and twirled the contents to face the desk.

General Avia Portilla's mouth dropped open. Inside, neatly stacked, was row after row of American hundred-dollar bills.

"Money," the bearded man said. "That's what all men seek. Excuse me—sometimes it is power as well. But most realize that one rarely comes without the other."

Portilla continued to stare. Never in his life had he seen so much money. "How much is there?" he asked.

"Five hundred thousand dollars," the bearded man said. "Two thousand dollars is to go to each of the men who have survived your struggle so far. They are to be sent throughout the countryside to recruit more, and each new man is to receive one thousand dollars. Tell them they will receive another thousand every month until we are no longer in need of their services."

Portilla suddenly realized he was gaping like an idiot. He clamped his teeth shut. With money like that, the recruits would come in thousands. He looked up from the briefcase into the bearded face. "We will need more money. With an offer like this I'll raise an army second only to the Chinese."

"There will be more as it is needed," the bearded man said. "You'll raise this army of which you boast and prepare to march on Mexico City."

Portilla felt a jolt of adrenaline burst through his body. He could do it. It was now possible. He could overthrow the Mexican government, and anyone who stood in his way would crumble.

"I'll stay in touch," the bearded man said. He closed the briefcase, set it back down on the floor and stood to leave. "You must have these men ready quickly. They must be able to march on the capital at a moment's notice. Timing is everything to our plan." He turned toward the door.

Portilla had stood with him. "Sir," he said hesitantly, and the bearded man turned back. "May I ask a question?"

"Of course."

Again, Portilla hesitated. Finally, choosing his words carefully, he said, "Our goal is the same. We both desire the overthrow of the current form of government. But our reasons for seeing it overthrown are different. I'm an idealist, I suppose. I seek a government where all men truly are equal under the guidelines set out by Karl Marx." He paused, considering again how to phrase what he was about to say next. "But you, your ultimate goal is...money itself, is it not?" He waited anxiously for the answer.

The bearded man surprised him by laughing. "And power," he

said. "As we spoke of before. When we are finished, I shall be even more rich and powerful in this country than I am now."

"For me, this money is a godsend," Portilla said. "But how, when your goal is money itself, can it be cost-effective to give away so much?"

The bearded man laughed even harder this time. "Your view of the world is so limited, General Portilla," he said without trying to hide or even soften his contempt. "Five hundred thousand dollars now? Perhaps five million dollars before we are through? It's nothing compared to the money I and my government will make when we have accomplished our goals."

Without another word, the bearded man disappeared through the doorway.

7

The Krazy Kolonel's Kombat Korner was busier than Lyons had hoped it would be. But maybe that was good. Ever since he'd decided that the only answer to their predicament was to procure more arms and ammo, he'd been trying to design the safest way to go about it.

Now he knew. A simple "stick up your hands, this is a robbery" was out of this question. With this many people in the store—many of whom, since it was a gun store after all, would be carrying firearms—someone would decide to play hero. And they'd get killed. Lyons couldn't let that happen. No, the Able Team leader thought as he led Schwarz and Blancanales through the front doors, subterfuge was the only answer.

Lyons led the way past the counter. Several rows of shopping carts stood just to the right, and an area devoted to boots and outdoor clothing lay to the left. They moved on through a forest of gun safes, past a wall of holsters and other ballistic nylon gear, and into an area of pistol cases. Spotting a young clerk who didn't appear to be occupied with a customer, Lyons reached into the briefcase and pulled out his U.S. Justice Department credentials. "I need to talk to your floor manager," he said.

The young man to whom he had spoken wore a green safari vest and jeans. He glanced at the badge case suspiciously, then said, "You ATF?"

Lyons chuckled. Among other things, the U.S. Bureau of Alcohol, Tobacco and Firearms monitored all federal firearms licences. That had never made them particularly popular, even with legitimate gun stores, and in the past few years the abuse of power by several of their agents had inflamed that antagonism even more. "No, kid," Lyons said. "We're not ATF. Justice field agents. We're just running short of supplies. Now, can you get the manager for me?"

The kid nodded, walked between two glass counters full of pistols and disappeared somewhere into the back.

A few moments later, a tall thin man appeared. He wore a black vest identical to the kid's green one, and Lyons remembered seeing the garments, in a variety of colors, hanging in the clothing department when they'd passed.

"Can I help you?" the manager asked.

"Sure can," Lyons said. "Like I told your young friend, we've run short of supplies. I've got official purchase orders and the tax exemption number with me. How about we start getting what we need and then we'll do the paperwork?"

The man in the black vest nodded. "Sounds good to me," he said, motioning to the younger man in the green vest. "Don, help these guys out. When they've got everything, bring it back to the wholesale area and we'll take care of the paperwork there."

Lyons, Schwarz and Blancanales returned to the front of the store and each got a shopping cart. They began moving about the showroom, picking up weapons, ammunition and other supplies. The Able Team leader set his briefcase in the top compartment of the shopping cart where toddlers usually rode. He moved first to the clothing section where he picked up a dozen camouflage bandannas which could be rolled into sweatbands; it would be hot where they were going and he didn't want sweat ruining anyone's vision. Moving to the rifles, he pulled five AR-15s—the semiauto civilian version of the M-16 often favored by police—from a rack and lined them up in his basket. In the police equipment section, he picked up a pair of Peerless handcuffs.

"Boy, you guys did come unequipped," the man called Don said.

Lyons saw the suspicion on his face. He wasn't surprised. Heavy arms and cuffs weren't something a federal agency was likely to buy over-the-counter at retail prices—not when they could get them cheaper from the huge lots the government bought directly from the factories. The Able Team leader hurried on. If they wanted to avoid problems that might escalate into violence, they needed to finish and get out of the store quickly.

Blancanales had a shopping cart full of ammo boxes by now. Schwarz had loaded five canvas backpacks and various other gear into his cart. Lyons looked at them and nodded. Both men nodded back. "Guess we're ready to check out and get out of your hair," Lyons told the young man.

The clerk's eyes were full of suspicion now. He didn't know exactly what it was, but something didn't quite add up. He looked up at Lyons, then shrugged as if to say, "it's not my store, I just work here." "Okay. Follow me."

The men of Able Team pushed their carts through a pair of swinging back doors, through a large storage room packed high with crates, then into an office complex. A man wearing thick spectacles, a short-sleeved white shirt and a tie said, "These the Justice Department guys?"

"Yeah, Bob," Don answered. He gave Lyons and the other two men one final not-so-sure-about-this look then said, "I better get back on the floor. Commissions, you know."

"Okay, gentlemen," the office worker said. "I'll need the forms and your tax numbers."

Lyons pulled his briefcase out of the shopping cart and began shuffling through it. A moment later, he frowned and turned to Schwarz. "I must have left them in the car. Want to run out and get them for me?" he said. Turning back to the man in the tie he said, "Good thing my head's tied on, huh Bob?"

It wasn't a particularly funny joke, and certainly not original. But Bob didn't look like the sort who'd have laughed even if it had been. He pushed the first of the shopping carts to a desk that had an adding machine and began totaling the items.

Schwarz had exited through a door to the side parking lot. Able Team's electronics man reentered the wholesale area a few minutes later. Bob looked up briefly as the door opened then resumed his task.

Several minutes later the man in the short-sleeved white shirt hit the total button, sat back and whistled through his teeth.

"Well," he said. "That should be our biggest sale of the day." He tore the receipt from the adding machine. "The total is $14,297.88. Now, if you'll just give me your tax exemption number and the government purchase order so we don't have to worry about the waiting period—"

He looked up to see a .357 Magnum Colt Python aimed at his nose. "That's a problem," Lyons said. "You see, we can't seem to find the purchase order."

"Look, just take the stuff," the clerk said, his voice trembling. "Don't hurt me."

"We have no intention of hurting you, Bob," the Able Team leader said. "At least not if you cooperate."

His hands were trembling as well as his voice. "What do you want me to do?" he asked.

Lyons reached into the briefcase and pulled out two stacks of bills wrapped in brown paper bands. He counted out dollar bills from one stack, then pulled more from the other. "Keep the change," he said.

"You're...paying for it?" the clerk gasped.

Blancanales gave him an expression of mock hurt. "Do we look like thieves?" he asked.

"But...why the gun?" He asked as he looked back at Lyons's Colt Python.

"Because we don't have paperwork and we don't have time for the waiting period to pick this stuff up," Lyons said.

"You aren't really with the government, either, are you?"

"Actually, we are, but it's too long a story to get into," Blancanales said. "Probably bore you to tears anyway, Bob." He turned to Lyons. "Ready to load up?"

The leader nodded. He kept the Python trained on the clerk as Schwarz and Blancanales propped open the door. Through the opening, the Able Team leader could see that Schwarz had pulled the Suburban around. The rear doors were open.

A few minutes later, when the gear was almost loaded, Lyons looked the man in the eye and said, "Grab the handcuffs." The clerk's shaking hand pulled the cuffs from the bottom of the shopping cart. He tried to hand them to the Able Team leader but Lyons shook his head. "Run them through the handle on that bottom drawer," he said, nodding at the desk. "Then put them on."

The man did as ordered.

Lyons stepped in and gagged him with one of the bandannas. "Now it's not going to take you too long to get loose," he said. "The drawer will be a little tough to get out but you'll be able to do it. When you do, just get up and go in the front. I'm sure the store sells handcuff keys, and by the time you get out there we'll be long gone."

The man nodded. He tried to say something behind the gag but Lyons couldn't understand him.

Blancanales returned and together the two Able Team warriors loaded the last of the equipment. They were on their way out the door when the clerk started gurgling behind the gag again.

Lyons walked back and lowered the bandanna. "What is it?" he asked.

"I was just trying to thank you."

"For what?"

"Well, for paying for everything, I guess."

"You're welcome." Lyons started to replace the gag.

"And for not killing me," the clerk added.

"Don't mention it."

"Don't forget your receipt," he said, his eyes moving toward the adding-machine tape.

"We don't need it." Again, Lyons started to replace the bandanna.

"Thank you for shopping at the Kolonel's."

BOLAN AND KATZ dived out their doors to opposite sides of the alley as a second round blasted through the windshield of the Mercedes. By the time he'd rolled behind a garbage heap, the Executioner had his Desert Eagle in one hand, the sound-suppressed Beretta 93-R in the other. Gunfire opened up from both ends of the alley, then he heard the distinctive pops of Katz's Beretta 92 return fire.

But none of the Mexican police officers visible in the direction the Israeli was shooting fell to the ground. They did, however, scatter.

The Executioner couldn't help taking time for a grin. Katz wouldn't shoot cops any more than he would. Which put the men from Stony Man Farm at a distinct disadvantage. Somehow, they had to get out of the alley and to safety without harming any of the men trying to kill them.

One of the officers had located Bolan and sent a volley of pistol fire into the garbage heap. The Executioner was forced to burrow deeper, out of sight, into the foul-smelling mess. Sticky paper wrapping and coffee grounds stuck to his skin as his mind raced for a plan of action.

Bullets continued to explode all around him as he formulated his plan. Mexican police, Bolan knew, were underpaid and overworked. That combination rarely instilled loyalty in a man. What it did breed was the corruption for which they were famous. Even the feds at *Los Pinos*—with the exception of Juanito Oliverez—had proved that fact time and time again to the Executioner.

But how to play it? An environment full of flying lead was hardly the time to shout out the offer of a payoff. No, Bolan knew he would first have to create some lull in the action. He had an idea. It just wasn't a very good one. And it could only succeed if Katz was able to partially at least read his mind. But it was the only plan he could come up with at the moment.

Rolling to the side through the rubbish, Bolan jammed the sound-suppressed Beretta back under his shirt and drew both backup Desert Eagles. What he needed now wasn't silence but noise. All of it he could get. Instead of hiding, now, he wanted to draw attention.

He took a deep breath. What he was about to do was one hell of a risk. Would Katz catch on in time to play his own part in the charade? He was betting both of their lives on that intangible bond formed between warriors who have fought side by side so long they think almost as one.

Rising suddenly from the center of the garbage heap, the Executioner aimed both big .44 semiauto pistols toward one end of the alley. His fingers snapping the triggers at light speed, he sent a cluster of hollowpoint rounds down the narrow passage. Uniformed men ducked and dived as the powerful slugs struck the police cars around them. Metal crunched and screeched. Car doors caved in, and sparks flew through the air as lead met steel. The putrid stench of the garbage in the Executioner's nostrils was now replaced with the near-narcotic scent of cordite.

Before the Mexican cops could react, Bolan pivoted and aimed his weapons toward the other end of the alley. He repeated his performance, firing until the slides of both Desert Eagle's locked back empty. But halfway through the assault, he had seen Katz rise from behind a trash can on the other side of the alley and add his Beretta 92 to the fire.

The entire ruse had taken less than three seconds from the time the Executioner had appeared from under the garbage. But the next phase seemed like an eternity as Bolan stared down at his empty guns as if not knowing what to do next. He wasn't only counting on Katz following his lead, there was another fundamental aspect of his plan that he would have to leave in the hands of God.

He had to stand there, in full view of the men trying to kill him, long enough for at least one of them to recover from the shock of the attack and return fire. And he had to pray that the sudden panic he had instilled in them caused them to miss.

Several rounds finally came from both ends of the alley. Dropping the Desert Eagles, Bolan clutched his chest with both hands and toppled to the ground. Facedown, he heard Katz let out a blood-curdling scream and then a body hit the ground not far from him.

The Executioner waited as more rounds flew down the alley, striking the ground all around him. Then, suddenly, the explosions died and for a few moments the alley was bathed in silence.

Finally, a voice spoke in Spanish. "I got him! I got the big one! I saw my bullets hit!"

"No, you fool!" another voice cried. "I was the one who shot the American!"

A few more such comments flew, then were cut off by a voice that rang with authority. "Silence! We don't even know if they're dead yet."

The voices fell to hushed whispers. Bolan waited, wondering if Katz's scream of death had been faked or real. If his long-term battle companion and friend had indeed taken a bullet, the Israeli's death would ride on the head of the Executioner for all eternity. But nothing could be done about that at the moment. The primary question right then was what would the police do next? Would they walk cautiously down the alley to inspect the fallen men as Bolan hoped? Or would they fire more rounds into the bodies to make sure?

Another seeming eternity went by. The Executioner had kept his eyes open in his feigned death, fighting the urge to blink. From the position in which he had fallen, he could see only one end of the alley. Finally, uniformed men began to show themselves from behind whatever cover they had taken. Then he heard the soft patter of footsteps moving slowly toward him.

But from the other end of the alley.

One man? No, at least two and perhaps more. He waited, his hands still clutched to his chest beneath his prostrate body.

Close to the shoulder-holstered Beretta 93-R.

The footsteps stopped directly behind the Executioner. He felt a hand reach down timidly and gently shake his shoulder. In the other hand, he knew there would be a gun aimed at the back of his head.

Moving swiftly, Bolan rolled to his side, reached up and grabbed the hand holding the .45 caliber Government Model. As he moved, he saw the captain's bars on the shoulders of the Mexican police officer's tunic, and guessed it must have been him who had stopped the argument over who had been the "hero" of the shooting. Wrapping his fingers around the hand holding the pistol, Bolan twisted with all his strength and the captain screamed. The .45 pistol fell to the ground.

Bolan held on to the man's wrist as he snatched the Beretta from beneath his shirt. Tugging hard, he jerked the captain down on top of him. The pull on the man's injured wrist elicited another shriek of pain. Suddenly the Executioner and Mexican cop were nose to nose on the ground. The captain's body shielded him from the fire of the other officers, and the sound suppressor attached to the barrel of the Beretta 93-R was jammed into the side of the man's neck.

A collective gasp went up from both ends of the alley.

"Nobody move!" Bolan shouted at the top of his lungs. He paused, then hearing nothing, said, "Katz! You okay?"

"Me?" the Israeli's voice came back. "As you Americans like to say, 'I'm right as the rain.'"

The Executioner breathed a silent sigh of relief.

"Took a little nap while we waited," Katz went on. "And I'm still a bit groggy is all. Of course, this wasn't exactly the way I'd envisioned retirement. What satanic force gave you the idea for this plan?"

They weren't even close to being out of danger yet, but Bolan couldn't help but chuckle. "You close to your gun?" he asked.

"In my hand," Katz said.

"Good." Bolan raised his voice again. "Listen closely!" he called out. "Your captain can die, or he can live! It's all up to you!" While he gave the other officers a moment to let it sink in, he spoke to the captain in a whisper. "We can all get out of here safely," he said. "And there'll be some money in it for you and your men."

Even in the face of death, Bolan saw the greed come into the man's eyes. "How much?" he asked in a trembling voice.

"Under the circumstances does it really matter?" the Executioner couldn't help saying. He continued before the man could respond to the rhetorical question. "I've got ten thousand American. I'll give it to you. You keep whatever you think is fair and distribute the rest among your men however you see fit."

The captain's face took on a strange look that could only be described as a blend of covetousness and terror. Slowly, he nodded.

"Then tell them to follow my orders," Bolan said. He dug the sound suppressor a little deeper into the man's neck to remind him it was there.

"Men!" the captain called out. "Do as you're ordered! There has been a terrible misunderstanding...they aren't criminals!"

Bolan waited for him to go on. When he didn't, the Executioner wasn't surprised. If possible, the captain planned to keep all of the ten thousand dollars for himself. "Tell them about the money," he ordered the captain.

"These men have very generously agreed to give each of us fifty dollars!" His voice lowered to a whisper. "It's all they should have," he said. "I know them. With more, they would just get into trouble."

The Executioner shook his head in silent disgust. There were five men at one end of the alley, and the same, at the other. The captain would go home with the lion's share of the ten thousand.

"Katz," Bolan said. "Have them lay their weapons down and gather them all at one end of the alley. What kind of shape is the Mercedes in?"

"Looks like the PLO got word I was in it," the Israeli said simply.

"Any of the cop cars unmarked?"

There was a short lapse in the conversation while Bolan imagined Katz scouting down the alley at the vehicles. Then the retired Phoenix Force leader said, "Doesn't look like it. All black-and-white units."

"Then pick out whichever's in the best shape and get it ready." The Executioner heard Katz's footsteps as he took off down the alley. A few moments later, Bolan heard the sounds of cars being moved.

Five minutes after that, a black-and-white police car pulled down the alley and Bolan looked up to see the Israeli behind the wheel. Katz got out, walked over to the two men on the ground, and helped the Executioner haul the captain to his feet. All of the Mexican cops' weapons had been stacked in a pile at one end of the alley, and the men stood at the other. Still, Bolan and Katz were careful to keep the captain between them and his men.

Throwing the captain into the rear of the police car, Bolan left Katz to cover him while he retrieved his fallen Desert Eagles. Katz took the wheel and Bolan slid into the back with the captain. The police car rolled slowly down the alley to where the officers stood waiting for their payoff.

Bolan rolled down the window as the car came to a halt. "I believe the captain promised you each fifty dollars?" he said.

The men at the front of the group all smiled and nodded.

"Well, you did your jobs so well I'm going to give you a hundred instead," the Executioner said. "Line up."

Greed covered the men's faces. A few mouths even fell open.

Bolan reached into his pocket and pulled out a thick roll of hundred-dollar bills. As each Mexican cop paraded by the window, he handed the man one. When the last man had his money, the Executioner said, "Now, just to be safe, we're going to keep your captain with us for a little while. We'll let him out a few blocks away."

One of the men, a sergeant, frowned into the back seat. "How can we be certain he will be safe?" he demanded.

The captain leaned across the Executioner toward the window. "It's all right," he said. "Do as they say." When he had leaned back out of the man's sight he gave the Executioner a conspiratorial smile.

Bolan returned it with a wink.

Katz threw the police car into gear and they drove out of the alley.

"It was a wise move," the captain said. "Giving them a hundred each. And it won't make that much difference to me." When Bolan didn't respond, he said, "And I thank you."

"For what?"

"For not giving me the rest of the money in front of the men. They would, of course, have expected even more."

"No problem," Bolan said.

Katz left the neighborhood and drove several blocks to a shopping center. He pulled in next to a phone booth and stopped. "There," he said, turning in his seat and resting an arm over the back. "You'll be able to call for a ride."

The Mexican police captain nodded enthusiastically, then looked to Bolan, his eyes filled with anticipation.

Bolan reached into his pocket and pulled out the money again. He held the thick roll of bills in front of him. "You lied to your men," he said.

"No," the greedy captain said. "I just didn't tell them the entire truth." He grinned shrewdly. "Like I said, too much money at one time gets simple men into trouble. I'll keep the rest for them so it will be safe, and hand it out to them little by little." He hadn't expected the Executioner to believe it and now he giggled like a teenage girl.

Bolan pulled two hundred-dollar bills off the roll and tossed them into the captain's lap. "Here you go," he said. "I figure the leader should get a double share."

The captain's eyes opened wide. "No, no. You promised me ten thousand dollars!"

The Executioner shrugged.

"You lied!"

"No, I didn't lie anymore than you did to your men," Bolan said, his face deadpan. "I'm going to keep the rest for you so it'll be safe. I don't want it to get you in trouble."

"Maybe we could put it in a college fund for his kids," Katz said with a smile.

The two hundred still resting in his lap, the captain made a lunge for the rest of the money in Bolan's hand. The Executioner back-handed him across the face, leaned across the man and opened the car door. Bolan's boot sent the Mexican cop sprawling onto the shopping center parking lot.

As Katz pulled away, the Executioner watched the man crawling madly after the hundred-dollar bills that had been caught by a gust of wind.

ALL DAVID MCCARTER knew at this point was that they were going south. By air. Flown by Charlie Mott, one of Stony Man Farm's pilots.

McCarter looked across the cockpit to where Mott sat behind the controls. Wearing a California Angels baseball cap and mirrored sunglasses, he whistled softly as he flew.

"Thinking about that girl young enough to be your daughter, I suppose?" McCarter gibed. For some time now, Mott had been keeping company with a former Miss Alabama who had been runner-up in the Miss America pageant and was now trying to break into show business.

Mott smiled and turned toward the man next to him. "Tsk, tsk," he said in an exaggerated British accent that mocked McCarter's. "Jealousy doesn't become you, old boy."

"Where are we, Charlie?" McCarter asked, changing the subject.

Mott glanced through the window, then looked back to the control panel in front of him. "You want the smart pilot's coordinates or the dumb guy's version?" he asked.

"Just give it to me in English."

"Just passing the Canal de Salsipuedes," the pilot said. "Look over there. That island you see is San Lorenzo."

McCarter nodded. He checked the cellular phone in his lap for perhaps the fortieth time since they'd taken to the air, made sure the light was on and the battery was working, then glanced over his shoulder. In the rear of the plane, he saw Calvin James, Gary Manning and Pompei stretched out on the floor between the seats taking naps. Seated around them were Rafael Encizo, Leo Turrin and Toro. Their eyes were closed as well.

The Phoenix Force leader turned back to the front of the plane and let his own eyelids drop. The wise warrior, he knew, took advantage of every opportunity to catch up on sleep. He never knew when the action would begin and he'd be awake for days on end.

McCarter tried to relax but it didn't come easy. His mind kept drifting back over all the transformations that had taken place in the plan they'd worked out to locate Scott Hix, Ronnie Quartel, and the other hostages. He didn't like the *Legitimas* changing the location of the fight from Tijuana. Neither did Turrin. While McCarter had been on the phone in the office, Turrin had been handsomely paying off a cantina owner to allow them to have the fight in his place and ask no questions. The Stony Man crew was all set up to grab Scott Hix and his guards the moment they arrived, whisk them away from the scene for questioning and then force the kidnappers to lead them back to the other hostages. With advance knowledge of the premises, they could cover all entrances and exits and dominate their environment. Stony Man Farm was even sending the men of Able Team down to help.

But now they had lost those advantages. They had also been forced to leave before Lyons, Schwarz and Blancanales could arrive. McCarter had advised Stony Man Farm of the change of plans but the relay hadn't made it to Lyons and his men. Able Team's last orders were to meet with their fellow warriors at the Toro Enterprises office in Tijuana.

Able Team had, at least temporarily, dropped from sight.

McCarter didn't know exactly what had happened. But he did know there were times during any mission when immediate communication just wasn't possible. Able Team was tied up doing something and couldn't be reached. When they got to the office in TJ, they'd find a note. But they still wouldn't know where to go because McCarter himself didn't know where they were going yet.

The Phoenix Force leader shook his head. Containment of the fight between Hix and Toro was now out of the question. Who knew where it might take place? In a another bar somewhere here on the Baja peninsula? If so, it would be a location with which they weren't familiar. The fight could be in the open desert, for all McCarter knew. If that was the case, they would have to concentrate on getting Hix and whichever of the revolutionaries they could, and do their best to make sure none of the other kidnappers got away alive. If someone did escape, it would take only one phone call for Quartel and the other hostages to be moved to a new location.

No, McCarter thought unhappily, there were holes big enough to drive trucks through in this new plan. Things weren't looking nearly as rosy as they had before. But he saw no better way to handle the situation. Their only choices had been to go along with the changes or abort the mission.

The former British SAS officer let his eyes open again. They had passed the island and to his side he saw only the clear blue water of the Sea of Cortez. McCarter had spoken to the man he assumed was the *Legitima* leader again right before takeoff. They had been directed to follow the eastern coast of the Baja peninsula south. The mysterious voice on the other end of the line had noted their time and the speed at which they planned to fly, and informed them they would get a cellular call when it was time to land.

McCarter felt a hand on his shoulder and turned to see that Turrin had leaned forward to talk to him. The stress was evident on his face. Whispering so as not to wake the other men, Turrin said, "I like this less and less the more time passes, David."

McCarter nodded. "I know, Leo," he said. "The farther away we get, the harder it's all going to be."

Turrin shook his head. "That's part of the problem but not the main part. What bothers me the most," Turrin said, his voice still low. "Is that we're running on borrowed time."

McCarter frowned. "I'm not sure I follow you," he said.

"The CDML aren't a stupid group," Turrin said. "But they're operating very stupidly at the moment. You see, we're the ones offering the five million. Which means we carry all the weight. We should be telling them the rules; where and when the fight should take place and even what they have to wear, if we decide to. We hold all the cards but we aren't playing them. Right now, they want the money so bad they're overlooking that fact. But sooner or later they're going to wake up and realize something's wrong. The longer all this takes, the more time they have to do that."

"So what do we do, Leo?" he asked.

"Okay, I've been thinking about it. I think we need to beat them to the punch. What I mean is, get our answers out before they even think of the questions. Head them off at the pass, so to speak. It might just keep them from scrutinizing the situation as close as they would if they come to their senses on their own. In other words, keep telling them, in one way or another, that you're getting tired of this mess and thinking about calling it off altogether."

"And what if they agree?" McCarter asked.

"They won't. They want the money. But they need to be reminded that we're on the verge of backing out every step of the way. It's our only chance."

The Phoenix Force leader took a deep breath and held up the phone. "Why don't you talk to him next time?" he said.

Turrin quickly shook his head. "No, you've already established a relationship with him, David. And that's as important as anything in an undercover op. It's better that you stay on it. Besides, you're doing fine."

McCarter was about to respond when the phone in his lap finally rang. He let it ring again, then thumbed the button and said, "Hello?"

"Welcome to the Baja," the same voice he had spoken to several times already said. "I trust your flight has been enjoyable?"

"Why don't we skip the pleasantries," McCarter said. "It hasn't been particularly enjoyable, and I'm wondering why I let you talk me into this in the first place."

There was a pause on the other end of the line. McCarter waited, then finally said, "Are you still there or should we turn back and find another man who's not afraid to fight in TJ?"

"No," the voice said. "And again, I apologize for the inconvenience. But you're very close now. Do you know Loreto?"

"Loreto?" McCarter said, glancing at Mott.

The pilot nodded.

"Yes, we know Loreto."

"Excellent," said the *Legitima*. "Three miles to the west of the town, you'll see a landing strip. There will be cars waiting for you there. Reservations have been made for you at the Villas de Loreto—a beautiful place."

A sudden thought crossed McCarter's mind. He decided to deal with it up front. "In case you have any ideas of ripping us off when we land," he said into the phone, "forget them now. We're well armed and don't have the money with us anyway."

"Sir, you hurt me with your accusations."

"I don't care," McCarter said bluntly. "You're a pain in the arse with all your changes."

"May I assume some arrangement for the money to be delivered has been made?"

"Assuming your man earns it, it will be there."

"Loreto dead ahead," Charlie Mott said at McCarter's side.

"We'll contact you once you are settled," the voice on the other end of the line said, then hung up.

Mott banked the plane slightly and began to drop it through the air. Not far in the distance, McCarter could see the mountains. A few moments later, the landing strip appeared. Two cars were waiting to the side of the strip. As the wheels hit the ground, the Phoenix Force leader saw the decals on both limousines—four palm trees sprouting below the elaborate *V* that advertised the resort, Villas de Loreto.

Mott brought the plane to a halt and the men of Stony Man Farm stepped out onto the Baja peninsula, their hands near their guns. Though several miles inland, the salty smell of the Sea of Cortez was thick in their nostrils. McCarter scouted the area quickly. The two limos appeared to be the only vehicles in the area. Only the heads of the drivers were visible through the glass as the cars rolled toward the plane.

Two Hispanic men jumped out of the cars, "Welcome to the Baja!" one of them said. He and the other man helped the Stony Man crew stow their bags in the two trunks, then they all climbed inside. McCarter rode with Calvin James, Turrin and Pompei in one of the cars, and listened to the driver exhort the charms of the resort where they'd be staying. The man either knew nothing of their real purpose for being there, the Phoenix Force leader concluded, or he was one hell of an actor.

The procession entered the city, then turned south again over a bridge spanning the Rio Loreto. A few minutes later, they pulled into the resort.

The driver jumped out again. "You have already been checked in by your friends," he said, and pulled several keys from his pocket. "You need only get settled and have a restful time." McCarter and the other men took the keys and, with the help of the drivers, carried their bags to the rooms. McCarter gave each driver an American ten-dollar bill and received grateful nods in return.

Finding himself in a room with Calvin James, the Phoenix Force leader glanced quickly around. The resort was a blend of old and new—Old World architecture combined with modern plumbing.

James broke into his thoughts. "Well David, what now?"

McCarter shrugged. "Wait on them to call, I suppose." He lifted the cellular phone and dropped it into his pocket. "In the meantime, let's change clothes and take a walk. I want to talk to you about something."

A few minutes later the men were wearing shorts. McCarter jammed his Browning Hi-Power into the waistband and covered it with the tail of a tank top. James, he noticed, did the same with his Beretta 92 but also added the customized Crossada fighting knife across his back and wore a heavier cutoff sweatshirt to conceal it.

The Briton led the way out of the room and through a deserted courtyard. Palm trees rustled overhead as they followed a pathway down to the beach. Straight ahead, the peaceful waves of the sea lapped at the sand. The two men walked in silence for several minutes. Phoenix Force had no official number-two man—any of them were capable of taking charge if necessary or they would never have been recruited by Stony Man Farm. But over the years, McCarter had learned to value Calvin James's common sense and battle wisdom, and James just seemed to be the right man with whom to discuss the current problems.

Finally, James said, "Okay, David. Enough of the beautiful scenery, spill it. Something's really eating at you."

McCarter took a deep breath. "Several things," he said. "But right at the top of the list is the simple fact that we don't have enough men."

Out of the corner of his eye, he saw James smile. "So when was the last time we did?" the knife expert asked.

"Good point," McCarter said. He stepped over a conch shell in his path and walked on. "But with T.J. out of commission, we're even more shorthanded than ever. The real problem is that we're trained to operate as a five-man team. Not four. Everybody has his jobs—his specialties, and his cross training. When we lose one man, we've lost more than *one man*." He stopped and turned to face his friend. "You understand what I mean?"

James nodded. "Of course. But we do have Leo, Pompei and Toro," he added.

McCarter shook his head. "They have their own duties on this mission," he said. "Toro has to act like a fighter while Leo and Pompei have to play trainers." He reached down to the sand, picked up a flat seashell and sent it skipping out over the water. Turning back toward the Villas, the two men started walking again. "I'd counted on Lyons and his crew showing up to take up the slack," he said. "But that's a no-go now. This will all go down before we can even let Able Team know where we are, I'm afraid."

They walked in silence, returning to the path that led back up from the sea before stopping again. Finally, James said, "So we do what we always do, David. We go with what we have and do the best we can."

McCarter nodded. "I just wish we had our fifth man along."

"We could try to get Katz to fly over," James said.

McCarter thought of his last communiqué with Stony Man Farm and shook his head. "He's tied up at *Los Pinos*. I understand he and Striker haven't been letting any grass grow under their feet."

"They never do," James said with a smile.

The two warriors made their way up the path to the courtyard. McCarter saw that it was no longer vacant. The open-air bar had come alive for business and several people sat around the tables beneath large umbrellas. His eyes were somehow drawn to a couple near the center of the courtyard who were sipping drinks. The man had short-cropped steel-gray hair sticking out of the sides of his baseball cap. He was shirtless but wore a pair of black running shorts and sandals. Several scars covered his chest, and middle-aged as he might be, he looked to be in top physical condition.

The Phoenix Force leader's eyes didn't stay on the man very long, however. Seated next to him was one of the most beautiful women McCarter had ever laid eyes upon. Long blond hair fell to her shoulders and framed a face that had to have been the result of handpicking only the most lovely genes ever found in the Scandinavian gene pool. He started to walk toward their room but James reached out suddenly and grabbed him by the arm.

The two men stopped just short of the cobblestones. McCarter turned to James and saw a wide smile spreading across the knife expert's face.

"I can't magically heal T.J. for you, David," James said, staring past him to the man and woman at the table. "But I think I just found somebody who can temporarily take his place."

CALVIN JAMES, Phoenix Force's top knife player, had never met Richard Stevens. But he had seen his picture in every issue of *Defensive Knives*—a bimonthly periodical that Stevens edited— since the magazine's inception several years before. And over the issues, through Stevens's editorial column entitled "The Edge" and other articles the editor had written, James had put together enough about the man to know Stevens was a Vietnam vet who had been a member of a long-range patrol team in the 75th Ranger Infantry and later a paratrooper in the famous 82nd Airborne Division. Still an avid adventurer, the *Defensive Knives* editor often field-tested blades for his magazine while on kayaking, hunting, fishing and cross-country skiing trips with his wife.

With both the Sea of Cortez and the Loreto River within spitting distance of the Villas de Loreto, James was guessing it was kayaking that had brought the two to the resort.

David McCarter nodded his head in understanding as James related all this to the Phoenix Force leader. "Okay," McCarter said. "You're the knife guy. You go break the ice. We could certainly use a man with his experience." James watched McCarter take a final glance at the blonde. "But if you ask me, he'd be a fool to voluntarily leave a woman like that to go off and get shot at with us." McCarter took off toward the room.

James crossed the cobblestones of the courtyard to the open-air bar. Behind the small wooden structure, a young Hispanic man wearing a Villas de Loreto T-shirt stood polishing shot glasses. James had the man pull a Red Stripe beer from the refrigerator, as he dropped some money on the counter and turned toward the Stevens's table. He took a sip, caught the seated man's eye, and smiled.

Walking over to the table, James said, "Excuse me? Aren't you Richard Stevens?"

The man looked up and smiled. "Guilty," he said pleasantly. "But call me Dick." James couldn't help noticing that Stevens's hand had moved inconspicuously over the left-hand pocket of his shorts. The Phoenix Force knife expert had noticed earlier that what looked like a left-handed version of the Benchmade Advance Folding Combat knife was clipped there.

James smiled inwardly. The movement increased his suspicion that Stevens was the man they needed to fill the void left by T.J.'s absence. Getting ready to draw the Benchmade if necessary might be considered paranoid to the average citizen who had never faced danger. But to Calvin James it was simply the behavior of a trained warrior. He doubted that Stevens even consciously realized what he'd done.

"Just wanted to tell you I'm a fan of the magazine," James said. "I've learned a lot from it."

Stevens continued to smile. "Thanks," he said. "That's what makes it all worthwhile." He nodded to an empty chair across from him. "Care to join us...er...?"

"James. Calvin James."

"This is my wife, Inge-Marie," Stevens said. He stuck out his right hand to shake James's. But the Phoenix Force warrior noted his left still stayed over his pocket.

"Pleasure to meet you, ma'am." James shook Stevens's hand and sat in the vacant chair, placing his Red Stripe on the table in front of him.

Inge-Marie smiled and turned to her husband. "I don't want to seem rude," she said. "But if I'm going to look even halfway presentable tonight, I'd better start getting ready."

James was tempted to tell her that she already looked far more than "halfway" presentable. But he didn't know either of them well enough, and didn't want to take the chance that what was meant as a simple compliment might be taken as flirtation.

Dick Stevens laughed. "What she means is she's afraid the conversation is going to be about nothing but knives from here on out," he said.

Inge-Marie turned to James. "My husband, among other talents, is a mind reader, I'm afraid," she smiled.

"You aren't a knife expert yourself?" James asked.

Inge-Marie laughed. "I like them," she said. "I'm just not obsessed the way some people are." She glanced back to Stevens who chuckled.

"It was a pleasure to meet you," James said.

"Likewise," said Inge-Marie. She stood, then disappeared across the cobblestones.

"Beautiful lady," James said when she'd gone.

Stevens shrugged. "Some of us are luckier than we deserve, I guess." He paused, then his eyes narrowed. "There's more to this meeting than the fact you read my magazine," he said.

James was a little taken aback. For a split second, he wondered if there might even be some truth to the joke Stevens's wife had made about mind reading. "Well, yes," he said. "But how'd you know?"

Stevens smiled. "You're wearing a sweatshirt instead of a T-shirt. People who do that in this kind of weather are either nuts or they want the heavier material to hide something they're carrying. You don't seem nuts. At least no more then me."

James started to reply but the man continued. "Oh, don't worry. Nobody else around here will have noticed. No one pays that much attention to other people. But when you sat in the chair, there was about a half second where something pushed your shirt about a half inch out on the right-hand side. You appear to be right-handed. My guess is it was the handle of a Bowie."

James couldn't help smiling. "You're half right," he said. "A Crossada." The Crossada fighting knife, which had become James's favorite, was a cross between the Bowie knife and Arkansas Toothpick.

"That's a big blade meant for serious business," Stevens said. "Few men carry one on the beach to clean the sand out from under their toenails." His eyes fell to James's waist. "Don't know what it is, but there's something hiding up front there, too."

James glanced around quickly. Although the eyes of several men had strayed their way when Inge-Marie had still been with them, now that she was gone their table held no interest to anyone. He turned back to Stevens. The man was sharp. He had spotted the weapons that only a trained warrior would even look for. And he didn't seem surprised in the least, and certainly not offended or put off.

Common ground from which to work had been established. James decided to just come right out with it. "Beretta," he said. "92-SB."

"Decent gun," Stevens said. "Not my personal favorite but it's okay."

A waitress appeared at their table and asked if they'd like another drink.

James shook his head.

Stevens looked down at his glass, then said, "No, I've got a sneaking suspicion I should keep a clear head the rest of the night."

"At least the rest of the night," James said as soon as the girl had left.

"Okay," Stevens said. "We've been fencing long enough. What is it you want from me?"

James knew he was a good judge of character. And even in the short few minutes he had known Dick Stevens, he had decided the man was trustworthy. So he told him.

The warrior-editor's face had remained unchanged throughout the revelation. When James finished, he said, "You know, Calvin James, I said earlier that you didn't seem nuts. Now I'm not so sure." He leaned closer across the table. "Are you for real? Or are you one of those drugstore-mercenary nuts who writes me letters every issue asking things like the best way to cut the throat of the neighbor's pesky Chihuahua?"

James didn't reply.

"This sounds like something out of a James Bond novel," Stevens said but James could see that the man's interest had been aroused. The editor sighed. "But okay," he said. "Take me to this McCarter guy you mentioned and let's find out."

"Will your wife understand?"

"Of course not. Would yours?"

"Never had one."

"Then there's no use trying to explain." Stevens stood. "Inge-

Marie's the best woman I know," he said. "Which means no, she won't understand. But she'll accept."

Side by side, the two men walked across the courtyard toward James and McCarter's room. James glanced at Dick Stevens out of the corner of his eye as they walked.

The Phoenix Force warrior was pleased to see the editor of *Defensive Knives* had finally let his hand fall away from his pocket.

8

The drug tunnel to which Pancho Montoya led the men of Able Team had sounded as if it was similar to the ones Carl Lyons knew Phoenix Force had destroyed a few days before. He saw one major difference, however, as he pulled the Suburban up a small hill, then down into an arroyo.

This tunnel was big enough to drive a vehicle through.

Lyons pulled the Suburban to a halt just to the side of the cavernous entrance half-hidden by cactus and other desert shrubbery. Schwarz and Blancanales didn't need orders—they jumped out with flashlights and disappeared into the hole. A few minutes later they came back smiling.

"They must have known we were coming," Schwarz said. "It's not paved, but the earth's been packed down so much by the traffic that it's almost like a highway in there."

Lyons nodded. Once in a while, even the men from Stony Man Farm seemed to get a stroke of luck. The tunnel not only solved the problem of crossing the border without having to lug all the equipment on their backs, its size meant they'd still have wheels when they reached Mexico. The Able Team leader stared at the dark opening. It did create another problem, however.

Montoya voiced that problem now, as he had earlier. "I must warn you again," the captured drug smuggler said. "There is every chance we will run head-on into a drug shipment coming this way."

"And I must warn you again," Lyons said. "Shut your mouth until I tell you to speak or I'll shut it for you." He turned to his team members who still stood just outside the window of the Suburban. "Each of you grab a rifle. I want you to take the scout position on foot. You pick up any light sticks back at the gun store?"

"All I could fit into the basket," Blancanales said.

The Able Team leader nodded. The soft green glow of the light sticks would illuminate the tunnel enough to see but wouldn't be as visible at a distance to anyone coming from the other direction. "Take a walkie-talkie and stay a hundred yards or so ahead of us," Lyons went on. "That should give us time to get ready if we meet resistance."

"Get ready to do what?" Schwarz asked. "That tunnel's only big enough for one vehicle at a time. If we meet any cartel runners coming toward us all we can do is shoot or put it in reverse and pray."

"We'll do both," Lyons said. "Now grab your weapons and let's move out."

While Blancanales and Schwarz slid into load-bearing vests and jammed extra CAR-15 magazines into the pockets that covered the front, Lyons, Keener and Harsey did the same. Harsey stayed in the back of the Suburban to guard Montoya while Keener got into the shotgun seat next to Lyons. Five minutes later, Schwarz and Blancanales entered the tunnel. Lyons gave them thirty seconds head start, then slowly let the wheels of the Suburban creep into the darkness after them.

The sunlight faded quickly once they were inside the passage. Lyons kept his headlights off, keying on the bobbing soft green glows that preceded the Suburban down the tunnel. It was slow going, tedious and nerve-racking. The Able Team leader had to keep their speed down both to pace the two men and avoid scraping the sides of the tunnel. The passageway had been dug hurriedly and wasn't well reinforced. Only a few rotting boards every few feet supported the dirt walls. The possibility of a cave-in was constantly on the mind of the Able Tam leader.

"Where's this thing come out, Montoya?" Harsey asked in the back seat.

"Perhaps a mile on the other side of the border," the captive answered. "Only a mile or two east of Tijuana."

Once they were in Mexico, Lyons knew things would speed up. They'd rendezvous with McCarter and his team at the offices of Toro Enterprises, then set up the cantina where the fight was to take place. After that, grabbing Scott Hix and his revolutionary escorts should be a simple enough task. But first, they had to get through the tunnel and past any cartel drug shipments that chanced to be heading their way.

Most of the time the men rode in silence. Occasionally, the quiet was broken, but only by whispers. The dark tunnel created an ambience of mystery and malevolence that cautioned the men to keep their voices low. And the fact that the sides and roof of the passageway were so poorly fortified added to their desire to remain noiseless. Voices alone weren't likely to bring down walls but, like men bending low beneath a helicopter blade ten feet above their heads, they still whispered from instinct.

Most of the time, the tunnel led in a straight line. But occasionally it bent to one side or the other. On those occasions, Lyons could see the striations of rock through the dirt and sand on the walls, meaning the diggers had come up against rock formations easier to work around than dig through.

Lyons guessed they had covered roughly two underground miles when Schwarz's voice came over the radio. "Able Three to Able One," the electronics wizard said. "Come in, One."

Lyons lifted the walkie-talkie, guiding the Suburban with one hand. "Go Three."

"Something coming, I think."

"You see lights?"

"No, no lights. And we haven't heard anything yet, either. But the ground's started to vibrate and it's getting stronger. Something heavy—vehicles—heading our way."

Lyons slowed the Suburban. There was no way they could turn in the narrow confines of the tunnel, and they were too far in to try to back out now. With the Suburban in reverse, whatever was headed their way would overtake them long before they reached the exit.

The walkie-talkie spoke again. "We can hear them now," Schwarz said. "At least one truck. Probably more. Wait...okay, yeah. A light just came around a curve about a quarter of a mile down.''

"Get your butts back here on the double," Lyons said.

"You don't have to tell me twice," Schwarz answered. Over the walkie-talkie Lyons heard both Able Team men start running before Schwarz let go of the transmit button.

Lyons stomped on the brake, threw the Suburban into park and turned off the ignition. He and both Texas Rangers were getting out when they heard Pancho Montoya's trembling voice. "Señors, give me a gun, please!"

Lyons had stopped with one foot outside the door. "Right, Pancho," he said. "Maybe you'd like a couple of frag grenades, too?"

Montoya reached over the back seat and caught Lyons by the arm. "But señor!" he pleaded. "There will be shooting. What am I to do?"

"I'd try keeping my head down, if it was me," the Able Team leader said and shook his arm away.

The ex-cop stood in the open doorway as running footsteps sounded in front of the Suburban. Ahead, in the darkness, he could see the eerie green light sticks bobbing up and down. A moment later, Schwarz and Blancanales appeared. "They aren't far," Blancanales said.

Lyons, Keener and Harsey had pulled their CAR-15s out of the vehicle and stood awaiting orders.

"Pick out positions around the Suburban," Lyons said quickly. "I'll stay here and turn the headlights on as soon as they get near. As for now..." He turned back into the car where the dome light had come on when the door opened. With no time to remove the cover and take out the bulb, he swung the stock of his CAR-15 up against the roof of the Suburban and smashed the light.

Schwarz and Blancanales had disposed of their light sticks and now the tunnel was cast into total darkness.

Ninety seconds later, the sounds of the approaching vehicles became clear. The Able Team leader waited. He needed to estimate the distance by sound. For full effect, he had to wait until the vehicles were as close as possible without being too close to stop before they crashed into the Suburban. With his boot still inside the car, he leaned forward and stomped on the high-beam-light button on the floor.

The Able Team leader didn't expect it to work like catching deer in the headlights. But he had to hope it succeeded in giving him and his men at least some advantage.

Harsey had taken up a position somewhere on the other side of Lyons. "This ain't as bad as it could be," the young Ranger whispered. "They're as penned in as we are. It's going to be like shooting fish in a barrel." He paused. "For both sides, of course."

"Getting shot isn't my main worry, Junior," Bud Keener's voice came from somewhere behind Lyons. "Shooting a bunch of rounds that bring down the walls and seal us in like King Tut seems a likely end to my brilliant career right now."

The vehicles came closer. Finally, with a deep breath, Lyons gripped the forefront of the CAR-15 in his left hand and stuck his right back into the Suburban. He jerked on the light control and suddenly the tunnel lit up like the sun. The sudden sound of brakes and tires skidding across packed dirt met their ears.

Carl Lyons watched the Chevy S-10 pickup fitted out with a camper shell jerk to a halt ten feet in front of him. In the lights, he could see the surprised faces of two men in the cab.

Behind the pickup, a Plymouth Grand Voyager churned up dust as it skidded to a halt, and to its rear a third vehicle, unidentifiable in the darkness, did the same.

The Able Team leader aimed the CAR-15 between the Suburban's door and frame and sighted down the barrel at the pickup's windshield. "Throw out your weapons and step out of the truck!" he ordered. "Put your hands in the air!" His voice echoed off the walls of the tunnel and moved down the shaft.

For a moment, no one moved. Then Lyons saw the two men in the pickup exchange words. A moment later, the doors on both sides of the S-10 opened. The men got out as they'd been told to do. They even raised their hands like Lyons had ordered.

The only problem was, their hands had guns in them.

Lyons was about to depress the trigger on his assault rifle when, suddenly, the entire tunnel lit up from behind him. He whirled 180-degrees. To his rear, stood at least twenty Hispanic men armed with various assault rifles, shotguns and other weapons. At least half also held flashlights and lanterns.

The man who had ridden in the shotgun seat of the pickup now walked forward, holding a Glock-21 ahead of him. Lyons turned to face him. The man wore an expression that was part amazement, part disgust. "I don't know who you are," the man said, shaking his head in mock sadness. "But I'm afraid you're trespassing. The tunnel belongs to us." He reached out and ripped the Colt from the Able Team leader's hands, turned and handed it to the man who had driven the pickup.

Lyons watched helplessly as men from both in front and behind them walked forward and disarmed Keener, Harsey and Blancanales. But when two men approached Schwarz, who had taken up a place against the tunnel wall on the other side of the Suburban, the big man shot a fist into the nearest man's face.

No! Lyons wanted to scream. Not now, Gadgets! Not yet! But he didn't have time.

The man next to the one Schwarz had punched pointed his pistol at Schwarz's chest and pulled the trigger twice.

BOLAN DROPPED KATZ off two blocks from *Los Pinos* and drove quickly back to the warehouse. As soon as he had pulled the bus through the door, he locked it behind him and climbed back into the home-on-wheels. Taking a seat on the couch in the back, he switched on the lamp and pulled out the old woman's address book.

A bearded man. A description that might apply to half the Mexican men over the age of fourteen. With an accent. Which could mean foreign, or simply that the man with the beard came from a different area of Mexico and had a slightly different pattern of speech. Those two clues, and the address book, were all he had to go on.

The Executioner opened the tattered leather volume and started with the As. Scanning down the pages, he saw that some of the entries were names with numbers. Some had addresses as well. Others were numbers only, or had undecipherable letters in front of them that appeared to be some code. He considered calling

Stony Man Farm and having Aaron Kurtzman get busy decipher-
ing the cryptology with his computers. It would likely be a simple
task. But without the actual book in front of him, some vital aspect
might be missed. And Bolan didn't have time to send the book all
the way to Stony Man Farm.

The writing was difficult to read—the letters and numbers had
been scratched down by the old woman's aged hand. The soldier
studied the pages for a few more moments, then moved back to
the storage trunks. Searching through the contents, he came up
with a plastic package of colored highlighting pens. Resuming his
seat, he began color-coding the entries. Numbers only were high-
lighted in pink. Coded numbers became green. Those with actual
names attached he marked in yellow.

Bolan pulled out his cellular phone, opening the address book
to the As once more. Playing a hunch, he started with the coded
numbers. Some didn't answer. With the ones that did, he immediately asked for Maria Rodriguez if the voice sounded older, and
Roberto or Santiago if it was the voice of a younger person. Some
of the people on the other end simply told him he had called the
wrong house. Others gave him the Rodriguez's home number. A
few were skeptical about saying anything, which confirmed the
Executioner's suspicion that the code was used for numbers related
to the Rodriguez family's criminal and witchcraft endeavors.

But nothing gave him anything that pointed to the bearded man
with the accent.

Two hours later, the soldier had called all of the numbers except
those with actual names attached. He began on them, asking for
the party in the book and finding most were accurate. After the
eighth call, he stopped. These were simply the numbers of friends
or associates that didn't matter if the book fell into the hands of
the law. He wouldn't find what he was looking for in those numbers with a name attached.

His eyes had grown tired. Bolan dropped the book in his lap,
switched off the light for a moment and closed his eyes. Something
was eating at his mind, trying to rise from his unconscious. What
had he seen that had registered but refused to surface? The feeling
that he had come across something of value had been with him

almost since the moment he first opened the book. That feeling
had grown as he made the calls. But still, he couldn't identify it.
He rubbed his eyes, then turned the light back on. Wearily, he
opened the book again to the beginning.

Staring at the yellow highlights, he began going down the numbers with names again. It didn't seem likely that the old woman
would enter the bearded man's name when she could use whatever
code she had worked out. Then again, the bearded man would be
the person be far more incriminating than Roberto or Santiago's
criminal friends, and would therefore warrant extra protection from
prying eyes. So was he hiding in plain sight? Did she assume that
if the police ever found the book they would use the same logic
as Bolan had and concentrate on the nameless numbers and the
codes, overlooking the obvious?

Bolan didn't know. But there was only one way to find out.
Starting with the *A*s again, he began to call all of the numbers
with names. The task took another hour and a half. And accomplished nothing.

The Executioner fought the urge to turn off the light again and
sleep. The answer to who the bearded man was could be found in
this book; he felt it in his soul. He had no idea where the thought
came from. But for some reason, his exhausted mind suddenly
reminded him that an old woman who could invent one code could
invent two. The bearded man was listed in the names somewhere.
In another simple code unrelated to the other one.

The Executioner's tired eyes were hard to focus as he moved
them down the first page again. The names he saw before him
were primarily Hispanic. There were also the usual number of
German and Irish names that anyone who had studied Mexican
history would also expect.

The Executioner suddenly stopped halfway down the second
page. Señor Jose Abrab, the name read. A number followed, but
no address. Abrab? It sounded Middle Eastern. Was it? Was it
even a real name at all? Bolan reached across to the table and
lifted the Mexico City phone book. He found no such name.

The soldier tapped the numbers listed after the name into the
phone. He got a recording telling him the number was no longer

in use. He stared at the name. What was it? Something was there, right in front of him. He saw it, but he didn't see it at the same time.

Bolan reached up and switched off the light again. He needed rest, and his mind was too tired now to do him any good. Closing his eyes, he settled into the chair and fell asleep.

When he awoke a half hour later, the address book had fallen to the floor. Upon reaching for it, he saw that it was upside down but still opened to the page he had been studying. It was then that it came to him, looking down at the inverted and reversed letters. *Abrab.* Backward, it spelled *barba.*

Barba was Spanish for beard.

Fully awake now, Bolan snatched the cellular phone and looked at the number again. The name had been entered backward. Did that mean the number had been, too? Quickly, he tapped the buttons and waited for the answer.

The phone rang three times, then a voice with a foreign accent said in Spanish, "Iranian Embassy."

Bolan hung up and sat back in his chair, his head swimming. Ideas were racing at the speed of light. He was putting together bits and pieces of information in his brain that he had not suspected, up until now, were connected. He waited patiently for the cluster of eclectic thoughts to take shape, then lifted the phone again.

This time, the Executioner called Stony Man Farm.

THE MEN OF PHOENIX FORCE, with former airborne Ranger and magazine editor Dick Stevens standing in for T. J. Hawkins, were ready to go.

All they were waiting on was a call.

McCarter glanced up as James opened the door of the room at the Villas de Loreto. The black warrior stepped back and Gary Manning and Rafael Encizo walked in carrying two six-packs of Coca-Cola. The Canadian and Cuban handed them out to the men already assembled on the beds and chairs, then found seats themselves.

McCarter glanced around the room. All of the men but Toro

were dressed in jeans or slacks, with traditional loose-fitting shirts hanging over their belts to conceal their weapons. Toro wore his skintight sweat shorts and a tight-fitting sweatshirt in preparation for the fight. Everyone, including Stevens who had been equipped by Phoenix Force, carried Beretta 92-SB semiauto pistols. Everyone except McCarter. The Phoenix Force leader favored the Browning Hi-Power. He had learned to use the Hi-Power with precision during his days as a British SAS officer and continued to rely upon it ever since. The only conciliation he had made was to switch from the traditional 9 mm version to the larger .40 S & W model when it had become available a few years earlier. He lost a couple of rounds of firepower in the trade, but the ones he had carried a far more potent punch.

"Any word from Lyons?" Gary Manning asked.

McCarter shook his head. As soon as they had arrived in Loreto, he had called Stony Man Farm to see if they had found Able Team. No luck. He had then phoned the offices of Toro Enterprises and left a message on the answering machine. When Lyons and his crew arrived to meet them, at least they would know where Phoenix Force had gone.

The former-SAS man glanced at the telephone between the beds. He had a bad feeling in the pit of his stomach. A feeling that told him Loreto wasn't their final destination.

McCarter looked to Dick Stevens. "You get everything you need?" he asked.

Stevens nodded. "James got me a Beretta, and I understand there are long arms out in the vehicle."

"Yes, M-16s," McCarter answered. "I assume you understand how they operate." As a Vietnam vet, Stevens would be more than a little familiar with the weapon.

The editor smiled. "I've shot it once or twice," he said. "I've also brought my own blades with me." From a sheath underneath his shirt he pulled what looked at first to be a simple USMC Ka-bar. But when he handed it to McCarter for inspection, the Phoenix Force leader noted the subtle differences. Based on the Ka-bar, it was slightly longer and made of one-quarter-inch 440C steel. The custom maker's name on the blade read Don Mount.

McCarter handed back the knife. "Did James get you a backup pistol?" he asked.

Stevens shook his head. He lifted his shirt again and this time a tiny little Seecamp .32 came out. "Had my own."

The Phoenix Force leader grinned inwardly. The penalties for tourists bringing guns into Mexico were severe. Of course Dick Stevens knew that. The Vietnam vet also obviously knew that the penalty for not having a gun when you needed one was even more severe.

McCarter was about to speak again when the phone between the beds suddenly rang. He lifted the receiver and said, "Hello?"

"Good evening," the voice on the other end said. "Are you and your man ready, señor?"

"We're ready," McCarter said. "Where's the fight to be held?"

"Do you know how to find the docks?"

"In a town this size I'd suppose it could be done."

The voice on the other end either missed the tone or ignored it. "Please go there now. Our men will find you and lead you to the location."

McCarter looked to Leo Turrin, seated in a chair across the room. Although Turrin couldn't hear the other voice, he had guessed what had been said. He scribbled quickly on a piece of paper and held it up to McCarter's face.

Argue. But agree.

"I don't like this idea," McCarter said into the phone. "How do we know you don't plan to just rob and kill us?"

The *Legitima* laughed good-naturedly. "Will you have the five million dollars on you?"

"Of course not."

"Then why would we want to rob you? To get the few hundred, or thousand even, that you carry?" There was a short pause, then, "No, señor, we want the five million. And the easiest way to get it is simply to go ahead with the plan we have all agreed upon."

When McCarter said no more the man continued. "Our representative will meet you at the docks in fifteen minutes. In addition to Toro, you will be allowed to bring two trainers. A total of four men."

"All right, dammit!" McCarter suddenly shouted into the phone. "I've had enough. I'm bloody sick and tired of being told what to do when I'm putting up the money. The fight's off." He slammed the phone back into the cradle wondering if he was doing the right thing. He looked up at Turrin questioningly. "Will they call back?" he asked the undercover expert.

Turrin shrugged, then grinned. "Would you for five million bucks?"

The phone rang again almost immediately. McCarter picked it up. "What?" he said.

"My apologies for overstepping my boundaries, señor. How many men will you be bringing with you?"

McCarter glance around the room. With the four Phoenix Force men, Stevens, Toro, Turrin and Pompei, that made eight. But he had bounced the psychological ball back into his court now, and he decided to keep it there. "As many as I bloody well want," he said. "We'll see you in fifteen minutes." He hung up the phone and stood. "Everybody set?" he asked.

THE EXPLOSIONS threatened not only to deafen the men in the tunnel but to bring the roof down on top of them. Carl Lyons watched helplessly as Schwarz clutched his chest and fell forward onto his face.

The man who had taken Lyons's rifle clapped his hand, then spoke as soon as the noise settled. "Enough!" he ordered. "We don't need a cave-in!" He stuck his Glock into his belt, drew a long dagger from a sheath on his side, stepped forward and pressed the tip into Lyons's jugular vein. "I'll offer you and the rest of your men the chance to live until we leave the tunnel," he said. "We won't shoot you until then. But if there is any more resistance from any of you, we'll cut all of your throats immediately. Is that understood?"

Lyons felt the nausea rising in his belly as he stared across the tunnel at Schwarz's body. The Able Team leader strained to see his friend's chest rise and fall, even slightly. It didn't. Schwarz lay motionless, sprawled at an awkward angle.

The Able Team leader stared at the man with the dagger. The

drug runner was around fifty but still slender, his long hair tied back into a ponytail. He wore small perfectly round eyeglasses through which Lyons could see the broken red lines of his bloodshot eyes. For a moment, the ex-LAPD cop almost grabbed the dagger away and plunged it into the man's heart. It could be done, he knew, before the bullets of the other men struck him down. Perhaps their rounds would even bring down the tunnel roof and get all of the cartel smugglers as well; then they would all—both good men and evil—rest for eternity in a massive unknown grave.

Lyons took a deep breath and stared at the man holding the knife. Right then, with Schwarz's lifeless form not ten feet away, he didn't care if he lived or died. But he was responsible for Keener, Harsey and Blancanales, too. If there was any chance to get them out of this alive he had to take it. He couldn't indulge his own desires; couldn't allow himself to give into the temptation for immediate revenge no matter how strong it might be. "Yeah, we get you," he said.

"Search the Suburban," the man with the ponytail ordered.

A moment later, several men pulled Pancho Montoya out of the back and brought him to their leader.

The eyebrows of the leader lowered. "I know you," he accused.

"Señor Santana," Montoya cried. "They kidnapped me! You have saved me!" He dropped to one knee and kissed the man's hand.

The leader smiled wickedly. "Stand, Montoya," he said.

Able Team's informant did as he was told.

"You led them here."

"No, boss! They knew about the tunnel themselves!"

"They couldn't have known, Montoya," said Santana. The smile widened. "But I forgive you. I'm sure they forced you."

"Yes!" Montoya cried out in relief. "I had no other choice!"

Slowly, paternally, Santana, reached out and patted Montoya on the head. He left his hand on top of the man's hair as he said, "I understand, Pancho." He paused and the smile vanished. "I hope you do, too."

In one swift motion the cartel man grabbed a handful of Montoya's hair and brought the blade away from Lyons's throat and across that of the informant. Crimson blood shot from Montoya's neck as if propelled by a fire hose. He was dead before he hit the ground.

The knife moved quickly back to Lyons's throat and the Able Team leader felt Montoya's blood drip from the blade onto his neck and chest. Santana looked past him to address the men who had come up behind them. "Where did you park your vehicles?" he demanded.

"At the other entrance," answered an unseen voice. "When we saw these men enter the tunnel, we followed on foot so we wouldn't be heard." Behind him, Lyons heard a chuckle. "They didn't even think to look behind them, Santana. Only ahead."

Lyons mentally kicked himself. The man was right. His concentration had been to the front and he hadn't even considered the possibility that two groups from the cartel might meet to make the drug exchange inside the tunnel. That error in tactical judgment had already cost Schwarz his life. And would most likely kill Blancanales, Keener and Harsey as well.

The Able Team leader ground his teeth together silently. He couldn't change the past but he could affect the future. He didn't know how he'd do it yet but before they died he swore to himself that he'd kill Santana and as many of the cartel men as possible before the rest of them went down.

"All right!" Santana shouted. "Disarm these men, tie their hands behind them and take them to the flatbed."

Now that the tunnel was lighted, Lyons could see that the third vehicle that had come from the Mexican entrance of the tunnel was a medium-sized Chevy 60-series truck. Its flatbed was loaded almost to the roof of the tunnel and the cargo was covered with a tarp. The outer edges of the truck cleared the underground passage's walls by less than a foot on each side.

A moment later, the Able Team leader felt both his .45 and .357 pistols yanked from the holsters. His hands were pulled behind his back and bound. Men from both sides grabbed his arms and dragged him back to the truck, then threw him on top of the tarp. He was less than six inches from the roof of the tunnel.

"Don't breath too deeply," laughed a voice from below.

A moment later, Keener, Blancanales and Harsey joined Lyons on top of the tarp. All three men had their hands tied behind them as well.

The men who had come up behind Able Team and the Rangers now jockeyed for seats in the other vehicles. Those who lost out stepped onto the truck's running boards or prepared to walk behind the procession. Slowly, the convoy took off toward the American side of the tunnel.

As they moved out, Carl Lyons looked down from the top of the flatbed and saw Schwarz. The Able Team electronics expert's body had been pushed to the side of the tunnel. He still wasn't moving, and Lyons knew he never would again.

9

"Everything back in place?" the Executioner asked.

"If you mean Fierro Blanco," Katz said. "Yes, he's back from his latest mysterious disappearance. Has a smile on his face that makes me think it was the actress again."

"It probably was," Bolan said. "I don't think it's his beard we're looking for."

"You've learned something?" Katz asked quickly.

"I think so. And it's starting to look like Fierro Blanco is clean. Stupid, granted, and probably not one hundred percent clean, but he's not the force behind all the problems going on." The Executioner paused a moment. "It's a little complicated and I don't have time to explain it all right now. I'll fill you in when I see you." His mind drifted to the captain in charge of Fierro Blanco's protection team. He hadn't seen Juanito Oliverez since the Rodriguez brothers had kidnapped him, and like the rest of Mexico, the captain assumed he was dead. "Is Oliverez nearby?" he asked Katz.

"He was with *el presidente* a few minutes ago."

"We're going to need his help, Katz," Bolan said. "Find him and mentally prepare him for my ghost rising from the grave."

"I'll be delighted to," Katz said in a wry tone of voice. "You're his hero, you know. He hasn't talked about anything else since your death. 'Mike Belasko did this, Belasko did that. Belasko would have done it this way.' I'll be more than happy to resurrect you for him, Striker. To be honest, I'm getting pretty sick of hearing about how wonderful you are...were."

Bolan smiled. Katz had always enjoyed teasing him, and it was always good-natured. "Just find him. Tell him I'll call back in five minutes." He disconnected the line.

Tapping more numbers into the phone, Bolan listened to Barbara Price, Stony Man Farm's mission controller, lift the receiver and say, "Hello, Mack."

"Hi, Barbara." The Executioner ran down the latest developments to her. In return, he got the update on Able Team and Phoenix Force. He noted that her voice had a trace of concern in it when she said, "Able Team was on its way down to join McCarter. But we've lost contact with them now for several hours."

Bolan felt the same concern but said, "It happens, Barb. Any number of things can cause that." He paused. "Patch me into Kurtzman, will you?"

A moment later, the computer genius was on the line. "Well, Striker," he said. "You've been a busy boy as usual."

"Bear," Bolan said. "Get on your magic machines and get me an update on activity in Iran."

Kurtzman didn't hesitate. "Don't have to, big guy. We've been keeping tabs ever since Phoenix Force left. The troops they had massing at the base in Shiraz—the one McCarter and his boys blew to kingdom come—have all been moved farther south. They're regrouping around Bandar Abbas." He took a deep breath. "We knew all along that blowing the base wouldn't stop them, just slow them on whatever it was they were up to."

"Any idea what that might be?"

"We're getting some bits and pieces of intel from the CIA, DOD and other sources that make it look pretty bad. We think there's a full-scale invasion planned."

Bolan knew the answer to his next question. But he asked anyway. "Where?"

"My guess, and I'd say it's more than an educated one, Striker, is that they're going across the Strait of Hormuz and into Oman and the United Arab Emirates. Maybe Bahrain and Qatar as well." The computer wizard paused and Bolan heard him take a drink from the ever-present coffee cup he kept on his computer console. "If they can take over the Strait, the local armies aren't even likely to put up a fight and they'll control the whole Persian Gulf. Which means they'll control the world price of oil.''

"What do we have in the area?" Bolan asked.

Kurtzman laughed out loud. "The skeleton crew still leftover from the Gulf War in Saudi and Kuwait. In other words, nothing."

"How about ships?"

"A couple," Kurtzman said. "Not enough to do much more than make noise." He took another drink of coffee. "The Iranians know about our military cutbacks and downsizing as well as we do. They also know about the massing of troops along the Mexican border."

"Is Hal there, Bear?"

"He's at the White House, Striker. The CIA just got word that the *Marxistas* are amassing an unbelievable army in the south. There's even rumors that they're going to invade Mexico City. Military intel thinks they've even rolled over a good number of the Mexican army and navy commanders. The question is, how'd they—the *Marxistas*—get so many men so fast?"

"Money," the Executioner said. "That's the only possible answer. They're paying the local farmers and workers to fight for them."

"Ah, we're back to Iran, I see," Kurtzman said. "Like they say, always follow the money. It's all starting to make sense now that we've got this bearded man linked to the Iranian Embassy."

"Get hold of Hal," the Executioner said. "Fill him in, and tell him he has to talk the President into withdrawing our troops from the Mexican border and sending them toward Iran right now."

"I'll do that, but whether or not Hal can convince him—"

"Dammit!" Bolan said in a rare moment of profanity. "He's got to! If the Iranians take the Strait we'll be paying ten dollars a gallon for gas before you know it. You have any idea what that's going to do, not just to the U.S., but to the world? By comparison, the violence in Mexico will seem like an argument on a grade-school playground!"

"I'll call Hal," Kurtzman said. "Anything else?"

"Not for the time being." He paused, thinking of Able Team again. "Any idea why nobody can find Lyons?"

"Not even a guess. Last we talked to them, they'd just procured more armament and were about to head across the border to Tijuana to back Phoenix Force. We haven't been able to raise them since."

Bolan shook off the concern. It wouldn't accomplish anything. Lyons, Schwarz and Blancanales were big boys. They could take care of themselves as well as any three men on the planet. "I'll keep the cellular phone handy," he told Kurtzman. "Keep me updated."

"Will do," Kurtzman said and hung up.

A few seconds later, the Executioner had Captain Juanito Oliverez on the line. "You could have told me you were alive," he said, his voice sounding hurt. "Didn't you trust me? I could have helped."

"You're probably the only man in Mexico I do trust, Juanito," Bolan said. "But it was a need-to-know basis."

"But I need to know now?" Oliverez said.

"You do," Bolan said. "I need electronic surveillance equipment, Juanito. Car bugs and a tracking device. The best you've got and as many as you've got."

"I can have all you need in two hours," Oliverez said. "They won't be state-of-the-art but they will be the best in the government armory. Where should I meet you?"

Bolan remembered the furniture store a few blocks from *Los Pinos*. It was as good a place as any to meet. "Katz will recognize the bus," he said.

"I will see you then." Oliverez hung up.

Walking to the back of the bus, the Executioner opened one of the equipment trunks Grimaldi had flown down from Stony Man Farm. He dug through the contents until he found what he was looking for.

Then, as his mind raced to put together the plan that would guide him the rest of the night, the Executioner began to remove his clothes and step into the skintight black combat suit.

THE VILLAS DE LORETO was only too happy to provide limousine service to the docks.

The men got out of the vehicles, tipped the drivers and stood alone on the wooden platforms as the limos drove away. McCarter stared after them, then looked back inland toward the streets of Loreto. Where were the cars that would come to get them? It had been almost fifteen minutes since they'd left the room.

The Phoenix Force leader took a deep breath of the salty night air. His instincts told him that the fight would be set up nearby. The *Legitimas* needed money—that's why they were risking the fight in the first place. And they already had a decent amount of venture capital invested in travel expenses getting from wherever the hostages were being held to Loreto. He didn't think they'd go to the additional expense of moving the site yet again.

Then again, McCarter reminded himself, he could be wrong. He reached under his shirt, past the .40-caliber Browning Hi-Power to the cellular phone clipped inside his pants. If they wound up in some isolated place and vastly outnumbered, would he have an opportunity to contact Stony Man Farm for help? He didn't know. Would Able Team get word of where they'd gone to arrive in time? Highly unlikely. No, they couldn't count on Able Team arriving like the cavalry, and they couldn't count on being able to use the cellular phone.

They were on their own.

Calvin James stepped up beside McCarter and glanced at his watch. "They're late," he said.

McCarter nodded. "They know we aren't going anywhere without them." Both men turned toward the sea, staring out across the water to where several tourist ships had docked. Rowboats and other smaller craft were tied up in the slips along the quayside, obviously used to transport the passengers to and from the port. Beyond where the big ships rested in the gentle waves, barely discernable under the quarter moon, McCarter saw the tips of several masts appear above the horizon, as a ship neared.

"Looks like a four-masted bark," former-Navy SEAL Calvin James said.

McCarter turned back toward the village. But as he did, a sudden sinking feeling filled the pit of his stomach. He had been wondering where the fight would take place, and hoping it would be nearby rather than far away and isolated. There was a possibility that hadn't crossed his mind until now, and that was that the site could be both nearby and isolated. He was about to turn toward the sea when the caravan of cars appeared.

The vehicle in the lead was an aging Lincoln Continental. It came to a halt ten feet way from where the men from Stony Man Farm stood and the passenger door opened. The bandit who had made the *Legitima*'s first contact at the Toro Enterprises office in Tijuana stepped out and walked over. He bowed slightly, and the same dank odor of tequila and body odor McCarter remembered invaded his nostrils.

"Allow me to introduce myself," the bandit slurred drunkenly. "I am Pablo Huertes. Are you gentlemen ready?"

McCarter had suspected it hadn't been this man's voice he had spoken to on the phone. Now he was sure of it. "We're ready," he said. "You have enough room in your cars for all of us?" He glanced back at the vehicles who had pulled in after the Lincoln, hoping it was indeed cars they would be going in.

"We don't need cars."

McCarter's spirits fell as his new, and worst, fear was confirmed. He knew suddenly exactly where the fight was scheduled to take place. In fact when they got there they would be even farther from help than if they'd been alone and on foot a hundred miles deep into the desert.

"We need boats," the fat man said, and turned to the vehicles behind them.

Car doors opened and heavily armed men emerged. Many looked as filthy as Huertes but others seemed to be cut from a different mold. Their appearances—perhaps their clothes, perhaps the way they carried themselves or perhaps both—led the Phoenix Force leader to believe they were the true CDML revolutionaries while the dirtier men were the bandits that Pompei had learned were linked up with them.

James still stood next to him and now the former-SEAL spoke in French, assuming that Huertes wouldn't understand. "This isn't good, David."

James had assumed correctly. The bandit stared at them stupidly, then shrugged and took another swig from the tequila bottle.

McCarter, James and the rest of the warriors watched as the men from the cars walked past them and down the steps that led to the boats. A few were even police officers—wearing their uniforms.

"I thought you said your man Sykes couldn't show his face around the cops," McCarter said.

Huertes frowned, as if searching his mind for words someone else had told him to say. "That's only in Tijuana," he recited like an actor in a bad high school play. "Here, they don't care."

By now the men from the cars—perhaps thirty in total—had gone aboard the small transport boats. The purr of outboard engines filled the air above the sound of the waves. Huertes extended his hand like an usher at a movie theater and announced, "Gentlemen, shall we?" He led the way down the steps to the boats.

The men from Stony Man Farm climbed into the small craft and pulled away from the docks. McCarter found himself seated next to Dick Stevens. "Sorry to get you into this, old boy," the Phoenix Force leader whispered.

Stevens's grin was slight but present. "Don't mention it," he said. "Not that any of us is likely to ever get a chance to mention anything, anywhere, again." A sarcastic chuckle jerked his chest, then he said, "Of course if we do get out of this alive, you owe me, you know."

McCarter nodded. He truly did feel bad that he had allowed Stevens to be recruited on this mission. He had thought it would help. But as things were turning out one man more or less didn't look like it would make much difference. "Name it, and it's yours," he told the magazine editor.

"You explain this to my wife when we get back, McCarter," Stevens said. "I promised her I'd be back in time to take her to brunch tomorrow." He paused and grinned, this time wider. "And she scares me a hell of a lot more than these clowns in the boats."

McCarter couldn't help chuckling himself. But that faded quickly as he looked out across the waves and saw the four-masted bark anchored in the Sea of Cortez.

CARL LYONS wondered what the cargo was they were riding on. Drugs of some type—probably cocaine. But whatever it was, it was piled high enough that he found he was better off rolling onto his stomach and burrowing his head as deep into the tarp as he could. On his back, faceup, every time there was even the slightest dip in the tunnel ceiling it scraped his nose and sent clods of dirt down into his face and eyes.

But that wasn't the Able Team leader's predominant problem at the moment. He had only until the slow-moving convoy of drug smugglers reached the exit on the American side of the tunnel to come up with some plan of escape. Otherwise he, Blancanales, Keener and Harsey would be as dead as Schwarz.

The thought of his body lying cold behind them in the tunnel returned the fury to Lyons's soul. Again, he had to fight to keep from letting his hatred overcome his judgment. Slowly, he maneuvered his head so he could see the tunnel behind them. The voices and footsteps of the men following the truck on foot could be faintly heard. Once in a while he could even make out a shadowy form in the taillights. He tried to count. As best he could make out, there were six of them. They seemed to be walking in pairs.

None of the cartel smugglers had mounted the cargo on top of the flatbed to guard the prisoners; none of them wanted to bang against the roof of the tunnel like Lyons and the others were doing. And there was really no need to do so. If one or more of the bound prisoners rolled off the truck behind the convoy, it would be impossible for them to be missed by the walkers, who'd cut their throats immediately.

The Able Team leader felt one of the other men moving on top of the tarp. He heard a few muffled grunts, then Bud Keener's voice whispered, "Ironman? That you?"

"It's me."

"I've got a plan."

"I'm all ears."

"Well, you better be all hands," Keener said. Lyons could tell by his voice that the Ranger, although he had rolled up next to him, was facing the other way. "In the back of my underwear,

I've got a pocket knife. I'm tied too tight to reach it. Can you give it a try?''

Lyons wormed closer and felt his hands brush against the back of Keener's gun belt. The Texas Ranger's shirt was tucked into his pants but by using the fingers of both hands together he was able to grasp the material and tug it out.

"I'm going to suck in my gut and lean forward," Keener whispered. "Then, if we're still alive to talk about it, we aren't going to tell anyone about this next part."

Lyons almost smiled. "I'm not looking forward to it any more than you are," he said. He wiggled slightly forward on top of the tarp, trying to get his bound hands down the back of Keener's pants. It wasn't easy. Finally, he had them inside Keener's jeans and felt a hard metallic object. He dug deeper and wedged it between two fingers—at the exact moment the truck hit a bump on the tunnel floor. The small knife fell from his grasp.

"Shit," Keener said.

Lyons strained further, locating the knife again. This time he got a firmer grip, and then slowly worked his hands back out over Keener's gun belt. He could tell by touch that what he had in his hands was a small multiblade knife. Carefully, he transferred it to one hand and began trying to work one of the blades out. He had to force himself to take his time. If he dropped it, the knife would likely bounce off the tarp and be lost.

Lyons got the blade out but cursed softly under his breath.

"What's wrong?" Keener whispered.

"I just opened the nail file."

"There's a can opener and screwdriver next to it," the Ranger answered. "Turn it over. The blades are on the other side."

Lyons turned the knife upside down and felt along the edge. The larger of the two blades seemed to be on top. He opened it and found it was sharp against his thumb. He pressed it to the ropes that bound Bud Keener's hands and started to saw, then suddenly stopped.

A soft thud had sounded somewhere behind the truck. Two more similar noises followed almost immediately. The Able Team leader strained his eyes through the darkness, trying to see the men behind them. He could see none of them now but he still heard voices talking. Was it his imagination, or did their number seem fewer?

The Able Team leader went back to work. The knife was sharp, the ropes were old and the restraints came apart fairly easily. As soon as Keener was free, he rolled toward Lyons and the Able Team leader turned away.

Five minutes later, Lyons and Keener had freed Blancanales and Harsey. The four men crawled to the center of the tarp as the drug convey continued to make its way through the tunnel. Lyons was about to speak when he heard the strange thuds behind him again. He waited a few moments but nothing else happened. Then, before he could say anything, Texas Ranger Mark Harsey's voice whispered across the tarp. "What's next, Ironman?"

The Able Team leader hesitated. Except for the small pen-knife, they were still unarmed. What would they do when they got to the end of the tunnel?

Carl Lyons didn't want to say it out loud because a good leader never said anything he knew would dampen the esprit de corps of his men. But to himself, at least, he had to admit it.

He didn't know what to do next.

HE FELT HANDS grab him under the armpits. Others lifted his feet. The man facedown on the ground went as limp as he could, holding his breath and praying that they didn't check for a pulse or turn him over to check his wounds.

If they did, he really would be dead.

Silently, Hermann "Gadgets" Schwarz thanked God that even in the bright headlights from the vehicles, he had fallen into the dark shadows at the side of the tunnel. Otherwise, the lack of blood from the two rounds he had taken in the chest would have been too obvious too ignore.

Schwarz watched through slitted eyes as the cartel men bound Lyons, Blancanales, Keener and Harsey, and threw them on top of the flatbed truck. Just before Lyons went up, he saw the Able Team leader look his way. In a rare moment of sight into the man's soul, Schwarz saw the sadness in the Ironman's eyes. But he also saw the rage, and he prayed that Lyons wouldn't let it overcome his discrimination in the minutes to follow.

The vehicles pulled out. Schwarz was forced to jam himself farther against the walls of the narrow tunnel to keep from being run over. Had anyone seen him move? No, the wheels where still rolling. Men who hadn't been able to find seats in any of the vehicles fell in behind the flatbed. Schwarz watched them break off into pairs, chatting as if they were on their way to a cantina.

A few moments later, the truck's taillights faded down the long narrow tunnel.

Schwarz rose painfully from the ground. He felt as if someone had struck him in the chest with a hammer. Were any of his ribs broken? It felt like it. He ripped off his already-torn shirt and dropped it to the ground. His fingers traced along the ragged outer layers of the Kevlar vest until he found the shallow holes. The vests he had come across back at the Krazy Kolonel's Kombat Korner had been level three—they'd stop anything up to a .44 Magnum slug fired from a six-inch barrel. He had tried his on before picking one up for each of the other men, then found it easier just to put his shirt back on over it rather than take it off again. The other vests were still in a duffle bag in the Suburban, and he kicked himself mentally for forgetting to tell Lyons about them before they entered the tunnel.

If they'd all been wearing bullet-resistant vests, it might have given them the edge when they ran into the smugglers. And it might, even now, give them an advantage in escape.

Schwarz put the negative thoughts out of his mind. He had made a mistake. It was over, and there was nothing he could do about it now except try to make up for it by helping his comrades.

The Able Team electronics expert took off down the tunnel after the convoy, keeping his footsteps as light as he could. The tunnel was pitch black so far behind the lights of the vehicles, and at first he had to drag a hand across the wall to find his way. Then, as he began to catch up, the taillights reappeared. He saw the shadows walking behind the vehicle, and began to formulate his plan.

It looked like the men on foot had spread out farther during their trek, each pair walking behind the next. They had taken

Schwarz's weapons, of course. He knew he could overcome any of the men with his bare hands. But the time it took might well give each man's walking partner a chance to sound the alert. Then his element of surprise would be gone.

Schwarz stopped long enough to rip one of the wooden supports from the tunnel wall and waited breathlessly, hoping the sudden jerk wouldn't bring the tunnel down on top of him. He hurried on, feeling the board in his hands. The plank was roughly six feet long. Too clumsy to swing. He ran his hand along the board as he continued to pick up his pace, feeling the large knots in the wood. Cheap lumber. And it had started to rot.

Stopping again, Schwarz hesitated. Would the men ahead hear what he was about to do? Probably. The real question was, how would they interpret the sound? Schwarz took a deep breath. He didn't have time to wait and let them get out of earshot. He would have to take a chance.

Swinging the plank as hard as he could, the Able Team warrior struck another of the reinforcement boards at the side of the tunnel. The plank in his hand snapped loudly, echoing down the passageway.

Again, Schwarz held his breath, listening. He could still hear the men's voices, though he couldn't make out their words. But there didn't seem to be any change in their tone. Feeling the piece of the board still in hand, he found he now had a decent-sized club. The board had splintered to about three inches in diameter and four feet in length. The end he hadn't held had even broken into a relatively sharp point. Not a perfect spear or club, but serviceable.

The electronics expert quickened his pace then. The closer he got, the more chance he took of the men hearing him. But the roar of the trucks grew louder as he neared, too, and muffled his footsteps.

Another two minutes and Schwarz found himself ten feet behind the pair of men at the end of the convoy. He looked to the side of the tunnel rather than directly at the men's backs. It was an old clandestine-approach trick originated by the Thuggees of India. Men could sometimes "feel" the eyes of an attacker approaching them. No one could explain it scientifically, but it had been proved in battle too many times to be disputed.

With yet another deep breath, Schwarz suddenly darted forward. When he was three feet behind the men, he swung the board like a baseball bat and struck the first man on the back of the neck. He heard the drug smuggler's skull crunch inward.

So did the man walking next to him. He turned to face his partner and Schwarz ran the pointed end of the stick into his throat.

The Able Team warrior went to the ground on top of the men, freezing in place, staring ahead to see if the other men had noticed. He was close enough to understand what they said now, and heard the next pair laughing and discussing two prostitute sisters with large breasts they planned to visit when they returned to Tijuana. They continued to walk, undisturbed by what had taken place behind them.

Quickly searching the men beneath him, Schwarz came up with an old .45 automatic and two knives. But his smile widened when he checked the man with the stick still in his throat. He found Lyons's beloved Colt Python. The man also had a machete strapped to his belt.

Schwarz looked up as he pulled the long blade from its canvas sheath. He didn't know exactly how far they were from the end of the tunnel, but they had to be getting close. For his plan to work, he needed all of the men walking behind the convoy out of commission before they got there.

Jamming all of the weapons into his belt except the machete, the Able Team warrior rose from the tunnel floor and stalked on.

IT HAD TAKEN Bolan, Katz and Oliverez most of what remained of the night. But they had gotten the job done.

The three men sat in the old bus which was parked two blocks down from the Iranian Embassy as the sun came up over the city. A few of the men and women who worked at the embassy—mostly Mexican employees hired by the Iranian government—had already arrived for work. As daylight broke, a few more early birds began to arrive and show their credentials to the Revolutionary Guardsmen who stood at the doors. Bolan watched through binoculars as the men, wearing the red scarves that signified their commitment to the Shiite Muslim rebellion that had overthrown the shah, checked each ID carefully. Both soldiers wore AK-47s with folding stocks on slings around their necks.

"I thought they had us for a moment during the night," Oliverez said to Bolan.

After infiltrating the Iranian compound and entering the parking area where the embassy's motor pool was located, the three men had crawled through the lot attaching the homing devices Oliverez had secured from federal supplies. The mission had gone smoothly until they had almost completed it. Then, for no apparent reason, one of the guards had suddenly changed the route of his rounds. He had walked directly past them, even pausing to light a cigarette beside the vehicle under which they had scrambled for cover. Bolan had known that to take him out would have drawn suspicion the next morning. So they had held their breath and waited. Finally, the guard had moved on.

"You guys do this sort of thing all the time?" Oliverez asked.

"He does." Katz grinned. "I'm retired."

The next plan, Bolan thought, if they were to follow the bearded man, meant cosmetic changes to the outside of the bus were a must. The vehicle had served the Executioner well during his stay in Mexico City, making him appear to be the burned-out expatriate American he wanted to look like. But the bus would be too easy to spot and remember during this next leg of the game. He had considered appropriating a more common vehicle, but the average car wouldn't hold all his equipment and the other two men. So he and Katz had left Oliverez at the embassy to watch while they hurried to the nearest bus station. Several buses had been waiting while the drivers drank coffee inside. They had left with a magnetic sign with the Spanish equivalent of Chartered—and another that said The City of Oaxaco.

The stroke of luck had come as they had driven back toward the embassy when Katz noticed the darkened windows of a clothing store. Mannequins of men, women and children dressed in the latest fashions stood facing the street. Ten minutes later, the store had suffered a "break-and-grab" burglary and the mannequins were on their way to the bus. A little rearrangement in seating and a few nails later, and from the outside it looked like the bus held fifteen passengers on their way to Oaxaco.

Bolan handed the binoculars to Katz and picked up the cellular phone. A few moments later, he had Kurtzman on the line. "How are we coming with the Iranian personnel files?" he asked.

"Slowly," Kurtzman said. "I didn't have any trouble hacking into their system. The problem is, they're so disorganized. It's a nightmare trying to make sense of it, Striker. It looks like the program was put together by a ten-year-old with a Nintendo game."

The Executioner glanced out the window again. "We're running out of time, Bear," he said. "It's almost time for the embassy to open. I'm afraid we'll miss whoever it is if we don't get that intel soon."

"Then let me get back to it," Kurtzman said a little testily. "I'll fax it your way just as soon as I can put something together."

"Affirmative," Bolan said and disconnected the line.

Embassy workers continued to arrive. Bolan did his best to memorize the descriptions of each one, and even had Oliverez taking notes on their appearances. By the time the portable fax machine began to click and hum, at least half a dozen men wearing beards had arrived for work.

The Executioner stepped over to the machine as the pages began to roll out. When they were finished, he found three complete files, abbreviated versions of top-secret Iranian intelligence personnel dossiers of clandestine operatives currently stationed in Mexico and posing as diplomats. Before he could look at them closer, however, the phone rang.

"Hello?" Bolan said.

"Kurtzman. You got it?"

"That's a 10-4. Nice work. Thanks."

"It gets better," Kurtzman said. "The minute I tapped the Send button, Tokaido came running up the ramp. I had our Japanese junior computer genius monitoring all the latest intel, and you can ignore two of the files." He paused, then went on. "Katz's old buddies, the Mossad, spotted two of the men in Jerusalem last night. They're history. Concentrate on Reza. He's your man.''

"You're amazing, Bear. So amazing, I forgive you for being a little short-tempered earlier.''

Kurtzman laughed. ''Go get him, Striker.'' The computer wizard hung up.

The Executioner lifted the stacked sheets from the fax machine and sifted through them. He discarded the top and bottom files, and stared at the pictures on the last page of the remaining file. Amir Reza. In all but one of the pictures, Reza wore a beard of varying lengths. In one picture, in which he looked to be around ten years younger than the others, he had only a mustache.

Katz had moved over to the fax machine. ''What do we do when he gets here? If he gets here?'' the former-Phoenix Force leader asked. ''We got into the parking lot last night. But we aren't going to get into the offices. At least not on this short notice without planning.''

"We wait for him to leave," Bolan said. ''Then we follow.''

Oliverez had taken the binoculars from Katz. Now he dropped them from his eyes and turned to face the men from Stony Man Farm. ''What if he spends all day in the office?'' he asked.

"He won't," Bolan said confidently. ''He's the Iranians' contact to the *Marxistas.* My guess is he's footing the bill for the army they're raising. He's going to be out and about, checking on things.''

Oliverez wasn't satisfied. ''But what if he doesn't come in?''

Bolan shrugged. ''Then we go to Plan B.''

"Which is?" the captain asked.

"I don't know yet."

As Oliverez turned back to the window with the binoculars, he said, ''Another bearded man.'' He held the lenses out to his side. ''Take a look.''

Bolan pressed the binoculars to his eyes. He saw a man wearing a lightweight beige suit with an open collar walk up the sidewalk and turn toward the front doors of the embassy. The two guards saluted as he neared, then dropped their hands as he walked past them without bothering to show any credentials.

Katz had lifted another pair of binoculars and watched along with the Executioner. When the man with the beard had disappeared into the embassy, he dropped them and said, "We have an old saying in my country that fits situations like this."

"What's that?" Oliverez asked.

"Bingo," said Katz.

Oliverez looked confused. "I thought that was an American expression. From the game they play of the same name. It's what they say when they win."

The Israeli shook his head. He glanced at Bolan, winked, then turned back to the captain. "Don't you believe it," he said. "Americans try to take credit for everything."

10

The ship's name was painted on the side, near the bow: *Señorita Malvada—the Wicked Lady.*

McCarter followed the rest of the men up the rope ladder from the transport boats and boarded the ship. The first thing to catch his eye was the boxing ring set up on deck. Then he turned his attention to the thirty or more men moving about the ship. While the *Legitimas* who had met them at the dock had been a combination of true-believing revolutionaries and simple Mexican *bandidos,* the ship's crew were all *bandidos.* Dressed in ragged clothing and openly sporting pistols, knives and even a few cutlasses, they looked like eighteenth-century buccaneers beneath the sails of the *Señorita Malvada.*

The captain, who stepped forward to speak with Huertes, didn't wear an eye patch, but he should have. The ghastly, gaping hole to one side of his nose where an eye had once been stared hideously at McCarter as the man glanced his way.

Huertes grunted at whatever the captain had said into his ear, then turned toward McCarter. The one-eyed captain shouted orders to his crew. The men pulled anchor, unfurled two of the sails and the ship began to slowly glide away from Loreto, out to sea.

Huertes then walked over to the Phoenix Force leader. "I'm sorry," he said in a voice too syrupy to be sincere. "But the captain has insisted that all of your men be checked for weapons." He paused for another shot of tequila. "We're all to be confined here in close quarters and engaged in a sporting event that will be quite emotional. He fears violence might occur if you're armed."

"I suppose he's going to disarm your men and his as well?" McCarter said, knowing the answer ahead of time.

"No, señor," Huertes said, grinning. "He knows us. He knows we will control ourselves even if the fight doesn't go to our satisfaction. But you are...and please don't take this personally, a...how do you say it in English? An unknown quality?"

"No, that's not how we say it, but I get your drift," McCarter said sarcastically. He saw Calvin James and Gary Manning watching him, waiting for a cue. Was it time to call a halt to the whole charade right now and just get things over with? Should they chance the possibility that they could kill enough of the *Legitimas* to end the fight and still have someone left to lead them back to the hostages? The odds were heavily against all that falling neatly into place. They were vastly outnumbered, and confined to the ship where there was limited combat maneuverability.

No, an armed conflict now wasn't the answer. The fight between Toro and Scott Hix would have to go on.

McCarter withdrew his Browning Hi-Power and handed it to Huertes. He slipped the dagger out of the back of his pants and gave him that as well. Maybe if he gave up the weapons willingly, they wouldn't frisk him and find the other weapon he had under these circumstances—his cellular phone.

He wasn't that lucky. Huertes, reeking more of body odor and alcohol than ever, stepped in and patted him down. He found the phone clipped inside McCarter's waistband. "I'll hold this for you as well," he said. Across the deck, the Phoenix Force leader saw the other men from Stony Man Farm being disarmed. When the weapons had been collected, the men who had taken them disappeared below deck, then returned empty-handed, wearing only their own guns and knives. The captain shouted more orders and the sails were trimmed. The anchor went overboard and the ship stopped. McCarter turned toward Loreto. The lights of the little village were barely visible across the water.

All eyes now turned to the boxing ring. Lights had been suspended from the masts, and the tails of the fully trimmed sails fluttered beneath them, sending strange shadows jumping across the canvas. McCarter looked back to Huertes. The drunken sot couldn't be the true leader of the *Legitimas*—that would be the voice on the phone. But Huertes was obviously in charge there. Maybe he was sent as the front man while the real leader stayed back to keep watch over the hostages?

The bandit pointed to a corner of the ring where a stool had been set up. "You may go to your corner now, and prepare your fighter," he said.

McCarter led his men that way. Leo Turrin, still playing the part of fight promoter and head trainer, stepped through the ropes and held them for Toro and Pompei. McCarter, Manning, James and Dick Stevens took up places just outside the ring. Again, McCarter lamented the fact that T. J. Hawkins wasn't with them. One more gun might not make any difference but... The Phoenix Force leader stopped suddenly in midthought.

Where was Encizo?

McCarter turned away from the ring, his eyes scanning the crowded deck. He half expected the little Cuban to step out of the crowd of men to join them. But he didn't. Where the bloody hell was he?

The Briton's eyes returned to the ring as a roar suddenly went up among the men crowded around it. He saw the mass part as a man wearing only soiled khaki slacks was led to the ring. In his mid- to late-thirties, muscles rippled from his sweat-covered chest. He wasn't nearly as big or muscular as Toro but he moved with the grace of a jungle cat. The Phoenix Force leader looked at the man's face. Although older, with more lines from the stress he had been under, there was no mistaking Scott Hix from his pictures.

SCOTT HIX HAD MOUNTED the ladder from the bowels of the ship ready to fight.

But it wasn't the face of the man calling himself Toro he wanted to pound into dust. It was the men who had brought him to the ship; the men who had kidnapped him, Normandi, Ronnie and the others.

The men who had, at the last minute, gone back on their word and refused to allow Normandi to accompany him to the fight.

Hix came on deck and squinted under the bright lights that had been hung from the masts. At first, his vision was blurry. Then it began to clear and he saw the men surrounding the ring. Inside it, across from him, was a huge muscular man who might have been black and might have been Mexican or maybe a cross between the two. Who was he, though? CIA? FBI? Maybe even U.S. Army Military Intelligence who had entered the investigation because of Hix's past record with them? Scott Hix didn't know and he didn't care. It was enough to know they were the "good guys."

When he had sent the message by using the name Rex W. E. Sykes, he had suspected that it was the American government in some form behind the fight. Why would anybody in their right mind offer five million bucks to someone who could stay in the ring three minutes? Now, the suspicion was gone and he was certain that Toro and his entourage were there to locate the hostages. No syndicate would have put up with the shit. It didn't make sense. Only the *Legitima*'s greed had kept them from seeing that.

But there was another thing of which Scott Hix was certain. Toro and his fellow American agents hadn't planned on actually going through with the fight. Their plan would have been to grab him and the guards who accompanied him and force them to lead the way back to Quartel and the other hostages. Now, they'd been backed into a corner. The fight would have to take place.

Hix began to jump up and down, staying loose. So what was he to do? he wondered as he looked across the ring and saw Toro doing the same thing. If he didn't last the three minutes, he suspected he, and Normandi West, would pay the price. But could he kill a man who had been sent to rescue him?

The American didn't know.

Hix took a seat on the stool in his corner as the man in the center of the ring made his announcements. Looking both ways to be sure he wasn't being watched too closely, he shifted the Applegate-Fairbairn combat dagger still hidden in his underwear. He didn't want it falling out during the fight. He didn't know what was about to happen, and things certainly looked grim at this point, but it still might come in handy somewhere down the line.

The ship's captain stepped into the center of the ring. With no microphone at his disposal, he held up his hands to quiet the roar of the spectators who were busy placing side bets. When they had calmed, he shouted, "Gentlemen, in this corner—" He pointed to where Turrin and Pompei were standing next to Special Agent Martinez. "The champion of Tijuana, Mexico, Toro!"

There were several boos and no applause.

Turning his attention to Scott Hix, the captain said, "And in this corner—" The men on deck went wild, screaming and clapping. A number of pistols were even fired into the air. "From the United States of America but representing the people of Mexico..." He let his voice trail off dramatically. "Mr. Rex. W. E. Sykes!"

Now it seemed like every gun on board boomed, sending lead into the air to fall into the Sea of Cortez.

Turrin was directly behind Toro, just behind the corner post. As the cheers died, he heard the big man say in his Shirley Temple voice, "Leo, what am I supposed to do? I don't want to hurt this guy."

Turrin glanced over his head at McCarter. The undercover man didn't look rattled. But he didn't look happy, either. "Any ideas, David?" he whispered.

The former-SAS commando fought the temptation to remind Turrin that he was supposed to be the undercover ace. But this was no more Turrin's fault than anyone else's. "We'll have to go through with it," he said. He leaned through the ropes. "Try to knock him out quick. Get it over with *inside* three minutes. If they think we owe them five million dollars, our troubles are only starting."

Toro turned on his stool to face McCarter. "Hix wouldn't be doing this if they didn't have some kind of hammer on him," he whispered. "Which means he's going to try to win himself. And I read his file. He's not some drunken TJ brawler. He's a close-quarters combat expert. According to the reports, he's the best the Army's had since Rex Applegate himself."

McCarter tried to think of something to say. Before he could, though, his thoughts drifted back to Encizo. Where was the man?

As soon as the answer hit him, McCarter looked at his watch.

Time was their only ally now. Somehow, they would have to get around the three-minute problem.

"Don't take him out," McCarter said.

"I don't know if I can take him out," Toro said. "Didn't you just hear what I said?"

McCarter ignored the man's lack of confidence. "Forget the three minutes. I've got a plan. But it depends on making this thing last as long as possible."

Toro shrugged. "I'll do my best," he said.

All faces looked back to the center of the ring. The captain nodded somewhere on the side of the deck, and the ship's horn sounded. "Let's rumble!" he said in English.

LYONS, BLANCANALES, Keener and Harsey were free.

The only light during the slow trip had been that from the vehicles. But now, Lyons realized, a little more illumination was starting to show up ahead. Not much. Just a little.

Another of the mysterious thumps sounded behind the flatbed. This time it was followed by what sounded like a soft whimper. Lyons wondered if his ears were playing tricks on him, but then Keener whispered, "Did you hear that?"

Lyons nodded, knowing there was enough light now for the Ranger to see him. "Been hearing them for several miles."

"Me too," Keener said. "But that's the first time I heard somebody moan afterward."

"Does it seem like there aren't as many guys following us as there were?" Lyons whispered.

The Able Team leader began to smile. It could mean only one thing. He grabbed Blancanales and Harsey by their shirts and pulled them close in the middle of the tarp where they could hear. "Keep your hands behind your backs like you're still tied," he said. "But be ready to move at a moment's notice."

"What are we going to do?" Harsey asked.

"I don't know yet," Lyons said. "But we'll find out." He paused. "I'm temporarily turning over leadership of this mission to somebody else."

"Who?" Harsey said.

"To a dead man."

SCHWARZ HAD WORKED out a pretty good system by the time he finished off the last of the men walking behind the flatbed. From the second pair of men, he had recovered Carl Lyons's sound-suppressed Government Model .45 automatic. The big heavy handgun turned out to be an excellent club. And it hadn't been nearly as messy as the machete he'd used on the second two. So, to take care of the last two drug smugglers following the convoy, he had simply hit them over the head and then knelt next to them, cutting their throats with the folding knife he had also requisitioned.

As the dark tunnel began to lighten, Schwarz formed his plan. He knew it would work better if Lyons and the others knew ahead of time that he was alive. So, taking a calculated risk, he rose from the bodies of the last two followers and sprinted forward into the glow of the flatbed's taillights.

Schwarz stayed within the illumination only long enough to see four heads on top of the tarp acknowledge him. He also saw eight hands, free of restraints, rise into the air. The messages from both parties given and received, he dropped back into the shadows and continued to follow.

The narrow tunnel, and the fact that Able Team's Suburban had to be driven in reverse, had forced the convoy to drive slowly. But finally Schwarz saw the exit appear ahead and took a deep breath.

It was now or never.

Sprinting forward, the electronics specialist made it to the rear of the flatbed. The tarp was tied down but the knife quickly cut through three of the lines. He lifted the tarp high enough to see stack after stack of kilo-sized bricks wrapped in brown paper. The bricks were bound into larger bundles with metal bindings. There was a small vacant area—perhaps two feet wide—along the tail of the flatbed. Pulling himself up, he squeezed under the tarp and squatted on this ledge, turning back and reaching out to try to grab the cords he had severed. They flapped out of reach behind the truck.

One of the men on top of the load—Schwarz couldn't see who—leaned over the side and pressed down against the fluttering tarp. This brought the ropes within reach and he retied two of them. He had cut the third too short and was forced to leave it loose—and wonder if the cartel men would notice.

With Lyons's Colt Python ready in one hand, his knife in the other, the Able Team warrior waited.

The moonlight was faint but strong enough that Schwarz could tell when the flatbed exited the tunnel. Then the convey came to a halt and he heard the vehicle doors opening and shutting. He didn't know exactly what his next step was going to be; he would have to think on his feet. He did know, however, that his side was vastly outnumbered. And they were unarmed. So a blatant shoot-out was out of the question. He had to figure something else out, and he had to do it fast.

Footsteps and voices sounded around the truck. He heard Lyons and the other men being hauled down from over his head. He knew they must have re-wrapped their severed restraints around their wrists to make it look as if they were still bound, or else something would have been said about it.

"Señor Santana!" one of the cartel voices suddenly called out. "The tarp is coming unfastened at the rear!"

"Then fix it, you fool!" came the voice of the man with the ponytail.

Footsteps shuffled toward Schwarz. A moment later, just below the edge of the tarp, he saw a pair of hands grasp the severed cord. He set the Python on the bed of the truck next to him for a moment, then reached under the tarp and grasped a wrist. At the same time, he used the serrated edge of the folding knife to slit through the tarp between him and the cartel man.

A grunt of surprise had issued forth from the lips of the man when Schwarz's hand had grabbed his wrist. The noise had gone unnoticed among the other sounds around the vehicles. Schwarz pulled the man's arm, which jerked his face into the slit. The Able Team warrior held the jagged edge of the knife in front of the drug smuggler's eyes. Blood from the men who had been on foot behind the flatbed still glistened on the blade. "This is the blood of your friends," Schwarz growled softly through the hole in the canvas. "Do you want to add your own to it?"

The man shook his head.

"Then do as I say. Get Santana back here. Now."

The man's eyes were wild with fear. "But...what do I say?"

In a flash so fast the man couldn't react, Schwarz set the dagger down next to him and pressed the end of the Python into the man's forehead. "That's up to you," he said. "But if it doesn't work I'm going to turn your head into a canoe."

"Señor Santana!" the man cried out. "Come quickly! You must see this!"

It wasn't much but it worked. Footsteps pounded their way. "When he gets here, step back and tell him to look inside," Schwarz said. "And remember, this tarp isn't going to stop a .357 Magnum round."

The man nodded nervously.

A moment later Schwarz heard the leader's voice. "What is it, you fool?"

Schwarz dropped the other cartel man's wrist. The frightened drug runner stepped back and indicated the hole in the tarp.

Santana stuck his nose through the slit and Schwarz jammed the Python halfway up one nostril while he grabbed the ponytail with the other hand. Forcing Santana's head down tore open the hole in the tarp to the bottom. Schwarz jumped off the end of the truck, twisted Santana away from him and repositioned the revolver under his chin. "Here's the deal," he whispered into the man's ear. "All we want is out of here. We leave, we leave you alive and we'll even leave the dope with you."

So slow it was hard to see, Santana nodded.

"Tell three of your men to bring my team around to the back of the truck. Now."

Santana followed orders well for a man so used to giving them.

A moment later, Lyons, Blancanales, Keener and Harsey were pushed around the back of the truck by three men armed with rifles. They dropped their weapons without having to be told as soon as they saw the situation. The Able Team men and Rangers quickly armed themselves.

Schwarz, flanked by the other men, now guided Santana to the side of the truck. Several of the drug smugglers saw what was happening and froze in place, watching in awe. The others had begun readying the waiting vehicles for the drug transfer and didn't notice.

"Get them all over here, on this side of the truck," Schwarz ordered.

Santana called out and the men began to assemble, shocked looks on their faces when they saw the reversal in the balance of power. "Now tell them to drop their weapons, and explain things to them," Schwarz said.

"Men!" Santana called out. "Please drop your guns. Things aren't as bad as they seem!"

Some of the men were hesitant but they followed orders. Lyons, Blancanales and the Rangers gathered the fallen weapons, then led the men away from the guns. They shook the men down, finding several hideout knives and pistols. Those who had them got a rifle butt across the face, which caused a few men who hadn't yet been frisked to drop other hidden weapons.

"All they want is their lives," Santana called out. "And who can blame them, eh? Do as they say. They have promised to leave us alive and with our goods."

"You believe them?" one of the men shouted out.

"Do I have a choice?" Santana asked as Schwarz pressed the Colt tighter under his chin.

A few minutes later, Lyons, Blancanales, Keener and Harsey had assembled all the men on foot at the entrance to the cave. Schwarz turned the Python and Santana over to Lyons, who shoved the man into the Suburban. Harsey climbed in next to him, while Keener took one of the CAR-15s and climbed onto the hood of the vehicle to watch the cartel men as he rode.

Schwarz fumbled through the equipment bags in the rear of the Suburban until he found what he was looking for. Gathering it into his arms, he moved back to Lyons and spoke to him through the window of the vehicle. "Go ahead and get started," he said. "This won't take long, and you'll be going slow enough I can catch up to you on foot."

Lyons nodded. With the Suburban pushing them forward and Keener's CAR-15 aimed their way, the drug smugglers started walking through the tunnel.

Hermann "Gadgets" Schwarz moved quickly from vehicle to vehicle, doing what he did best. When he was finished with the cars and trucks that would have picked up the cocaine, he moved just inside the exit to the cave and performed a similar task.

All of the men's weapons had been piled on top of the tarp on the flatbed, and now Schwarz got behind the wheel of the truck and drove it into the tunnel, stopping ten feet past the opening. Grabbing his CAR-15, he began jogging toward the convoy, which was now headed toward Mexico again. He caught up to the Suburban easily.

Fifteen minutes later, Lyons pulled to a halt. Keener turned to face them through the windshield and the Able Team leader nodded.

"Okay, assholes, listen up!" Keener shouted out. "One at a time, you bastards make your way back past the Suburban to the other side. You try to go two at a time, or try anything else, you get a .223 bullet. Understand?"

The men made their way past the Suburban as Keener kept his rifle aimed their way.

"Now, we must walk back?" Santana said in the back of the Suburban.

"You can walk if you want," Schwarz said. "I'd suggest running, though."

A quizzical look came over the face of the man with the ponytail. "The truck, it is still outside the tunnel?"

"No, I pulled it just inside," Schwarz answered. "Didn't want anybody coming along and stealing your coke, you know."

Santana smiled. "Very considerate," he said.

"Oh, I wouldn't say thanks just yet," Schwarz said, returning the smile.

Lyons stayed behind the wheel. Keener climbed next to him. Blancanales, Schwarz and Harsey stayed in the back. "You might as well get out now," Schwarz told Santana. "You're free to go."

"Our weapons?" Santana asked.

"All neat and tidy on top of the dope on the flatbed. Just waiting for you."

"Again, I thank you."

"Whatever," Schwarz said.

The cartel leader exited the Suburban and Lyons pulled away down the tunnel toward Mexico. Five minutes later, Schwarz said, "What do you think, Ironman? About now seem right?"

"As good a time as any," Lyons said.

Schwarz pulled a small electronic device from his pocket that looked similar to a television remote control. He tapped a button, and an explosion roared far behind them. "Those were the vehicles outside the tunnel," the electronics ace said.

He waited a moment, then pushed another button. This time the explosion, though still far away, sounded three times as loud. "And there goes the flatbed, the dope, the guns and the exit."

The Mexican-side exit from the tunnel appeared a few minutes later and Lyons pulled through then stopped. Schwarz dropped down, moved back inside the entryway and applied more C-4 plastic explosives along the reinforcing boards holding up the walls.

Schwarz returned to the Suburban, and Lyons pulled a hundred yards from the tunnel, then stopped again. Schwarz pushed the button, and the tunnel that had supplied America with millions of dollars of drugs each day closed for good.

AMIR REZA emerged from the rear of the Iranian Embassy two hours later carrying a large briefcase in each hand. Oliverez still kept vigil on the front of the building from the bus, but Bolan and Katz had left on foot, taking up positions along the sidewalk where they could keep an eye on the parking lot. They watched the Iranian operative open the door to an embassy Mercedes and get inside before they hurried back to their bus.

"He's leaving," Katz told Oliverez as he pulled himself into the bus ahead of the Executioner.

The captain started the engine. "Could you tell which vehicle?"

Bolan shook his head as he climbed on board. "We'll have to try all of the frequencies," he said. "Which means keeping visual contact at least until we narrow it down." Already, two Mercedes had left the embassy that morning driven by other men. They had scratched them off the list of possibilities.

Oliverez let the vehicle pull through the gate and out of the parking lot, then gave it a block's head start before following. In the meantime, Katz was furiously flipping the dial of the receiver, trying to tune in the frequency for the bug that would monitor that specific vehicle. "Got him," Katz said. "Now just make sure he doesn't spot us."

Oliverez nodded. He let the bus fall farther back in traffic.

"What's the range on the transmitter?" Bolan asked.

"Roughly two miles," Oliverez said. "That's under ideal conditions, of course. In this traffic, and with all the electrical lines as interference, we'll be lucky to keep tabs on him at a half mile."

"A half mile should be enough in the city," Katz said. "What worries me is what happens if he leaves town. On the open road, if he keeps seeing us..." He let his voice trail off.

Bolan nodded. "It's a chance we have to take. But there's another problem. If he heads into the mountains they'll block the beeps worse than the electrical interference."

Oliverez turned in the driver's seat as the bus stopped at a stoplight. "You think he's going to the mountains?" he asked.

"I think it's a very good possibility."

Oliverez frowned. "Why?"

"Because that's where our intel people think the *Marxista* training compound is located. And somebody has to be financing all their new recruits." Bolan paused as he looked through the windshield of the bus toward the Mercedes ahead. "You saw the briefcases Reza was carrying. My guess is they had more money in them."

The light turned green. Several cars ahead, the Mercedes, which had been first in line, pulled out. The bus followed. Another bus, similar to theirs, pulled off a side street and Oliverez let it get between them, then pulled into a lane opposite so both vehicles could be seen.

Bolan nodded unconsciously. Oliverez had already proven he was a good fighter and this proved he was also a sound tactician. If Reza turned, or saw both buses in the rearview mirror, he would probably not even register the fact.

The Executioner watched the Mercedes as the miles went by.

Had he known that they would be tailing a vehicle, he would have ordered better equipment from Stony Man. The Farm had homing devices and receivers that included computerized maps that could be programmed for any part of the world. As it was, they would have to make do with the archaic surveillance gear Oliverez had been able to get from the government.

As they continued to follow, it became apparent that Bolan had been right—they were heading out of the city. The other bus pulled off, leaving them sticking up above the smaller vehicles, and as traffic began to thin, the Executioner instructed Oliverez to turn off the main thoroughfare, following the beeps from the receiver on a smaller road that ran parallel. When his instinct told him it was time to quit taking chances, they hurried back and saw the Mercedes a quarter mile ahead.

The procession drove through the outskirts of Mexico City proper and into the suburb of Puebla. Then Bolan watched Reza take the ramp onto the Inter-American Highway. They passed a sign telling them that Oaxaco lay 230 miles ahead. The Executioner relaxed slightly. No need to change the sign on the bus— at least not yet. If the Iranian was headed that way it only made sense that a bus with a sign advertising Oaxaco would take the same route. For once, they'd had some good fortune.

But what would happen later? Would they be that fortunate again? If the Mercedes left the highway and took off on one of the slow, winding mountain roads they'd be easy to spot. Then they would either have to stay close enough to keep visual contact with the Mercedes, or drop back and rely on the electronic bug that would be all but worthless in such an environment.

There was only one possible solution to the problem. And even as he picked up the cellular phone, the Executioner wondered if there was still time to put it into action.

RAFAEL ENCIZO, known for his strong swimming ability, rose from beneath the surface of the water as the last of the transport boats pulled away from the dock. He watched until it became obvious that the four-masted bark was their destination rather than one of the other ships anchored offshore. Then the little Cuban pulled himself back onto the dock and started running toward the lights of Loreto.

Encizo had been standing by the edge of the water when the vehicles carrying the strange combination of *Legitimas* and *bandidos* arrived, and he had guessed what was about to happen a split second before he saw McCarter do the same. Quickly checking to make sure he wasn't being watched, he had quietly slipped into the water and held on to one of the dock supports until he heard the transport craft leaving. Only then, after holding his breath for nearly three minutes, had he risen from beneath the dark waters and gasped for air.

Charting a course for the nearest lights, Encizo glanced over his shoulder to see that the sailing ship had pulled anchor and was setting out for sea. How far would they go? How easy would they be to find in the open sea? He didn't know. But he knew there was only one chance that any of his friends would live through the night.

A small grocery store, the windows darkened, was the first building Encizo saw. Would they have a phone? Not all small Mexican businesses, even in resort towns, could afford one. But what he could be relatively certain of was that they would have no burglar alarm. In any case, he didn't have time to check.

Drawing his Beretta 92 from his belt, Encizo grasped it by the barrel and crashed the butt through the window next to the doorknob. He reached through and opened the door, then sprinted past several rows of food items to the counter.

The phone sat next to the cash register. Two minutes later, he was talking to Barbara Price at Stony Man Farm.

THE SHIP'S HORN sounded and Hix rose from his stool. He advanced to the center of the ring where Toro stood before him. No shaking of hands before a match like this—it was not a game. It was life and death.

Hix raised his hands in a classic boxing stance and began to circle. He looked Toro in the eyes but didn't see the eyes of a murderer. The eyes were of a man who could kill if necessary, but also of a man who looked like he didn't want to be there any more than Scott Hix did.

Toro circled with him, keeping pace. Neither man made a move toward the other. It didn't take long for the men around the ring to grow impatient.

"Fight, dammit!"

"Do something!"

Toro moved in and threw a half-hearted feint. Hix blocked it easily—as he knew he had been meant to do. He threw his own three-quarter speed jab and let Toro brush it to the side. The two men continued in this manner for perhaps thirty seconds before the spectators lost patience again.

Hix suddenly thought of West and what would happen to her if he lost the money for the *Legitimas*. He made his decision quickly as a horrible mental image of the woman he loved, naked on the ground and surrounded by filthy leering bandits, crossed his mind. Without warning, he stepped forward and threw a right hook that caught Toro squarely on the jaw.

After the dance they had begun, the big man hadn't expected it. Toro went down, with Hix on top of him. A straight left to the side of the big man's face rocked his head into the canvas. But Toro wasn't one to give up easily. He rolled out from under the lighter man, sending Hix flying to the side. Before he could respond, the former intelligence operative felt a thick forearm wrap around his throat from behind. It dug into his windpipe, cutting off his breath. Hix felt the head of the man behind him press into the back of his hair for leverage. But then he heard a small, girlish voice whisper, "We've got a plan, Hix. But we've got to buy time. You're going to last the three minutes." There was a brief pause, then the tiny voice added, "Now elbow me in the ribs. Quick!"

Hix did as instructed and Toro grunted and stepped back. He bent over, clutching his side where Hix had struck. It couldn't have hurt that much, Hix knew. He had pulled the blow at the last second. But he, in turn, moved to the other side of the ring coughing and choking as if recovering from the stranglehold. Both men kept it up until the spectators began to scream for blood again.

They clashed, exchanging punches that reddened each other's faces but did little damage.

"Two minutes!" shouted a voice from outside the ring.

Hix saw Toro's eyes narrow. The man had the killer instinct, all right, and for a moment Hix wondered if he had forgotten that they were on the same side. Then Toro's face softened. The big dark-skinned man winked quickly back at Hix. Then he lowered his head like a bull and charged.

The tackle caught Scott Hix at waist level and drove him backward. He felt his back hit the canvas and the air rushed from his lungs. A series of punches rained down over his face and shoulders, which even though he could tell they were being pulled, felt as if they'd been delivered by a pile driver. He blocked, parried and occasionally even shot up his own strike between the fists that continuously came down at him. Toro had said they needed to buy time, and although he didn't know why, Hix knew each second they delayed was to their advantage.

A heel-palm strike from Hix to Toro's chin stunned the man long enough for Hix to grab his ear and drag him to the side. Scrambling on top of the bigger man, the American reversed the situation and began pummeling Toro's face with punches. He had the sudden bizarre feeling that he was a professional wrestler, just putting on a show for a crowd that expected entertainment rather than reality.

But this crowd was different.

Cries of "Fake!" and "Something's wrong!" went up from the men around the ring. "Finish him, you imposter!" and similar grumbles could be heard. Toro heard the cries too and, arching his back suddenly in a wrestling bridge, he sent Hix flying through the air.

Then, suddenly, the ship's horn sounded again and delirious cheers went up from the *Legitimas*. The three minutes were up. Scott Hix had lasted the prescribed time. And they were five million dollars richer.

Huertes entered the ring, grabbed Hix and hugged him. The bandit leader's odor hurt more than all of Toro's punches. Mercifully, Huertes let him go and turned to the other corner as one of the men who had come with Toro crossed the ring to join them.

Huertes didn't wait for him to speak. "We have won, and you owe us money," he said.

"No argument there," the man said with a British accent.

"We've arranged for you to be our guests on this ship until the money is safely in the hands of my associates," Huertes grinned. "There is plenty of food and drink. Perhaps you'll join us in a victory celebration, eh?"

"How would you like to turn your five million dollars into ten?" the British man asked.

Huertes's mouth fell open.

"I have a counteroffer," the man standing in front of Huertes and Hix said. "Your boy is tougher than I thought. He lasted three minutes but I don't think he can win. Let's go the rest of the way. Double or nothing. If you win, you go home with ten million instead of five."

The close-quarters combat expert could see the limited wheels inside Huertes's brain turning. The bandit knew that if he lost the five million dollars already won, Hidalgo would have his ass on a silver platter. But Hix could also see the man considering the fact that the additional five million could go to him. The *Legitima* leader need never even know of it. And as it already had so many times with the kidnappers, greed overcame intelligence.

"What we must do," Huertes said quickly, "is keep this as our little secret."

"Then it's on," the man with the British accent said. "Double or nothing. Only the three of us need know."

Huertes grabbed Hix with one hand, the Briton with the other and escorted them to the middle of the ring. Dropping their arms, he took a long swig from his tequila bottle, which emptied it, and threw the container overboard. He held up his hands for silence. *"Hombres!"* he called out. "We have won the money!"

Another round of cheers went up. When it had quieted again, Huertes continued, "But while we wait for it to be delivered, the fight will continue for your entertainment!"

This brought the loudest applause yet.

Huertes looked to the Briton. "Ten minutes of rest?" he asked.

The man looked at his watch. "I assume you're going to contact Toro Enterprises with the news and make arrangements for someone to get the money?" he asked.

"Of course."

"Then we've got all night on this ship. Give our boys an hour to mend. It'll make for a better fight."

Huertes nodded and pulled a new bottle from his pocket.

McCARTER RETURNED to the corner where Toro was sitting on the stool, holding a hand over one eye. "Good job," he told the federal agent.

Toro winced as he pulled his hand away from his face. His eye had swollen almost shut. "I'm glad the guy wasn't serious about all this," he said. "He packs a hell of a wallop even when he pulls his punches."

McCarter grinned. "We've got an hour before you fight again."

"What!" Toro said. "I thought—"

He was cut off by the roar of plane engines overhead.

All of the heads on the deck of the ship turned skyward as an unmarked F/A-18A Hornet suddenly dropped though the sky and buzzed the *Señorita Malvada*. It passed, then dipped a wing and began making a slow U-turn in the sky.

McCarter finally knew what happened to Encizo.

One of the ship's crew came scrambling up the ladder from below and yelled, "Captain! There is a call for you!" He held out the cellular phone that had been taken from McCarter.

The one-eyed captain took the phone and held it to his ear. A moment later his good eye widened and he began to tremble. "I don't believe you," he said. "Your men would also die."

There was a short pause, then the captain said, "I still don't believe you!" and hung up.

A moment later, the Hornet turned back. But this time, it followed a path roughly a hundred yards from the ship. Just before it drew even, a loud swishing sound came over the roar of the engines and then a Sidewinder missile flew through the air toward the water leaving a trail of white smoke in its wake.

The missile hit the water and exploded, sending waves across the sea that rocked the *Señorita Malvada*. A second later, the phone rang again. The captain answered. "I still don't believe your own men are prepared to die," he said. But this time he didn't sound as sure.

McCarter turned to Huertes, who was standing in the corner of the ring with Hix. The fat bandit didn't look sure at all. And if there was some way to convince Huertes, then he felt sure the captain would go along.

Scott Hix solved the problem himself.

As McCarter watched, the close-quarters combat expert suddenly reached down the front of his khaki trousers and pulled out an Applegate-Fairbairn fighting knife. Grasping the hilt like an ice pick, he suddenly reached around Huertes's throat with his other arm and hugged the man to him. The blade of the dagger pressed into the soft flesh beneath the bandit's flapping jowls. "The question isn't if their men are willing to die," McCarter heard Hix say. "It's whether or not you are, you fat fucking pig. Are you?"

Huertes wasn't. And he was several steps ahead of the game in what he'd be told to do. "Captain!" he screamed. "Tell your men to drop their arms! Raise the anchor and begin sailing to shore immediately!"

The captain shook his head. "No!" he said. "I, and all of my men, are wanted. I won't—"

McCarter hadn't seen Dick Stevens moving until he suddenly appeared right behind the captain. When he did, the knife-magazine editor suddenly performed a movement almost identical to that which Hix had accomplished. But the blade he held to the throat of the one-eyed captain was smaller—the spear-point blade of a Swiss Army knife.

"I don't know who all is going to die today," Stevens growled. "Or who all is prepared to. But we both know two guys who are about to start choking on blood whether they're ready or not, don't we, Captain?"

As if to punctuate Stevens's words, another missile shot from the Hornet into the sea.

The captain closed his good eye. "Sail for shore," he said.

A few minutes later, the men from Stony Man Farm, Scott Hix and Dick Stevens were fully armed and the *Legitimas, bandidos,* and pirates had been herded to the bow of the ship. All, that is, except Huertes.

McCarter left the rest of his men to guard the prisoners and he and Scott Hix took the fat bandit below deck. Hix had already told the Phoenix Force leader he'd been blindfolded when taken to and from the site where the hostages were being held, and that he had no idea where it might be. The two men dropped Huertes into a chair in the captain's quarters and stood over him. "We can do this the easy way or the hard way," the Phoenix Force leader said. "But you're going to lead us to Ronnie Quartel and the other hostages."

Huertes started to speak, but McCarter cut him off. "Don't talk yet. Let me explain the easy way first. That's where you just tell us where the hostages are, then take us there with no argument or tricks."

"What is the hard way?"

"Oh, that's unpleasant even to think about," McCarter said. "But since you asked...I go topside and leave you here alone with Mr. Hix. After what you've put him through, I suspect he'd prefer that method of interrogation. But I doubt you would."

Next to him, Scott Hix withdrew the Applegate-Fairbairn knife from where it had found a place on his belt.

"Tijuana," Huertes said quickly. "We drove for hours after leaving Mr. Hix's house to confuse them. But eventually, we returned to Tijuana." He went on to describe the location in greater detail.

The Phoenix Force leader pulled the cellular phone from his belt and tapped in the number for the Toro Enterprises office in Tijuana. There was always the chance...

Carl Lyons answered on the first ring.

"Where in the bloody hell have you been?" McCarter asked. "You missed all the fun."

"We found some of our own," Lyons said. "Where are you?"

"Never mind that now," said McCarter. "Just stay put. We're coming back your way."

The Phoenix Force leader disconnected the line and turned to Hix. "No matter how much you'd like to, or how much he deserves it," he said, "don't kill him. We might need him again later."

Hix nodded. He looked as if he'd love to disregard the orders, but McCarter knew he wouldn't. At least not until the hostages—including the woman Hix was in love with, the Phoenix Force leader had learned—were safe.

McCarter climbed the ladder to the deck in time to see the lights of Loreto grow brighter across the water.

11

The Mercedes was less than halfway to Oaxaco when it turned off the Inter-American Highway and started up the road into the mountains. Sitting in the bus a mile and a half back, Bolan looked at his watch. So far, he had heard nothing back on his call to Stony Man Farm.

"What do I do?" Oliverez asked.

"Turn off," the Executioner told him. "But don't get too close. We'll have to try to stay out of sight and rely on the transmitter."

Oliverez tapped the brake, slowing the bus. He waited until the Mercedes disappeared up a winding blacktop road before taking the exit ramp himself. The beep—every five seconds—remained strong over the receiver.

The bus followed, passing several side roads. Considering the unsophisticated tracking equipment, each intersection left a question in Bolan's mind. Was Reza still on the blacktop, or had he taken the turn? So far, all the roads they'd passed were dirt. There had been no recent rain and the earth was dry. So the Executioner kept the bus on the blacktop because he saw no dust clouds settling on the intersecting roads. But sooner or later, he knew they would come to a crossroad paved with concrete or blacktop. How would they decide their course then?

The Executioner's cellular phone rang and he thumbed it on. "Striker," he said into the instrument.

"Hey, big guy," said the voice on the other end. "Charlie Mott here, your eye in the sky with the latest surveillance report."

Bolan breathed a sigh of relief. There was still no guarantee that they wouldn't lose Reza in the valleys and side roads but the surveillance was a definite advantage. "Can you see him, Charlie?" the soldier asked.

"Yep. I can see you, too. Not much other traffic down there—a few old trucks scattered through the hills. So unless your boy gets down under some overhangs or something I should be able to keep him in view."

"Stay high enough that he doesn't spot you."

"I'm high enough."

"Good. Keep the line open. We're still beeping down here but I don't know how long that'll last."

They drove on, up into the mountains, down into the valleys and around the sharp curves. Oliverez kept the bus back even farther now that Mott was above them. The beeps remained strong for a while, then started to fade and finally stopped. Oliverez hit the accelerator and sped up. Thirty seconds later, the beeps returned.

"Okay," Mott said. "About a quarter mile from now you're going to come to a fork in the road. The Mercedes went to the left. Looks like he's angling toward Tlaxiaco."

"Tlaxiaco?" Katz said.

"It's a little mountain village," Oliverez said.

"Uh-oh," Mott suddenly said.

"What's wrong?"

"Well...he's not there anymore."

"What do you mean?"

"I mean, he disappeared."

Bolan gripped the phone tighter. He could still hear the beeps but they were faint. "He may have dipped into another valley, Charlie," he said. "Watch the spot where you lost him, then look up the road where he might come out."

"I've already done that," Mott said. "This isn't the first time he's disappeared. I just didn't want to give you a heart attack every time it happened."

Oliverez had sped up again but the beeps were still fading. "How long since you saw him?" Bolan asked the pilot.

"Two, maybe three minutes," Mott came back. "Like I said, it didn't seem unusual."

The Executioner glanced toward the monitor in Katz's hands. It had been silent now for maybe thirty seconds. Katz shook his head.

"Where'd you last see him?"

"There's a little valley ahead. You're almost to it—just past that fork in the road I told you about. He went down but he never came up the other side."

"Hold on," the Executioner said. He moved up to stand next to Oliverez as the bus took the left-hand fork in the road to descend into the valley. They slowed, with Bolan watching to the right, Katz's eyes glued to the left. They reached the bottom and had started up when Katz suddenly shouted, "Stop!"

Oliverez hit the brakes.

"Back up," Katz said.

The wheels of the bus rolled backward. "Stop!" Katz said again.

Bolan saw a long line of vegetation along the mountain. It looked little different than hundreds of other clumps of trees they had passed. But one thing did catch his eye. Several of the branches of the thick trees had been recently broken, and their clean white interior wood gleamed inside the green of the outer bark.

Oliverez stayed behind the wheel while Bolan and Katz dropped from the bus. Once on the ground, they could see the fresh tire tracks where the Mercedes had stopped, backed up, then driven forward, seemingly to disappear within the trees. Bolan led Katz forward. About ten feet into the trees, the hidden corridor into the mountains appeared. Just big enough to drive a car into, it looked like an old burro trail.

The Executioner and Katz returned to where Oliverez was leaning out the window. "The bus'll never fit," Katz said.

Without speaking, Bolan walked to the rear of the converted camper, opened the door and slid the ramp into place. He rolled the Harley-Davidson down to the ground and propped it onto the kickstand while he hopped back into the bus for his gear. To the Beretta 93-R, Desert Eagle and knives, he added a bandolier of extra magazines and his leather vest, then stared down at the SIG-

550 assault rifle and the Heckler & Koch MP-5K for a moment. Katz had followed him to the rear of the bus. Bolan made his decision, lifted the SIG and handed it to his old friend. He would be riding a motorcycle so it was the sling of the smaller MP5-K that went around his shoulders.

"So, I suppose you're going to ask me to follow you on foot?" Katz asked, grinning.

Bolan returned the grin. "I don't see any other way around it. Oliverez is young, though. He can carry you when you get tired."

Katz snorted. "We'll get there as fast as we can," he said, checking the action on the SIG and reaching into the bus for extra magazines. But we both know it's not likely to be soon enough to help."

The Executioner nodded. He knew that, too. Amir Reza, he was certain now, was headed for the *Partido Revolucionario Marxista* training grounds where thousands of men were preparing for their invasion of Mexico City. Reza had the money that would buy their support and, unknown to them, start a chain of events that would include an American invasion of Mexico and finally the takeover of the Strait of Hormuz by the Iranians.

The odds against the Executioner were however many thousands of men were at the camp—to one.

Kick starting the Harley, Bolan guided it through the trees and onto the old burro path.

IT WAS A deserted winery, by the looks of it. It lay in the heart of Tijuana. Even the shanties that surrounded it had been forsaken as those who had inhabited them found new scrap lumber and built better shelters farther away.

David McCarter drove the Suburban to the upper level of the Sears parking lot two miles from the site where the hostages were being held. Back at Loreto, the *Legitimas* and bandits, with the exception of Huertes, had been tied to various objects on board the *Señorita Maldava* and then the ship had been pointed out to sea running full sails. McCarter had made a quick anonymous call to the Mexican navy.

The next step had been the flight back from Loreto. Jack Grimaldi had been at the controls. Knife-magazine editor Dick Stevens had insisted on coming along too, stating flatly that he didn't like to start anything he couldn't see through. McCarter had agreed—the man had risked his life to help when they needed him and he deserved it. So after a quick phone call to his wife, they had all boarded the plane.

Able Team had been waiting at the airport, and taking a handcuffed Huertes with them, McCarter, Lyons and Scott Hix had done a quick recon of the old winery. Hix had been able to supply some intel on the building's interior, and what he couldn't, had been offered by Huertes. Pablo Huertes would have given up his own mother if he thought it would have helped him out of this jam.

The rest of the men got out of the rented vehicles that had brought them to the parking lot and gathered around the Suburban. "Not a lot to say," McCarter said. "There are two main entrances, front and rear. Three floors. Unless they've been moved, the hostages are in the basement—the old wine cellar. Ground floor's been gutted into two big rooms—one in the front, one right behind it facing the back. Barracks for the guards. The top floor was where Hix trained for the fight but it may contain hostiles by now, too." He paused, then went on. "Three teams. Ironman will take Able Team, Pompei and Toro in the back. Phoenix Force, with Turrin, Stevens and Hix, goes in the front. Once inside on the ground floor, we take care of whatever we meet. Then Able Team and Pompei head to the top. Toro, you break off from Able Team at that point and join Turrin, and Stevens in securing the first level." The Phoenix Force leader looked from face to face. "My boys and I will head down to the wine cellar." His eyes fell on Hix. "I'm assuming you'd like to accompany us?"

"Just try to stop me."

"There were two men perched on the roof," McCarter said. "Lookouts."

"I remember them," Lyons nodded. He patted the sound-suppressed .45 pistol beneath his light jacket. "They're mine."

"We'll use that as the cue," McCarter said. "When you hear

the sound of two suppressed rounds from the rear, we all go. Any questions?''

No one answered.

"Then let's do it."

THE EXECUTIONER kept the Harley's throttle twisted as far back as he dared, darting along the bumpy burro trail in pursuit of the man who wanted to start the war between Mexico and the United States. It wasn't a war in which Mexico was likely to fare well. But that wasn't the man's motive. The U.S., even after they'd won, would lose as well. They'd create an enemy south of the border if the American President invaded Mexico's solidarity. And they'd be spread too thin to stand in the way of Iran taking control of the Persian Gulf and, in turn, the world price of oil.

As the Executioner rounded a curve, the Mercedes suddenly appeared ten yards ahead of him. He saw the flat tire, the jack and the surprised face of Amir Reza at the same time, a split second before the Harley struck the Mercedes' back bumper.

Bolan flew over the car and landed on his back in the middle of the rocky trail. For a moment, he lay dazed, the wind knocked from him. Then he heard the footsteps of the man who'd been changing the flat and rolled to his side a second before a burst of fire struck the ground where he'd been. He looked up to see Reza grinning down at him through the thick black beard. The Iranian held a Skorpion machine pistol in his right hand.

"I don't know who you are," Reza said in the accent that sounded so strange in these Mexican mountains. "But I think you must die." He raised the Skorpion again.

The Executioner rolled as another burst came his way. One round caught the leather vest, skimming across the skin covering his ribs and making Bolan feel like he'd been seared with a hot branding iron. As he rolled, his hand wrapped around the grip of the MP-5K.

A third burst of fire was on its way by the time Bolan rolled to his belly and lifted the submachine gun hanging at his side. He pulled the trigger at the same time another trio of rounds exploded from the Skorpion. This time, one of Reza's bullets penetrated the leather at the top of his left boot. He felt the scorching pain again, but even as he did, he saw the Iranian jerk like a marionette on the end of his master's string. Both rounds from the hammer feature Kissinger had installed in the submachine gun took the Iranian in the heart. Reza fell to the ground.

The Executioner stayed where he was for a moment, the MP-5K trained on the fallen body. Then, struggling to his feet, he limped forward on his injured leg. He found Reza staring upward, his unblinking eyes open to the sky. Bolan dropped to one knee and felt for a pulse. There was none.

"I guess you'll never know who I was," the Executioner said under his breath as he rose. His eyes turned to the Harley. It was scattered in pieces up and down the canyon path. But the damage to the Mercedes was superficial—a big dent in the bumper where the motorcycle had struck was the only evidence of the collision. The Executioner moved to the car's open door. Inside, he saw the two black leather briefcases on the front seat.

The bullet across his side hadn't even drawn blood—just seared a painful burn into the skin. His calf wound was an "in and out," the bullet having passed through the flesh of his leg without striking bone, tendon or ligament. He took a piece of his T-shirt and knotted it tightly around his leg, then finished changing the tire.

Sliding behind the wheel of the Mercedes, the Executioner started on the mountain path once more.

But he had gone only twenty feet when he heard the rounds strike the rocks just to the side of the Mercedes.

NOT ONLY DID they hear the Lyons's sound-suppressed Government Model, the men at the front of the building saw both of the lookouts fall from the roof.

The structure had been built to be a winery, not a fortress, and the front door gave way easily to David McCarter's right boot. The Phoenix Force leader pushed an unarmed, screaming, handcuffed Pablo Huertes through the doorway, then sprinted after him. Immediately, he saw the twenty-odd men scattered around the big front room. Some were lying on bare mattresses on the floor while others sat around two card tables.

The men were surprised. But not too surprised to dive for their weapons.

As Huertes fell to the floor out of the line of fire, McCarter cut loose with a full-auto stream from his M-16. Manning, James, Encizo, Dick Stevens and Scott Hix had all followed him through the door and opened up with their own automatic rifles. Out of the corner of his eye, McCarter could see Stevens firing. The knife editor had a calm, expressionless look on his face.

Hix, on the other side, looked like a man finally obtaining much-deserved vengeance. His face was a mixture of righteous anger, hatred and...well, McCarter thought, satisfaction.

Again, McCarter saw that the men in the room were a mixed breed. Some looked like dedicated revolutionaries. The rest were filthy bandits. A few from both camps reached their weapons, but the men from Stony Man Farm had surprise on their side, and their opponents all died before they could return fire.

Gunfire sounded from the room behind them. McCarter raced that way. He found the men of Able Team, Pompei and Toro engaged in a similar one-sided battle with more of the revolutionaries. He stopped in the doorway to avoid friendly fire, then stuck his head into the room and nodded to Lyons.

The Able Team leader nodded back, then took off for the stairs leading upward.

The stairs to the cellar, according to Huertes, were the ones McCarter had already seen in the front room. Hurrying back that way, he saw the fat bandit still on the floor. Leo Turrin and Dick Stevens had taken up positions to cover the room, and now Toro followed McCarter into the area to join them as ordered. The rest of Phoenix Force and Scott Hix were already heading down the stairs.

"Wait!" McCarter shouted.

The running men froze.

McCarter jerked Huertes to his feet and prodded him along with the M-16. The bandit was crying, begging to be allowed to go back to the floor. He had been without his tequila now for several hours and McCarter saw his hands shaking. He pushed the man, nevertheless, down the stairs to the cellar.

As soon as the Phoenix Force leader had shoved Huertes into the room at the bottom of the stairs he heard a burst of fire. The bandit fell to the ground in the doorway. McCarter jumped over him, seeing the hostages chained to the floor and the guards above them at the same time. The Phoenix Force leader had grown accustomed to the dirty bandits and the cleaner revolutionaries, and had learned to spot them quickly. As Manning, Encizo, James and Scott Hix followed him into the room all the *bandidos* dropped their weapons and threw up their hands. The *Legitimas* opened fire.

But they all died. All except one.

In the far corner of the damp wine cellar, McCarter saw a figure crouching behind a blond woman. With his hand wrapped around her waist, he hugged her toward him and pressed a revolver into her temple. The woman stared ahead, her face blank. In it, McCarter saw no fear. What he saw was fatigue, a desire to end her ordeal one way or another.

To his side, the Phoenix Force leader heard Scott Hix whisper, "No...please...don't."

But before Hix or any of the men from Stony Man Farm could stop him, the man, who McCarter would later learn was Jesus Hidalgo, the leader of the *Legitimas* and the voice over the phone who had set up the fight in Loreto, suddenly screamed at the top of his lungs, *"Viva Mexico! Viva la Revolucion!"*

Then he stuck the barrel of the revolver in his mouth and pulled the trigger.

THE ROUNDS RICOCHETED off the rocky mountain wall next to him as Bolan instinctively drew the Beretta 93-R from his shoulder holster. He looked into the rearview mirror.

Behind him, the Executioner saw Yakov Katzenelenbogen and Juanito Oliverez standing in the trail.

Bolan stomped on the brake and waited as the two men came sprinting up to the Mercedes. The retired Phoenix Force leader jumped into the front seat next to the Executioner and the captain got in back.

"If we'd known it wouldn't take you any longer than that to

find Reza,'' Katz said. ''We wouldn't have hurried.'' The Israeli glanced down at the Executioner's leg as Bolan threw the car in gear again. ''You okay?''

Bolan nodded. ''No big deal,'' he said. He glanced into the rearview mirror and saw Oliverez smiling as he checked the chamber of the Skorpion machine pistol Reza had used. But what caught the Executioner's eye were the guns on the federal bodyguard's hip and under his arm. Oliverez had found the replacement Desert Eagle and Beretta 93-R, and the accompanying holsters in the back of the bus. He wore them now.

Katz saw the Executioner's eyes and guessed what he was looking at. ''Oh, yes,'' the Israeli whispered. ''We're a big boy just like our hero, now.''

The Executioner drove on along the winding path. ''There'll be sentries posted above us somewhere soon,'' he said.

Katz readied the SIG.

Bolan shook his head. ''You may have to shoot them. But first, let's see if we can't just keep our faces covered.'' He pulled down the sun visor in front of him. ''They'll probably recognize the Mercedes.''

Katz nodded as he pulled down his own visor. Behind them, Oliverez shifted to the center of the seat where he'd be harder to see.

The Executioner spotted the first sentry a hundred yards later. The man wore a multicolored serape and was armed with an AK-47. Bolan watched him checking them. But the Soviet-made rifle was never aimed their way.

A half mile and three more sentries later, they came to a huge valley hidden in the mountains. Bolan stopped the car and let the motor idle while he looked upon the scene. A small building he assumed served as headquarters stood in the center of the camp. Tents and other quickly built structures circled it for at least a quarter mile. He didn't take time to count. But the Executioner estimated there were at least three thousand men.

''Well,'' Katz quipped. ''Here's another fine mess you've gotten me into.'' He turned to face the Executioner. ''You take the ones on the right of the building. I'll take the left.'' Without look-

ing over his shoulder, he added, "Probably won't need you, Juanito. But stay ready just in case."

"I've got an idea," Bolan said, still staring down at the army
of the *Marxistas*.

"Well, I'd dearly love to hear it," Katz said.

Slowly, the Executioner drove down the road that led to the
headquarters building. As soon as the Mercedes came into view,
heads began to turn their way. Then, as they reached the outskirts
of the tents and other structures, they saw men bearing a variety
of arms—everything from captured Mexican army M-16s to old
.22 hunting rifles. Some of the new recruits carried only machetes,
and a few even had pitchforks or other tools. What they did have
in common were the sun-dried faces and callused hands of the
hard-working Mexican peasants.

The Executioner's heart went out to them. They struggled their
entire lives, scraping a pitiful existence from the earth for themselves and their families. They never knew from where their next
meal would come, and at night they listened to the cries of their
hungry babies. All the while, they knew that the patrons who ruled
them grew fatter each day on the riches of the country's wealth.
So was it any wonder they could be induced to come fight for a
cause that offered them money?

Bolan pulled the Mercedes to a halt directly in front of the
building. He saw a man wearing a uniform with general's stars on
the epaulets walk out smiling. Then the smile faded as the man
looked inside the car.

"Don't get excited," the Executioner said, holding up one of
the briefcases. "Reza couldn't make it. He sent us."

The man's face relaxed. Looking beyond the Mercedes, he
called out, "Paz! Frederico! Come here!"

As Bolan, Katz and Oliverez got out of the car two men came
running toward the building. One of them carried a leather swagger
stick.

"I am General Avia Portilla," the man who had greeted them
said proudly. He stuck out his hand.

Bolan shook it and smiled. He pictured the man out of uniform,
wearing white peasant clothing and a ball-fringed sombrero. In his

mind's eye, he saw Portilla at *Los Pinos* when the presidential mansion had been overrun, then at the president's summer house when the Executioner had feared Fierro Blanco and his entire family had been burned alive in the basement while their house went up in flames. "I've been waiting a long time to meet you, General," Bolan said. "Shall we go inside?"

"Yes," Portilla said.

Katz and Oliverez carried the briefcases inside the building. Portilla indicated that they should take seats around the room, then dropped into the chair behind his desk. Katz and Oliverez set the briefcases on the desk. It was only then that Portilla suddenly recognized the captain. His hand went immediately to the pistol on his side.

Bolan held up a hand. "Relax," he said in a calm voice. "Oliverez has finally seen the light. He's on our side, now."

Portilla shook his head in wonderment. "My congratulations to you then. I tried everything with this man. Money, threats. Nothing worked." He began laughing. "Whatever you did," he said, looking to Bolan, "my sombrero is off to you." There was a sudden pause during which Bolan knew the man behind the desk was trying to place him. Portilla knew there was something familiar about the big man but he couldn't quite put his finger on it.

"Reza didn't get a chance to fill us in on all the details," the Executioner said. "Tell me exactly what kind of deal you cut with these men."

Portilla shrugged. "All of the men who survived the attacks on *Los Pinos* and Fierro Blanco's summer house received two thousand American dollars. New recruits were promised one thousand. Some have been paid, but many in camp are still waiting." His eyes moved to the briefcases.

"Go ahead," Bolan said. "Look inside."

Portilla did, and his eyes grew wide. "Five-hundred-dollar bills?" he gasped. "All of them?"

"Two for each man here," the Executioner said.

Portilla threw back his head and laughed again.

He was still laughing when Bolan drew the Beretta and shot him in the chest.

The smile on the *Marxista* leader's face turned to shock. Bolan watched as the man stared at him, finally understanding. "You..." he choked out. "Belasko..."

"Me," Bolan agreed, then put another sound-suppressed 9 mm round into the man's head.

The man with the swagger stick rose from his chair and fumbled for the big Government Model .45 on his hip. The Executioner swung the Beretta toward him and fired a 3-round burst into his heart. Paz fell to the floor.

The Executioner turned to the third man—the man Portilla had called Frederico. He had the same weathered face and hands of the other men they had seen when they'd entered the camp. But what stood out now was the fact that his face reflected no shock or fear. He looked more as if he had expected something like this to happen; like he knew the offer of a thousand U.S. dollars couldn't possibly be true. "Do you lead the new men?" Bolan asked.

Frederico's face remained impassive. "I was elected to represent them," he said.

"And they're willing to march on Mexico City for the money?"

Frederico snorted through his nose. "You have seen them," he said. "They would march on the devil in Hell for that kind of money."

Bolan stared the man in the face. Still, there was no fear. Frederico had lived a hard life and he would continue to do so now that he knew the money had only been a pipe dream. He didn't care if the Executioner shot him or not.

"How would your men feel about just taking the money and marching back home to their families?" Bolan asked.

Finally, Frederico's face changed. He looked confused.

"The revolution's been called off," Bolan said. "Distribute the money in those briefcases to your men and tell them to make better lives for themselves." He stood and headed toward the door. "Now, if you'll excuse us, we've got a long drive back."

The weathered old Mexican was still staring at the briefcases as Bolan, Katz and Oliverez walked out of the building and got back into the Mercedes.

EPILOGUE

He waited a day before he did it. But waiting didn't mean the Executioner had forgotten.

Bolan twisted the key in the ignition and drove away from *Los Pinos*. He fell in behind the Mercedes in the heavy Mexico City traffic, unnoticed. At the Executioner's side sat Yakov Katzenelenbogen. In the back seat, Captain Juanito Oliverez and *Defensive Knives* editor Dick Stevens sat against the windows. Scott Hix was squeezed between them.

Hix had been the target for most of the other men's good-natured jokes while they waited outside the presidential mansion. He and Normandi West were getting married the next day.

There was good reason for the men's high spirits. Upon returning to Mexico City from the *Marxista* camp, the Executioner had called Stony Man Farm. In addition to Able Team and Phoenix Force rescuing all of the hostages, he had learned that satellite pictures, shoved in front of the American President's nose by Hal Brognola, had convinced the man in the Oval Office that the newly recruited *Marxistas* were scattering and the threat was over. The President had immediately begun evacuating the troops along the Mexican border and sending them toward the Strait of Hormuz. And although he had never met the man, Bolan was glad to hear that Dirk Anderson, the Houston PD detective who had assisted Able Team, was recovering from his bullet wound.

The only bad news was that Thomas Jackson Hawkins, the youngest member of Phoenix Force, still lay in the hospital in Tucson, his condition uncertain.

Bolan followed the Mercedes through a green light, then

glanced at the men around him. He and the other four men all wore police uniforms, and the car Bolan drove was a Mexican black-and-white marked unit. As they followed the Mercedes, Katz turned to speak to Oliverez, who had procured the illusionary props for them. "Do we get to keep the uniforms?" the former Phoenix Force leader asked innocently.

Oliverez laughed. "I'm afraid I'll have to return them before they're missed."

"Just wondering," Katz said. He turned his attention to Hix now. "It was you I was thinking of, Scott. The honeymoon won't last forever, and I thought if you had the uniform you could throw in a little kinky stuff eventually."

Hix took the ribbing with the same good humor he had all the previous comments. Since the fight on the ship, and his assistance in the rescue of the other hostages, he had become "one of the boys." Dick Stevens had proved himself as well. So with Able Team and Phoenix Force already heading for the Strait to join the new fight there, Bolan had decided both men deserved to see this Mexican episode through to the end.

The Mercedes took an access ramp and joined the traffic on the same thoroughfare Bolan remembered from when he and Able Team had followed President Fierro Blanco to his secret rendezvous with film star Margarita Felice. He glanced over his shoulder quickly as he fell into pace with the other vehicles. "Hear from your buddy Quartel?" he asked Hix.

The American close-quarters combat expert laughed. "He called last night. He's got a press session scheduled this afternoon. Same old Ronnie. By the time this is over, the ticket-buying public will think he's Sylvester Stallone." He paused. "You remember the single-action revolver I told you he brought down to TJ with him?"

Bolan nodded. "He used it in the last movie. Loaded with blanks?"

"Not anymore," Hix laughed. "His agent brought in live rounds and they fired four of them into a mattress or something. He'll be wearing the whole rig during the press conference."

The real warriors in the car couldn't help but laugh. "Guess that's showbiz," Dick Stevens said.

The Mercedes took an off-ramp into a part of town that Bolan also recognized. They followed close behind until the same motel where Fierro Blanco had met the famous Mexican singer appeared in the distance. Bolan shook his head. It looked as if *el presidente* wasn't the only one having a clandestine affair with Margarita Felice.

"I'm going to pull him over," Bolan said. "There's no sense getting the woman involved."

The Executioner hit the red lights on top of the car. The Mercedes pulled over and stopped along the curb.

"He'll recognize you, me and Oliverez," Katz said.

Bolan stared through the windshield at the back of the head of the man behind the wheel of the Mercedes. General Antonio de Razon had been Amir Reza's link to *Los Pinos*. Razon hadn't only tried to poison the Executioner, the general had set both Bolan and his own president up for the kill countless other times. Only the Stony Man Farm warrior's efficiency and experience had kept him and Fierro Blanco alive.

"Let me do it," Hix said. "He won't recognize me, and I owe him one. I owe them all."

"Keep it low-key and quiet," Bolan said. "We don't need anyone else noticing." He glanced up and down the busy street and sidewalk.

Hix got out of the car carrying a citation book. He approached the driver's-side window, and the Executioner heard him say in Spanish, "License and registration."

"Do you know who I am?" A self-important voice from inside the Mercedes boomed.

"I know who you were," Scott Hix said. A second later the Applegate-Fairbairn knife came sliding out from under the ticket book and disappeared through the window. The Executioner saw Hix's elbow pump up and down twice, then the dagger reemerged covered in blood and went back into hiding.

Hix returned to the car. "That quiet enough?" he asked.

Bolan nodded. He pulled away from the curb as Dick Stevens said, "That knife saved your ass more than once, huh?"

Hix nodded as he wiped the blade on the trousers of his uniform.

"Don't you think you ought to ditch it now that you used it?" Stevens asked.

Hix turned to him in shock. "Are you out of your mind?" the American close-quarters combat expert said. "This thing was a gift from Colonel Applegate himself."

Before any more could be said, the cellular phone on the seat between Bolan and Katz suddenly rang. The former-Phoenix Force leader picked it up and pressed it to his ear. Bolan saw his old friend break into a grin, then the Israeli turned and handed him the phone.

"It's Hawkins," Katz said. "He's pissed off that Phoenix Force took off for the Strait without him."

The ultimate weapon
of terror...

JAMES AXLER
DEATH LANDS
®

Dark Reckoning

A secret community of scientists gains control of an orbiting transformer that could become the ultimate weapon of terror—and it's up to Ryan Cawdor to halt the evil mastermind before he can incinerate Front Royal.

Book 3 in the Baronies Trilogy, three books that chronicle the strange attempts to unify the East Coast baronies. Who (or what) is behind this coercive process?

GDL48

James Axler

OUTLANDERS™

ARMAGEDDON AXIS

What was supposed to be the seat of power after the nuclear holocaust, a vast installation inside Mount Rushmore—is a new powerbase of destruction. Kane and his fellow exiles venture to the hot spot, where they face an old enemy conspiring to start the second wave of Armageddon.

Shadow THE EXECUTIONER®
as he battles evil for 352 pages of heart-stopping action!

SuperBolan®